Navajo Witchery. Treachery and trickery.

Social worker Jordan Bia finds a child who escaped her captors and a life in the sex trade, but four other girls from her small Mexican village were not so lucky. Smugglers hide their human cargo in the hoodoos of a remote canyon on the reservation—a place the Navajo shun, fearful of the witches who practice their black rituals and feast on the dark energy of evil. Mysterious rites, omens of death, and bodies litter the canyon passes...

When she meets Navajo police officer Sam Tohee, sparks fly fueled by the danger of hunting men who buy and sell little girls. Techno savvy Jordan plots to trap the smugglers and find the rest of the children, but unless she can find the power to defeat the witches she may not live long enough to save the girls.

Books by P.H. Turner

Winterkill

Death & Desire

Desert Heat

Desert Heat

Book 2 in The Nation series

P.H. Turner

To the extent that the image or images on the cover of this book depict a person or persons, such person or persons are merely models, and are not intended to portray any character or characters featured in the book.

ISBN-10:
0996844511
ISBN-13:
978-0-9968445-1-2
First Electronic Edition: September 2015

ISBN-10:
0996844503
ISBN-13:
978-0-9968445-0-5
First Trade Paperback printing: September 2015

To Marcia, Matthew, and Alison for your love and support. Always.

Acknowledgements

Kudos to my untiring editor, Corinne DeMaagd, for her savvy advice and to Renee Rocco for her gorgeous cover art and her formatting and publishing help.

A special thanks to my readers for joining me again on the Navajo Reservation.

Chapter 1

I walked down the center of the shadowy street, far away from men who might slither out of alleys and doorways and grab me, a lone female. The woman whose child I had come to check on lived over a bar when she functioned well enough to remember where she lived. She and the child were nowhere to be found. I had tarried too long, and the night hovered under the thin crescent of moonlight that marked the time between the dark moon and the new moon. Clouds scuttled across the moon, darkening the sky.

The puny glow from the single streetlight outlined two men slouched between boarded-up buildings, smoking and swigging from bottles sheathed in tattered brown bags. They catcalled and hooted, "We got whatcha want, girlie." I scurried faster to my old Honda Civic, parked a block away. My heart pounded and my calves burned from the effort to put distance between me and their drunken lewdness.

Soft crying, a sound more like a wounded kitten than a person, stopped me in the middle of the street. I cocked my head toward the dim alley but only saw shadows. The pitiful sound drifted out, forlorn and frightened. I scanned the street for movement. No one was there. I walked on my toes to the mouth of the alley. Nothing stirred. Tiny fingers of light trickled into the alley from the streetlight. "Who's there?"

The crying became snuffling, and then silence.

Footsteps rustled. I called into the darkness, asking if anyone needed help.

"*Si,*" the voice whimpered.

"Come out into the street." I backed up two steps toward the middle of the road and waited for someone to join me.

A small bag of rags shuffled to the mouth of the alley. The waif was poised to run.

"Hide! Hide!" she begged.

Her English was heavily accented, and I wasn't sure I had understood her. "Hide you from whom?"

"No," she shrieked and took a step back into the alley.

"Are you by yourself?" I was hyper-alert the girl might not be alone.

"*Si.*"

"Come out under the light," I demanded. I walked to the center of the street into a yellow pool of light, well away from the dark mouth of the alley.

She obediently shuffled to within an arm's reach of me. Thin dirty arms stuck out of a shirt that sagged below her knees, and her hair was filthy and matted. She wiped her nose on her sleeve, leaving a trail of bloody mucus. Rain washed her dirty, bare feet clean, and oh how she stunk of unwashed body and fetid clothes. She clung to the knotted cord tied around the ratty sweat pants that swallowed her small frame. She stared at me, chin up, and poised for flight.

"Do you live near here?"

She shrugged and hiccupped.

"Do you speak English?"

"*Si,* little," she whispered.

I wouldn't leave her, but God help me, I vacillated about putting her in my car. Who was watching?

"Come." I touched her filthy shoulder, and she flinched. I pointed to myself. "I'm Jordan. You'll be safe with me."

I knew they were the words she wanted to hear, and I hoped to hell I could keep her safe. I knew the system. I worked in it. We trudged toward my car. I opened the passenger side door of my beat-up junker.

"Get into the car." I motioned to her to get into the Civic. She slipped in, and I pulled the seatbelt taunt around her gaunt frame. "What's your name?"

"Sofia."

"How old are you?"

"Eleven." She turned her head from me, staring out into the darkness.

Eleven years old and alone. How did she come to be in the alley? "Where are you from?"

"Banamichi." She kept her body angled away from me, and her shoulders heaved with her heavy sobs. "Me friend Juanita...find..."

I pointed at the alley. "Your friend is back in the alley?"

She nodded her head and sniffled.

"I'll look for her, but then we're getting out of here." Suspicion crept up my back that maybe the girl was luring me into a setup.

I walked around the car and got into the driver's side, dredging up what little I knew about Banamichi, a tiny village in the Mexican state of Sonora, and remembered only trivia—they grew green chilies.

"Water?" I waved a bottle of water in front of her, and she grabbed it. I scrounged through the driver's side door pocket looking for a granola bar. I kept a stash for the days I was overbooked with clients. I unwrapped the small bar and handed it to her.

She drank long and hard from the water bottle, gulping it down. Balancing the bottle between her knobby knees, she shoved most of the food into her mouth.

I waited until she swallowed the dry bar and took another mouthful of water. "Where are your parents?"

"Dead," she said so softly I had to lean in to hear her.

"I can't help you if I don't know who you are and how you got here."

I pulled out of the dark street and drove a four-block grid, slowing to peer into alleys, and finally returned to the street where I found her. "We're leaving."

She scowled as I drove into a better-lighted neighborhood, put the car in park with the engine running, and demanded some answers from the girl. "Tell me what happened."

She arched her dark brows at me. "Me parents dead. Live with aunt."

"How did you get here? Did you run away?"

"No." She spat on the floor mat and muttered vehemently in Spanglish, testing the limits of my comprehension. "Montoya bought me."

I disciplined my face to remain neutral, shocked at her claim her aunt had sold her to a guy named Montoya. "Is he the man who brought you to Flagstaff?"

She shrugged her shoulders and looked at me bewildered. "Is Flagstaff?"

"You don't know where you are?" I asked.

She glanced at me warily and muttered again in a mixture of Spanish and English, claiming she was thrown in a windowless van in front of her aunt's house by a Hispanic man who drove them away.

"Me amiga...fr-friend," she stuttered and gulped in air. "Juanita and me runned. He kill us if he finds." She buried her head in her hands and sobbed.

"Then we can't let him find you, can we?"

She studied me through her lashes, as if debating with herself whether to trust me or not. She raised her head and announced timidly, "Me stay you?"

I knew she would bolt into the night if I told her our laws weren't going to let her stay with me. "You'll be in a safe place, and I will get to visit you." I had just promised more than Child Protective Services would let me deliver, but I knew the words would soothe her, and they did. She slid into a restless, moaning sleep before I reached the police station.

She struggled frantically against the seatbelt when we reached the bright lights of the police station parking lot. "Policia!" she shrieked. Her whole body tensed, and she slapped away my hand when I tried to soothe her.

I snapped off my seat belt, but not hers.

She pinned me with her angry gaze.

"You'll be safe from the man who bought you. You want that, right? And these are not the Mexican police—these guys are going to help you."

She nodded stiffly.

"I know these men. It's going to be all right, and they'll protect you."

Fear and her wish to believe me battled in her eyes. Slowly, her tension eased, and she relaxed against the seat back.

I kept my hand on her as I unbuckled her seatbelt, afraid she would make a run for it, but she was as docile as a defeated animal. I held her small hand all the way into the headquarters.

The desk sergeant stared at me before he slid his eyes to Sofia. He cocked his head at the trembling girl. "Who do you have there?"

"Sofia. I'm Jordan Bia with Navajo CPS out of Tuba City. I would like to talk to Captain O'Brien."

"She's not Navajo, and this isn't Tuba City."

I pulled myself a little taller and stared directly into his eyes. "I'm licensed by the state and I've worked with O'Brien before in my role as a CPS investigator. I found her in Flag. O'Brien, please."

He picked up the phone and barked, "O'Brien, we got a live one up here."

O'Brien looked like a man at the end of a long shift with his rumpled suit and a tie yanked down in a messy knot. He ushered us into an interview room. I knew I had started a legal process for Sofia that would change her life, maybe for the better, but maybe send her straight back to Mexico.

We sat around a battered gunmetal gray table in a grungy interrogation room. O'Brien reached into his pocket and handed Sofia a piece of gum. She snatched it from his hand, chewed vigorously, and gulped it down. O'Brien shot a look at me. He rose from his chair, dug in his pocket, and brought out a wad of bills. He jerked open the door and thrust the money at the officer outside. "Get the kid some food, will you?"

"She speak English?" he asked me as he returned to his seat.

"A mixture of Spanglish and some English, but she can tell her story. She understands more English than she can speak. She's Sofia, and she's from Banamichi." I smiled encouragingly at the girl. "I found her hiding in the alley behind the Back of Beyond bar. She claims her aunt sold her to a man named Montoya, and that she and her friend Juanita got away. I didn't see any sign of Juanita."

O'Brien grimaced. To Sofia he said, "What is your last name?"

She stared at him without blinking. To me he said, "You know her last name?"

I shook my head, and O'Brien leaned back in his chair and studied the child."Here's how this works, Sofia. I'm the best help you got. I need answers. Who are you running from?"

She shook her head. "A fat man," she whimpered.

"This fat man got a name?"

She shrugged."Don't know."

"Did this fat man bring you across the border?"

She nodded vigorously and, for the first time, offered information. She held up five fingers. "*Cinco* girls."

O'Brien muttered, "You know any of the other girls besides this Juanita?"

She glanced at me.

"Go ahead. It's okay," I encouraged her.

She shook her head."Juanita from my village." Sofia shuddered and turned to me pleading, "Find…find. *Por favor*." A thin stream of watery mucus mixed with blood ran out of her nose and down her lip.

I dug in my purse and handed her a Kleenex knowing that I couldn't promise her we would find Juanita, much less the other three girls.

Ignoring her plea, O'Brien tapped his pencil on the tabletop. "How much did your aunt pay the men to bring you into the States?"

"No, no!" the little girl shrieked in protest. She jumped up and overturned her chair, sending it clattering to the floor, vehemently denying that her aunt had paid a coyote to bring her across the border. "Montoya pay! He pay aunt," Sofia shouted.

"Nathan Montoya?" He sighed tiredly.

Sofia bobbed her head up and down.

I righted her chair and took her arm, easing her back into her chair.

"You know this guy she's claiming bought her?" I asked.

"Yeah, he did a stretch for running a flea-bitten whorehouse, got out about ten years ago." O'Brien leaned back and steepled his fingers. "He's about sixty now, and somehow he had the cash to reinvent himself when he came out of prison."

"Wait, are we talking about the Montoya who just made a sizable donation to the YMCA?"

"Yeah, owner of Montoya Trucking Company. Looks like he's still got a taste for the business."

I was reeling. Nathan Montoya was the epitome of a debonair, successful businessman with a blond trophy wife half his age on his arm.

"Do you have a picture of Montoya you can show her?" I asked.

O'Brien flicked his wrist at me. "Yeah, thanks, I still know how to do my job." He turned to Sofia and asked, "So what's this guy who drove the van look like?"

She stretched her little hands wide apart. "*Grande*."

"You're going to have to give me more than he's a big guy."

She ran her forefinger over her upper lip. "*Pelo*." She pointed at O'Brien's mustache and tapped under her nose.

The door cracked open, and the officer set a bag of food in front of Sofia. He retreated two steps to guard the closed door.

Rather than touch it, she looked to me for approval.

"It's yours," I assured her, unwrapping the straw and sticking it in the icy Coke. She peeked inside the grease-stained bag. Her eyes grew large as she dumped the hamburger and fries on the bare table. She wolfed the food down. O'Brien also recognized she'd had to fight for every scrap of food.

When she finished eating, O'Brien asked, "Think you could describe the fat guy so we can draw a picture?"

She belched and nodded at him.

O'Brien cocked his head at the officer who brought the food. "Get that artist guy in here and let's work with her while she's fresh."

The officer nodded and slipped out the door.

"Would you recognize the place where the van picked you up?"

She ran her tongue over her cracked lips. "No." She walked her fingers across the table. "*En el desierto*."

O'Brien explained to me, "If they walked through the Mexican desert to the border to hook up with the van, they probably came through the corridor."

"What corridor?" I asked.

"The smugglers' corridor. Runs right through all that empty ranch land from Nogales to Tucson and up here through the Nation." He plowed both hands through the stringy, gray-brown hair he had left. "Hell, smugglers have been going through there for a hundred years, but it's a high tech operation now. The Mexicans have spider holes full of lookouts in those hills equipped with satellite phones and supplies. And the Nation has lots of empty spaces to hide the goods until they're trucked out of the state."

"What are they smuggling besides girls?"

"What's hasn't come in?" he said cryptically. He leaned back in his chair. "Used to be mostly car parts and booze. Now it's guns, drugs, and people. I'd love to nail that old bastard. In the old days, not one damn thing came across the border unless the Montoya family wanted it to, and they made money, plenty of money. Doesn't matter what it was, the family had its fingers in it."

"So arrest him."

O'Brien thunked his chair back on all four legs. "You know it's never that easy." He wiped his hand across his face. "I can tell you right now, his accomplice is back across the border combing the villages for more girls, and Montoya's probably attending a symphony board meeting with that celebrity wife of his."

Sofia had fallen asleep, resting her head on her arm. Her belly was full, and two policemen in the room had lulled her into relaxing.

"You think he uses his trucking company to deliver the girls?"

He was incredulous. "Wouldn't you?"

"Yeah, when are you going to talk to him?"

He frowned at me. "Thanks. Still got a boss here. Montoya's turned himself into a model citizen, a benefactor of the arts in Flagstaff. I'll have my ass covered before I see him. You're free to go right up to his big house or his company and ask him what he's doing in Mexico snatching girls."

I ignored his jab. "What's going to happen to Sofia's aunt?"

He pinched the bridge of his nose. "She may not have long to live if the kid keeps talking, and I'm keeping her here to wring outta her whatever she knows."

"I'll contact Children of Border Violence and get the paper work rolling."

"Jumping the gun, don't you think?"

"No, she's going to need a foster family. By the time she rolls through the system and her case goes to court, years will have passed. And no court is sending a kid back to the relative who sold her."

He studied me for a moment. "I thought you worked on the Navajo Nation as an investigator. What are you poking around in this for?"

"You just said human trafficking was going though the Nation. She's my job now."

"I'm going to make today your lucky day." He scribbled on a note pad and held it out to me. "Tom Hellman is an old buddy of mine from my army days, and he ranches down south of Nogales along the border. Tom can tell you what's it like down there."

"Thanks. Why are you so interested in me talking to Tom Hellman?"

"You mean what's in it for me?" He hunched his shoulders. "Mebbe justice for a little kid."

I pocketed the card. I knew the Hellmans. Alice Bia Hellman was born for The Corn People, my mother's sister, and I had visited them many times.

A sharp rap on the door woke Sofia. A young, efficient-looking woman burst into the room and swiveled her head from O'Brien to me. "What's she doing here?"

"She found the kid, and the kid wants her here."

"Highly irregular," Maria Vasquez spat out. "Your desk sergeant called me."

"You two met?"

"Yes," I said. "Ms. Vasquez and I worked some cases that overlapped between the Flagstaff office and the one in Tuba City."

"I want it on record that I object to her presence," Maria said. "This is not her territory. It's mine."

"Got it." O'Brien sounded weary.

I knew Maria well. She was petty and felt challenged by any social worker newer to the system than herself.

"We need to take her to the hospital. You know that is the protocol." She slapped a sheaf of forms on the table in front of O'Brien. She snatched up Sofia's shirt, exposing her back covered with welts and stripes. Some were fresh and still oozed pinkish fluid. The others had scabbed over. Two small burns on her back appeared to be cigarette burns.

"No," Sofia wailed, flailing out at Ms. Vasquez. The social worker jumped back, and Sofia ran to the corner, her feral eyes darting from O'Brien to me. Sofia hung her head in shame, her cheeks flaming red.

"Sofia, you haven't done anything wrong." I took a hesitant step forward, and when the child didn't bolt, walked into her corner and gathered her in my arms.

"How do you know that?" Maria hissed.

"She's an eleven-year-old child."

Maria sniffed in disgust and shook her head. "Her story could be a load of crap. A lot these girls are in the trade, and when they get caught, they lie through their teeth."

Maria advanced on the corner where I cuddled Sofia and pinned me with a stare. "What *is* your game? You're an investigator for the Navajo!"

"I'm a licensed social worker in the state of Arizona. I found her, and she trusts me."

"She can trust me," Maria snapped.

"I trust you to do the right thing here. Make Sofia feel comfortable and safe."

"Hell, Vasquez, bend a little. The kid needs anyone she can find who is willing to help her," O'Brien said.

I locked eyes with Maria. She had the grace to break eye contact first.

Chapter 2

I sat in the parking lot of the police station and called Children of Border Violence to alert them that Sofia would need a long term placement, though I knew she would have to stay in the emergency shelter until her medical treatment and psychiatric assessment were completed. I wasn't so damned naive as to think I could save all the children, but surely I could help Sofia, Juanita and the other three girls. If I failed, they would pay a high price, sold into brothels as sex slaves. I tossed my phone in the console and headed for home.

When I unlocked the door to my tiny apartment, Chloe Jane rushed to meet me. I braced myself for her usual greeting. She stood waist high to me, nuzzled me under my chin, and slurped me a sloppy hello kiss.

My parents laughed and said Chloe Jane was my first successful case as a social worker. Chloe had been dealt a bad hand in life. She'd been found wandering on the rough side of Flag, dumpster-diving for scraps. The vet at the shelter had removed a shotgun pellet from under the skin above her left ear, claiming she was lucky; the load wasn't heavy enough to penetrate her skull. I had gone to the shelter on one of their adoption days looking for a pup that would never weigh more than twenty pounds. I came home with a three-year-old Great Dane, sitting in the front seat, riding shotgun all the way back to an apartment too small for the two of us.

I dumped my purse and briefcase on the table by the door and gathered Chloe's head between my hands. "Hey, baby love. I'm home." She woofed her appreciation, turning tight circles in the narrow entryway until I shooed her toward the kitchen with the promise of her dinner. My apartment was cramped, but I didn't have or need much. I chose the apartment because the front door faced east, and my people believed an east-facing door received the blessing of the morning sun from the Holy Ones.

Chloe Jane gulped her dinner. She followed me into the bedroom, stretching out her full length and taking most of the available floor space. I stepped over her, telling her Sofia's story. She lay quietly, her head on her crossed paws as though she understood and empathized with Sofia's plight.

Chloe whimpered, tracking me with her eyes as I rummaged through my closet to find my favorite jeans and a black silk shirt. She knew dressing up meant I was leaving her for the evening. I paired my clothes with my turquoise and silver jewelry, a gift from my parents. I had a blind date set up by my friend, Taylor, and would meet her guy, Trace, and the date in a downtown bar. After dealing with Sofia, I was in no mood for first date chatter or trying to get to know someone. The others would have to carry the conversation. I knew Taylor could hold up her end of the evening—she was a reporter with the gift of gab.

I ran a brush through my long black hair, gave myself a once-over in the mirror, and judged I was fine for the occasion. I hadn't dated much in the last two years. My mom, fearful I would never marry and give her grandchildren, accused me of living in the desert of broken dreams after a nasty breakup, but I hadn't shared with her the whole story of the man who I had loved deeply and lost painfully the last year of college. My parents were traditional, married before they were eighteen, never finished high school, and kept to the old ways of tending sheep and weaving, staying safely tucked between our four sacred mountains that marked the boundaries of our Nation.

I had disappointed them when I chose a different life, and their disapproval permeated our relationship. As I grew older, I understood, in not accepting their ways, I had made them examine their well-established lives and made them uncomfortable. They came to believe my choice was a rejection of them. Our relationship stymied, and our conversations became stilted based on topics we would least disagree on.

***

I called O'Brien on the way to the restaurant. He reported that Sofia's burns had been cleaned and bandaged at the hospital, and Maria had just dropped her off at the Children's Emergency Shelter. I would go by and see Sofia in the morning before going to the office.

"I've already talked to Children of Border Violence and they placed her on the list of children needing placements."

"Another day's work done and dusted. I'm outta here," O'Brien said and hung up.

Parking by the Weatherford Hotel lifted my spirits. I was off duty and this might be fun. The third floor Zane Grey Ballroom was a popular watering hole for the locals in downtown Flagstaff. The Grey was misnamed since it had never been a ballroom, but always a beautiful bar full of stained glass and gleaming wood. Antique photos of the hotel from its heyday in the late 1890s hung on the walls. The warped old stairs creaked all the way to the third floor where convivial conversation and laughter drifted out over the smoky sounds of jazz. My worries drifted away, and I had a tingle of anticipation. Maybe the blind date and I would walk out of my desert of broken dreams together.

I scanned the crowd for Taylor. She waved at me from a table adjacent to the carved wood fireplace. She and Trace sat beside a tall man with jet black hair, sculpted short on the sides and longish on top. The men stood as I approached. My date had a warrior's face, a hawk nose balanced by high cheek bones and a chiseled jaw. Taylor reached over and grabbed my hand."Hey, you look great." She jerked her thumb toward the warrior. "This is Sam Tohee."

Sam's hand was warm and calloused, his fingers thick and hard as he clasped my own. A grin tugged at the edge of his generous mouth, and when his eyes held mine, it became a slow contagious smile that spread across his face.

I was still holding his hand when Trace broke the spell. "And this is Jordan Bia." Trace continued the introductions. "Sam and I served together over in Afghanistan. He spent fifteen years in the Marines." He clapped Sam on the back. "Now he's come home to the Nation and the Navajo PD."

Sam pulled out my chair, and I sat down, surreptitiously studying him. He was at least ten years older than me and had the easy grace of a man who is confident with his ability to handle any situation. His smile pushed up into his eyes, softening the planes of his face. "I've heard a great deal about you. You're going to school and working out of the Tuba City office, aren't you?"

"Yes, I've worked a year as an investigator with Navajo CPS." The air between Sam and I thickened with interest.

Sam's warrior visage conflicted with his beautiful eyes. He had the eyes of an old soul, full of romance, a hint of passion, and a tincture of the unexpected, and they never once wavered from drawing mine to his. I had a sudden premonition, knowing we would experience thundering passion and gentle understanding like a thunderclap in the desert is followed by soothing rain.

Sam broke the silence. "Perhaps we'll get to work together. I've just transferred here from the Window Rock Tribal Police. My people are from the Window Rock area. I'm Cliff Dwellers People clan and born for Bitter Water people."

"I am Corn People clan, born for The Red House people. I've lived around Flagstaff all my life."

Our waiter broke the moment. "Welcome to the Grey. My name's Belinda, and I'll be your server tonight. What are we having to drink?"

Trace gestured to me, and I ordered first. "I'd like sweet tea vodka in lemonade."

A ghost of amusement shot across Sam's face. "Maker's on the rocks, please," he said to Belinda.

Trace followed Sam's lead and ordered bourbon, Taylor ordered a dry martini, and I fidgeted, feeling like a school kid with spiked lemonade.

"Do you want an appetizer with that?" Belinda asked.

Trace looked around the table. "Thanks, we're fine for now." He asked Sam, "What do you think the Lumberjacks chances are opening the season against the Utah Thunderbirds?"

Sam grinned. "We're going to be the team no one wants to face this year."

Taylor gave me an exaggerated eye roll. "Man-talk about basketball. They both played for the Lumberjacks. How are your last couple of courses coming along?"

Our server brought our drinks. "Anything else right now?"

Sam shook his head at the server and fixed his attention on me, suspending the basketball conversation and waiting for me to answer.

"Nearly done, and I'm ready to be out of school." I fiddled with my drink, debating whether or not to mention Sofia.

"What's on your mind?" Taylor's razor-sharp reporter's instincts honed in on me.

"I found a little girl this evening who claims she was bought in Mexico and smuggled across the border. O'Brien claims they hide the girls on the Nation before distributing them to the buyers. Do they?"

Fine lines of worry etched around Sam's eyes. "They do, and it's dangerous business. I've found some isolated places used by smugglers with lots of abandoned gear and...well...other evidence."

Taylor jumped on Sam's admission. "What other evidence are you talking about?"

Sam drained his drink and motioned across the bar to Belinda for another. He sized me up before he answered Taylor. "A burlap bag of heads."

"Wh-What?" I stuttered, astounded at his answer.

He pushed his chair back from the table and folded his arms across his chest. "I said it was dangerous business. It's brutal, too." Sam picked up his empty drink and fingered the condensation on his glass. He scrutinized me under the fringe of his lashes before he lifted his head and continued, "I found the bag of heads a month ago on an isolated stretch of the Nation. You need to be careful about poking into this. You could ask questions and raise the interest of some bad-ass people, and you're no match for them. In those poor Mexican villages where families can't feed all their kids, some of them are more than happy to take a few dollars for a daughter, and there are plenty of human traffickers to seal the deal with them."

A warning flag shot up. His authoritarian manner turned me off. My father had dictated *the way* everything should be done in our household. As a child, I had accepted his ways. When I matured, I realized my mom felt marginalized and infantilized by his commanding manner.

But now, I was being too judgmental. He only had shared the story and warned me to be careful.

"I investigate charges of child abuse. Do you know anything about Nathan Montoya? That's the man Sofia claimed bought her."

"Sure, the Montoya family has run women in northern Arizona for generations. Montoya boasted to one of our informants, 'I can sell a bag of drugs once, but I can sell a woman over and over.'" He rapped his knuckles on the table top. "And that tells you about the people in this business. They're the filth of the earth."

Before I could reply, two phones buzzed, and both guys answered. Trace stood and said, "Heading your way."

Sam spoke into his phone, "Be there in fifteen minutes."

"Well, that's all the guy time we're getting tonight." Taylor sighed.

Trace pecked a kiss on her cheek, "Don't stay up, might be a long one. Texas Jack has a gang fight out at Crazy Gal's Bar and Dance Hall."

Sam stood, casually placing his hand on mine. "Perhaps we could have dinner some other time?"

A flame of desire licked through me. I rummaged through my purse and handed him one of my cards. His fingers brushed mine and warmth crackled between us.

He cut quite the figure weaving through the crowded bar, long legs and broad shoulders eating up the tight space between the tables. The heat of his hand lingered on mine. When he reached the doorway, he turned and gave me a grin and a two finger salute.

Taylor waved her hand in front of my face. "Earth to you. So what do you think?"

"Sexy, definitely sexy, but I don't know. We'll see. So is this middle school, and you and Trace are going to carry messages back and forth between Sam and me?"

"Nope. You and Sam gotta take it from here."

"I think I can manage. You already knew about the bag of heads, didn't you?"

"Yeah, I thought maybe he'd found something else. They were all Hispanic girls, killed by smugglers out on the Nation."

"Why did they kill them?"

"I'd bet the transportation didn't show, and they didn't want to leave any survivors who could give a description of them."

"But they were valuable. The smugglers lost money killing them."

Taylor's lips thinned, and her smile was grim. "There's plenty more girls where they came from, and the smugglers probably learned to set up better transportation."

"Do you think the rest of Sofia's group is hidden on the Nation?"

Taylor traced her finger around the rim of her empty martini glass. "Maybe. And maybe they're dead. You know I want to do a story on Sofia. Will you give me an exclusive?"

"Sure, but you know all I know at this point."

"Keep me in the loop on what you find out. I'll do some digging on Montoya, and I'll share with you."

"Deal. You know anything about the bar the guys went to?"

"A bit. Texas Jack reopened Crazy Gal's Bar and Dance Hall a couple of years ago. It's got a good rep with the local crowd—good music and the drinks aren't watered down—but after the working people go home, a rougher crowd moves in and fights break out. Gangbangers hang there."

"Navajo gangs?"

"Yep, Texas Jack's bouncer is a Cobra, so there's usually a few of them around."

"And that doesn't bother the owner?"

"Not as long as the bar bill is paid. The Cobras don't fight among themselves. Trouble pops up when a Dragon invades their turf."

I must have looked worried because she added, "The guys will be fine."

I was still rubbing my hand that Sam had touched. "Do you get used to having your plans interrupted?"

"Used to it, yes, happy about it, no, but I'm crazy in love with Trace, and he's a package deal. I get him and the demands of the Navajo Police."

Chapter 3

On the way to my office the next morning, I veered off to the children's shelter to see how Sofia had fared during the night. The shelter was a nondescript converted fire house unidentified by any sign in order to provide privacy to the children needing an emergency placement.

A middle-aged, avuncular woman opened the door and smiled. Ruth had run the shelter for over a decade and knew all of the social workers in Flag and Tuba City and most of the cops.

"Hi Ruth."

"Thanks for calling me before you came. So many don't and, of course, we don't answer the door if we haven't received a call to expect someone."

I joined her in the cheery hallway that led back to a dayroom surrounded by rows of tiny bedrooms. "How is Sofia?"

"She's eaten everything we offered her. Poor little mite. She's been asking for you."

"Did she sleep well?"

"No." Ruth shook her head. "She had night terrors as soon as we turned the lights low. I moved her out of the room with the other girls. She scared them." She placed her hand on my arm. "That's not unusual, and she has the resiliency of youth on her side. She'll work through this in her own way. I'll be here to help her."

Ruth opened the door to a big, airy, room full of toys, books, and a television. "Sofia, you have a visitor."

Sofia hurtled herself into my arms and snuggled her head at my waist. "I knew you come." She smiled up at me shyly, so young, still believing people would always do as they promised.

I held her back from me, staring at her in amazement. She looked so different. Her hair was clean and glossy black, held back with a red ribbon. She wore faded old jeans, but well fitted to her slim form. She pointed shyly to her Barbie T-shirt and giggled.

"You look so pretty."

She blushed and twirled around in front of me. When she turned back to face me, she pointed at her feet and wiggled her toes in a pair of pink flip flops. She cocked her head at me and said, "You stay?"

"For awhile."

She motioned me to follow her to a small table covered with pages torn from coloring books and some well-used Crayolas.

I chose a green Crayola and shaded in a tree. She talked about last night. "I had bad dreams."

"Was it better after Ruth moved you to your own room?"

She bobbed her head up and down.

"She'll take good care of you."

She shivered and ducked her head, putting a few finishing touches on her picture. She held it out to me. "You take."

I smiled and took it from her. "It's beautiful, just like you."

Ruth came out of the office and called, "Snack time."

I hugged Sofia and she wrapped her thin body around me, clinging tightly. "I have to go, but I'll come back to see you."

Her big eyes beseeched me to stay. I scribbled my personal cell on the back of my card and handed it to her. "You can call me anytime. Ruth will help you call me." She gingerly took it and gave me a timid smile and a small wave. Ruth was zeroing in on her when I stepped out of the room. Sofia called after me, "Find Juanita."

I turned and faced her. "I'll do the best I can to find her." I blew her a kiss. I worried all the way back to the office on how I was going to make it happen.

***

The tires of my old Civic crunched the gravel in the parking lot in front of the Child Protective Services building in Tuba City where we offered adult, family, and children's services as well as a case management system for people with disabilities. We were spread thin, but we were hardworking and diligent about our cases. My manager, the middle-aged and perpetually sour Bessie Benally, ruled her roost with sarcasm and demeaning criticism.

I walked into her office.

"Morning, Jordan. Got your e-mail. How is the child?" Benally snapped.

"Doing okay. She's in the shelter, and I've alerted the Children of Border Violence folks that she'll need a placement."

"Good." She cocked her head at me. "I know you'll make this case your priority and spend the appropriate time on it—even after hours." She pinned me with her most severe look. "I can't spare a caseworker to help you. You're on your own with this one. You know how shorthanded we are. And I expect frequent reports from you."

"Will do, Ms. Benally, and no problem." I respectfully backed out of her office and walked to my small cubicle while brainstorming ideas, tossing some out and making mental notes to follow up on the rest. Time was of the essence. Either Juanita was terrified and wandering the streets, or the men had recaptured her and made an object lesson of the little girl by killing her in front of the others.

I called O'Brien. He told me Sofia had not recognized Montoya from his picture, and all they got from her session with the police artist was a nondescript sketch of a guy who could be forty or sixty.

"But she said Montoya bought her from her aunt while she was standing right beside them."

"Yup, she did. But no way she recognized him or gave us a good description."

"How about the van driver? Could you get a sketch of him from her description?"

"Nah, all we got is he's a fat Hispanic guy with a mustache. A bust."

"Anything on the truck?"

"She said the vehicle was blue and had a *D* on the back of it."

"License plate or brand?"

"I don't know. She's an eleven-year-old kid. I wrung as much out of her as I could. Before you rag my ass, we're looking for Juanita."

I thanked him and hung up. Why didn't she recognize Montoya's picture? Was she too traumatized to recall him? Maria Vasquez's words about girls in the trade lying when they were caught needled me. My gut told me it didn't apply to Sofia, but my gut was not evidence.

I followed up on O'Brien's suggestion and call my aunt who lived along the smuggler's corridor running out of Mexico. Just as I reached for my phone, it rang.

"Hello, Jordan." The vibrations of Sam's deep voice rumbled in my ear. "It's Sam."

Listening to his sexy voice, my attraction level ratcheted higher. Jeez, I was in full-blown arousal from two words. "Hi Sam, how have you been?"

"Good. How about dinner at the Weatherford tomorrow night? We might even finish the meal," he quipped.

"Wonderful, I'd like that," I said.

"Good. Seven okay with you? I could pick you up a little before then."

"Umm, I'll see you then. Oh, and my apartment house is the last one out on Ponderosa Trail. The address is five one seven, but you can't miss it. The road dead-ends into the national forest at the edge of the units. My apartment is number two-seventeen."

"Until tomorrow."

I wasn't sure we fit together, but he was hot and sexy, and my sensual side had stepped right into the opportunity. Oh hell, she'd *embraced* it, clamoring for the date.

Nearly two years had passed since I had abruptly broken up with Collin, ending the affair and my dating life. Surely, enough time had passed to gain some insights to what I wanted and needed. Dr. Collin Dickens had been my history professor. He had called me into his office and asked if I would like to do undergraduate research with him in southwestern cultures. He flattered me with his attention, saying I could be pivotal to his research because I was Navajo and spoke the language, while he was just a white guy from back east. I'd thought he was genuinely interested in my help.

Our research meetings turned into picking up a bite to eat, then going to his place for a drink at the end of long days. The work was interesting, and I was good at it. I could never pinpoint when I fell in love with him, but it wasn't long until we were lovers. I was seduced by the intensity of his attention and his panache. We regularly hiked the back trails around Snowbowl and camped out one long summer weekend at the base of the mountain. How dumb could I have been? He never took me out, claiming he wanted me all to himself.

I walked into his office one sunny afternoon, and a tall, slim blond woman holding a fussy toddler was deep in conversation with him. He had the grace to pale when he saw me. He grabbed the edge of his desk as the blond turned and stuck out her manicured hand. "Hi, I'm Collin's wife, Margaret, and this is Julia." She turned the baby so I could see her sweet face. "You must be one of Collin's students."

All I heard was the howling roar of the blood rushing to my head. I stared at Collin, and he ducked his head, picking at the cracked veneer on his desk. I took her hand and said, "Yes. I'm Jordan Bia." I dropped her hand and took a step back. "I just came in to resign. I can't work on the project any longer," I said to the top of Collin's head.

Collin smoothly stepped out from behind the desk, making no eye contact with me. He slipped his arm around his wife's waist, snuggling her close, beaming at her, and made cooing noises at their baby, putting his face close to little Julia's. "No prob, Jordan. I can find someone else."

I stepped out into the hallway just as the departmental secretary was on her way to her desk from lunch. She was smug when she commented, "They are such a lovely couple. He is so excited when his wife and baby come out to visit."

I kept walking through the doorway and waved my hand over my shoulder to her as I left the history department. My face was burning with shame, guilt, and anger, so *much* anger. He called, texted, left voice mails and e-mails demanding we talk, that he could explain. I ignored them all. Explain what? He was married with a wife and small child ensconced back in Boston.

I was shaken to my core that I could be so fooled by his duplicity and miserable with guilt that I fell in love with a married man.

I'd covered this same ground of recriminations a thousand times. Collin was old history, and I mentally shoved him aside and picked up a clean pad and pen. O'Brien's talk of smugglers had me worried for my aunt and uncle's safety on their ranch where they had 30,000 acres of dry land south of Nogales bordering Mexico. The last time I was there, they were running twelve hundred head of Charolais cattle and growing row crops along the shallow wash that separated them from the border. They would have been unable to make the ranch profitable without hiring illegals, the tent pole of the American border economy.

Hard work had honed both their bodies to sinew and bone. When I was a kid, I worked, too, helping Alice feed the Mexican nationals who crossed the border to pick the melon crop before they moved on to follow the harvest all the way up north to the berry farms in Washington state. They knocked on her backdoor and stood patiently outside while she and I slathered peanut butter on thick slices of bread. They drank from the hose and sometimes slept in the barn. Aunt Alice said you couldn't convince them to return to Mexico because there was nothing behind them. And my uncle would always growl, "Americans sure as hell won't do the stoop labor."

I called her on her landline and hoped she was in the house. Cell service in the remote ranchland was spotty at best.

"Jordan, how nice to hear your voice. I hope you're coming to see me."

"I want to. I've missed you..."

"It has been a long time since you were down here. Your mom tells me you've almost finished your master's degree. Tom and I are so proud of you."

"Thank you. It's been a ton of work, and I'll be happy to be done. I hope you can help me with a human trafficking case I'm working on with Captain O'Brien in Flag. He told me he knows you and Tom."

She was quick with her response. "He and your uncle served together. You want to know what's going on down here, right?"

"Yes. I'm worried for your safety."

"There's just night and day difference down here in the last few years. I was loading the dishwasher last week after lunch when a line of armed Mexican men with backpacks trudged past the end of our drive. Four young women walked between the men. The smugglers are brazen, acting out in the open now. I used to walk all over these hills with binoculars watching birds. I wouldn't dare now. Some lone hiker or bird watcher is one pair of eyes too many to the smugglers. Tom and I are never far from a gun. He's dropping feed right now, and he's carrying a shotgun. Tom's found a couple of bodies on our land, and once he found a severed head. These are different people from the ones you used to help me make sandwiches for. These people are running a business, and they kill and dismember anyone who disobeys them to terrorize the rest of us. They trash our land, cut fences, and steal everything they can lift."

"What's the border patrol doing?"

"Nothing that helps us. The government built a border fence with concertina wire on top. The illegals just walk around the breaks in the fences."

"Can't the Border Patrol stop them at the fence breaks?"

She laughed bitterly."There are too many of them. The Border Patrol puts sensors on the ground around the fence breaks, but the illegals do banzai attacks on one place on the fence line to suck up the border patrol resources while the real smugglers are wiggling through in a different place."

"What about the Sheriff or Homeland Security?"

She snorted. "America no longer controls southern Arizona. The state of Arizona has posted signs on highway eighty-six warning motorists to abandon the route through the southern part of the state."

"What?"

"Oh, yes, Governor Brewer stood by one of those highway signs and made a video asking Washington if they had ceded southern Arizona to Mexico. It's up on YouTube. Look it up."

Her voice softened. "Honey, you remember Evelyn and Stuart Ford? They ranched just east of us?"

"Umm, I think so."

"She's moved up your way to Flag and is living with her son. You remember Weldon? He was much older than you and my boys."

I had a vague memory of a tall, gangly, redheaded teenager.

"Please go see her for me. Stuart was shot to death out on their ranch. Her border collie found his body."

"Why?"

"Stuart called the border patrol office every time he saw a smuggler or a spider hole full of food and water on the ranch. The border patrol thinks he was shot to send a message to the locals to keep their mouths shut."

"The smugglers can monitor your communications? Is that what you are saying?"

"Tom and I think so—or they have informants in the border patrol. These are highly sophisticated, technically savvy businessmen, and they're ruthless."

"Aunt Alice! You and Tom need to leave. Have you talked to Mom about coming to Flag?"

"Of course, dear. O'Brien's also urged us to leave. But our home and our land don't have any value. We can't sell out and leave. Who would come down here and choose to live like this? Our boys aren't bringing their families back home and working the ranch like we always dreamed."

"But you could leave and be safe."

"Tom's not going to leave the family land, and I'm not leaving Tom. Please, go see Evelyn for me and give her my love."

Chapter 4

It was almost noon when I finished talking to my aunt. On a whim, I called Evelyn Ford. If she could see me, I would visit her during my lunch hour. She greeted me warmly and sounded delighted at the prospect of having company. She gave me directions to her house.

Evelyn's son lived in an exclusive gated community in north Flagstaff. I suspected the gate assuaged Evelyn's fears after the violent death of her husband. I punched in the code Evelyn had given me, and the gate arm slowly swung open. I checked my mirrors to be sure no car was nestled on my bumper in hopes of slipping through the security. The winding street was lined with lovely homes. Her son's house was a red tile-roofed Mediterranean-Spanish-style stucco house on a large corner lot.

She answered the door bell as soon as it chimed. "Jordan, my you're all grown up. I'm so glad you came to visit me." She led the way down the entrance hall to the den, perched on a floral print sofa, and patted the cushion for me to join her. She hadn't changed all that much since I was a kid. Her hair was still a pale blond, and she dressed in bright colors with vivid prints and wore large, clunky jewelry. When I was very young, she reminded me of an exotic butterfly, hovering over a chair before she alighted.

She twisted her fingers in the pleats of her skirt. "Alice called me last week. I miss them so."

"They send their love, and they miss you."

Her face contorted with pain, and she plucked a Kleenex from the box on the lamp table. "She told you about Stuart, how he was murdered?"

"Yes. I'm so sorry."

She thrust her chin up."I've lost my husband and my home..."

I took her small hand in mine. "Are you afraid?"

"No. Fear diminishes in proportion to what you have left to lose," she said grimly. "Stuart claimed we were forced to live like Afghanis stuck between the Taliban and the US forces. He found a body a hundred yards from the ranch house, and within the next twelve months, he found a dozen corpses or body parts on our ranch."

Evelyn's face hardened in angry lines, her mouth set in a scowl, and her eyes were small and bright in the loose folds of skin around her eyes. "He called the border patrol every time he found a body or saw a smuggler, but they couldn't get there in time to catch them. It's that remote out there. Stuart wasn't the only rancher shot. A rancher just west of us was killed the same week Stuart was. If you cross the Mexican smugglers, you're going to die. Both of them were hounding the local authorities about what was happening on their ranches."

"And you left the ranch after Stuart died?"

She nodded. "My son insisted I come live with his family. I hung a white flag of surrender at half mast over my ranch house. I can't live there, and I can't sell it. Everything I love is gone except my son. He's all I've got left." She grabbed my hand. "Don't work this case," she pleaded. "Stay away from it. Look what happened to us. You live up on the Nation where the corridor ends, and it's just as dangerous as our ranch is down there on the border."

***

On the way back to the office, I called Aunt Alice and left a voice mail telling her I had just seen Evelyn and her friend was doing as well as I supposed she could. Poor Evelyn, her dreams for their retirement gone, time spent on her beloved ranch and her friendship with Alice truncated by murder.

My phone had been on silent while I talked to Evelyn. I had missed a call from Taylor and noticed I had a new voice mail.

When I was back in my office cubicle, I listened to the message. Taylor wanted to talk in person, teasing me that she had more to share than what she had sent in her email. She suggested that Chloe and I meet her and Mac at the trailhead behind her house for a run with the dogs after five o'clock. I texted her we would be there. As an afterthought I added that Sofia couldn't ID Montoya as the man who bought her and added a frowny face.

I opened the attachments she had sent and clicked the link to a story in the *Arizona Republic,* headed by a picture of Carolyn wearing an exquisite dress. Montoya stood proudly behind her in a tux, resting one hand proprietarily on her sequined shoulder. With short, cropped white hair and a lantern jaw thrust slightly up, he had a haughty visage and, coupled with his military posture, looked like a successful and formidable businessman, not at an ex-con involved in a dirty business. I couldn't conceive of him sloughing through the dirt and squalor of Banamichi buying kids, and he certainly wasn't doing it for the money. The diamond choker his wife sported was worth plenty.

I scanned the accompanying story in the Phoenix paper. The occasion was the re-naming of the Fine Arts building at Northern Arizona University to the Nathan and Carolyn Montoya Fine Arts Building. The Montoyas had spearheaded a fund drive for the construction of the new facility for the arts program, plowing a substantial donation of their own into the university's coffers.

Taylor's second link was juicier, the story from thirteen years ago recapping Montoya's brush with the law. A jury found him guilty of sex with a minor and running a house of prostitution, a third degree felony. He served ten years and paid a substantial fine, which evidently didn't empty his bank accounts. Montoya had been out of prison three years, and in that short time he had restyled himself as a wealthy business owner-philanthropist and married a young society woman. Quite the turnaround for him, but why would she marry Montoya?

Ever the thorough reporter, Taylor included the link to his wife's Facebook page, which had no privacy settings at all, allowing me complete access to her photos and postings. Carolyn's page was a gold mine of information I would have kept private except to my friends. I scrolled through her timeline to her earlier posts from her college years. Interspersed with photos of her sorority sisters at football games and bars, she had tagged pictures of wedding dresses, flower arrangements, and wedding cakes covered in exquisitely piped flowers, enthusiastically commenting on the ones she wanted for her future wedding. Her friends had clicked, liked, and voiced their own suggestions. Long before she even met Montoya, she had been planning her wedding.

After college and before she married, she had taught elementary school in Tucson, and there were pictures of tearful children hugging her good-bye in her colorfully decorated classroom. From the timeline, it appeared that Carolyn had taught one year before her engagement. Scrolling through the photos, I found a picture of Carolyn and Montoya with the Eiffel Tower in background. Carolyn smiled a thousand-watt smile of joy into the lens. She had tagged the photo *We eloped! So romantic. Honeymooning in Paris*. She and Montoya had returned to Flag after a fairy tale honeymoon, documented with dozens of selfies. He must have been really persuasive to get her to forego her dream wedding. What had her parents thought?

The *Arizona Daily Sun* had a feature story on Carolyn's volunteer work with children in the local schools. She had organized a reading program for children reading below grade level. She must have hit the ground running when she moved here, and I was finding it hard to dislike her. After reading the Phoenix article and her Facebook page, I regretted jumping to the conclusion that she was a pampered poodle socialite who busied herself with couture and parties. The question hammering in my head as I drove home was *what the hell was she doing with Montoya?*

When I got home and changed into my running clothes, Chloe Jane barked and ran in circles around the living room. She was so excited when I put the leash on her, I had a hard time locking the front door behind us. I opened the car door, and she hopped right into the front seat wriggling with excitement. She loved going for car rides. She swiveled her big head from her dog-spit-covered passenger window to the front windshield. I drew the line at letting her hang her head out an open window, too dangerous for her and the side mirror of a passing car. Chloe woofed and pawed the dashboard in front of her when I parked in front of Taylor's Spanish-style stucco house. When I let her out, she bounded up to the front door, but sat down expectantly like the lady she was until Taylor opened the door. Mac was on his leash and ready to run, but first they indulged in an exuberant doggie reunion.

After Chloe Jane and Mac finished sniffing their approval of each other, we set a slow warm-up pace on the trail that paralleled the ravine behind Taylor's house. We had run it many times, enjoying the change of seasons and the opportunity for uninterrupted girl talk.

"Have you heard from Sam?" Taylor asked.

"Yeah, we're having dinner."

"A little enthusiasm on your part when you talk about him would be good."

"I'm not sure he's a good fit for me."

"It's just dinner. Get to know him. Trace thinks he's a stand-up guy. Are you going to invite him in after dinner?"

I rolled my eyes. "I have to see if either of us is silently planning an escape before we finish the appetizer."

"Not going to happen." She laughed. "Attraction hummed between you two."

I ticked off the reasons I didn't think we were right for each other. "He's older and much more experienced than me, and he has that whole, you know, *when I talk it's the last word on the subject* kind of attitude."

"Ten years is a decade, not a lifetime. Stop worrying about that. And maybe he's an expert about what he was talking about. I don't get a bad vibe from him." She hesitated, and Mac took the opportunity to mark a few trees."Sam did talk to Trace, and he commented that you have a degree and most of a second one. He practically went from Window Rock High to the Marines. I think Sam may be worried his lack of a formal education might bother you."

"Uh-oh. This is sounding like middle school. Sam talks to Trace who talks to you, and you talk to me."

"No, it's not. Are you concerned about his not having a degree?"

"Nope, I worry about the other stuff."

"Don't sell yourself short. Social work gives you plenty of gritty life experiences. He's interested. Don't blow it. Put on something sexy and put your hair up. You have great high cheekbones and eyes. Use that smoky eye shadow we bought at Ulta." She puffed as we went up an incline."What are you wearing?"

"What I always wear when I go out—the short black skirt I bought when you were shopping with me and a blue silk blouse."

"And heels," she finished.

"Umm."

"Heels, definitely, men love them. No matter how high the heels are, he's still going to be taller than you."

When we had reached the turnaround on the loop trail, we sat down to let the dogs rest.

Social chatter out of the way, Taylor got down business."So, Sofia couldn't identify Montoya?"

"No, nor the van driver."

"I'm not surprised, but I don't think that lets Montoya off the hook. Sofia must have been terrified with her aunt counting the cash in the doorway as he dragged her off. Her mind could have walled off the details while she fought for survival. Did you get to read the stuff I sent about the Montoyas?"

"Yeah, did you look at her Facebook timeline? She had been planning her wedding for years before she met him."

"I saw that. Her friends were all gung-ho about it, too. Made me wonder if she married because marriage was next on the bucket list after college."

"But to Montoya? He's much older, an ex-con, and she didn't get the wedding she was dreaming about."

"She doesn't seem to be the kinda chick who would do an Internet search on a wealthy businessman holding a big diamond engagement ring. If she was a daddy's girl and still missing him, she might have been ripe for the picking."

"You were here when he came back from prison. What do you know about him?"

"When he got out of prison, he sure as hell wasn't hurting for money. He moved into one of those big houses on the ridgeline that overlooks the canyon south of town."

"Where did get the money?"

"Gossip was he had a lot of cash the government never found during the trial—but there's no evidence it's true."

"What about the whorehouse? Did he sell it?"

"He did, right before he went to prison, and to Texas Jack for a huge price. At the time, Trace thought he paid way too much for the bar, and that Jack did it to help Montoya out with his legal bills, which were huge."

"What's Jack's story?"

"I don't know that anyone knows. He just showed up in Flag a couple of years before Montoya went to prison. He was a businessman, hunting opportunities. He had already partnered with Montoya in the trucking business before he bought Montoya's bar.

"Why would Jack hire a Cobra to be a bouncer?"

"Insurance. None of the small-time gangs are going to bother Jack's place and risk a war with the Cobras. The Dragons invade Cobra turf to strut their stuff, but the barkeep, Jack, and Big Man are all armed and can usually, but not always, take care of themselves."

"Any chance Jack is running women at Crazy Gal's?"

She laughed. "I don't think Trace thinks so. We should get the guys to take us out there some evening."

"Let's see how tomorrow night goes."

We enjoyed the spectacular view of the valley and let the dogs nose around, flushing the occasional ground squirrel. "I drove by Montoya's house and his trucking business and did a little snooping," Taylor said.

"And?"

"The house is a huge log home with sweeping porticos and porches. Bet he has a spectacular view of the San Francisco Mountains from the back deck. Carolyn came out and folded herself into a sharp little black Mercedes sedan and waved to a guy pushing a lawnmower. I slunk down in my seat as she backed down the drive and slid past me. I followed her over to the seedy side of Flagstaff where she parked in front of a dilapidated elementary school that's probably fifty years old. But the kids on the playground knew her. Several little girls ran to her and wrapped their arms around her waist."

"I bet that's where she volunteers. After I read the Phoenix paper, I had her pegged as a trophy wife. Then I read the Flag paper about her volunteer work, and now I'm not so sure. I'm going to get in touch with her and show some interest in her reading program. It'll be a good way to get close to her and learn something about both of them," I said.

"Good idea. She might recognize me from TV, but I doubt she would recognize you."

"I'll work on it. What's his business like?"

"Montoya Trucking covers a full city block on the east side of Flag. It backs up to the railroad tracks, and his yard is a large-scale operation that required a lot of money to get up and running, which gets us back to wondering why he would jeopardize his legitimate business and his marriage by trafficking girls from Banamichi into the sex trade."

"The thrill? The buzz of excitement and the anticipation while he plans the trip? Maybe he fantasizes how the girls will submit to him, or he thrives on the danger of pulling it off. Think about it. He went down for sex with an underage girl. When a man gets a taste for little girls, it doesn't just go away."

Taylor got up and stretched. "Believe me, if you talk like that to Sam, there's no chance he'll think of you as a little girl with no life experiences. Let's get back before dark."

Chapter 5

I putzed around dressing for my dinner date with Sam, conflicted because my body warmed to him, but my head was in a different place. My independent life suited me just fine and I didn't want anyone's long shadow darkening my choices, but I was probably too sensitive because of my experiences with my father. Taylor had suggested that Sam had his deliberate attitude only in his field of expertise, cop work, and she might be right. I needed to watch and let the situation play out.

Then there was the complication of dating someone I had to work with, but I was getting ahead of myself. I could always pair up with Officer Nez or the new female officer, Jessica Akee. I took Taylor's advice, brushing blush on my cheek bones, sweeping on a touch of taupe eye shadow, and finishing with a swipe of mascara and a tinted brown lip gloss. I preened in front of the mirror, liking the fit of my blue shirt. I didn't look quite so much like the earnest young social worker I was.

When I opened the door to Sam, his eyes widened, giving me a niggle of pleasure.

"You look beautiful."

I murmured my thanks and stood back for him to come in. As he brushed passed me, my traitorous body fired to attention. I ogled the jeans fitted to his long frame, topped with a button-down white shirt, the top open and revealing a long smooth column of throat. His well-cut jacket in navy wool snugged his broad shoulders, and well broken-in but highly polished pointed-toed cowboy boots made him even taller. Some women were turned on by dimples, some by crooked smiles, but with me, it had always been cowboys except for my foray with the loafer-shod, professorial Collin, which had ended poorly.

Luckily Chloe Jane took center stage, taking the limelight off me while I admired Sam. She inched closer to him with her ears perked forward and her eyes alert. Sam stared back at her. She met his penetrating gaze until she submissively stretched out on the floor, her belly tight to the tile.

Sam bent down and held his hand out for her to smell. "Who is your friend?"

"Chloe Jane. She's usually a good watch dog, but not tonight."

Without lifting her head off the floor, Chloe slid her eyes my way and thumped her tail.

A big grin split his face. "Chloe Jane, thanks for your tail-thumping approval." He reached down and stroked behind both her ears. He slid one soft, floppy ear through his fingers, and she licked his hand."You didn't have her ears docked."

"I rescued her from a shelter. She'd already had a painful life, and I couldn't bring myself to dock her ears and tail, even though she can clear my coffee table with her tail."

Chloe stood at attention by his side, bumping his thigh, seeking more attention, and he readily gave it to her. "She probably smells Jasper on me. He's my border collie. You'll have to meet him someday."

He took my jacket out of my hands and helped me put it on.

He stood close behind me. I felt the heat pouring off his body and breathed in the scent of his cologne. All too soon, he slipped my jacket on and stood beside me. His face flushed with a tinge of pink. He took a small step back and opened the front door.

"Yes, you stay Chloe." I walked out the door and turned the lock, hearing a little doggy whine of discontent.

His recent-model black Ford 250 pickup was still damp from the car wash. He held the passenger door and cupped my elbow as I stepped on the running board. When he walked around to the driver's side, I realized it had been a long time since a man had held a car door for me.

He put the truck in gear and pulled out of my parking lot. He chatted easily. "I made us a reservation at the Weatherford at Charley's Pub and Grill. We could go upstairs to the Grey for a drink after dinner."

"Perfect, and it's nice enough we can drink outside on the Grey's balcony."

Our table in Charley's was tucked in a back corner by the fireplace, the roaring fire providing most of the ambient light and casting flickering shadows on the walls. Sam seated me, and the hostess handed us menus. "Your server will be with you shortly."

"I'm having the Wyatt Earp's Turf." Sam said to me when she had walked away.

"You didn't even open the menu."

He laughed. "I come here often. It's a ten ounce New York Strip. What makes it special is the bleu cheese butter. How about the artichoke heart dip and French bread for the appetizer?"

I was intent on the menu. "Hmm. Fine."

Our server joined us and took our drink orders. Sam asked for Bourbon. No more sweet tea vodka in lemonade for this girl. I was so ready. I'd researched drinks on the Internet. "A cosmo, please." I'd get my vodka fix but had swapped the lemonade for cranberry juice, a dash of Triple Sec, and fresh lime. But it was all about the name, *cosmo.*

Sam ordered the appetizer. His hands were fluid, and his mouth smiled generously when he spoke to the server.

There was a good crowd of diners in Charley's. Couples waiting for tables in the foyer chatted nosily. I closed the menu.

"You decided?" he asked.

I nodded. "The tuna." He took my menu and laid it on top of his, precisely squaring the edges of both menus with the table. He was watching me as I watched him. The air between us was thick with the expectancy, hope, and the apprehension of a date with someone you didn't know well, didn't want to screw up, and in my case, wasn't sure we were a fit. His eyes were clouded with interest, and he leaned in toward me and ran his hand through his short hair, but for the moment, he seemed as tongue-tied as me.

Rummaging through my brain for something to say, all I could come up with was, "I like coming to the Weatherford. Zane Grey wrote *Call of the Canyon* here, and a famous artist painted while he stayed here." I had turned into a tour guide.

The server brought our drinks and the appetizer.

"Thomas Moran was the painter. The guys who bought the hotel spent buckets of money and nearly twenty years finishing the historical restoration, but they did a fine job."

I spooned the dip on the plate and took some bread. My cosmo was not as sugary as sweet tea vodka, but it was going to be my new drink. We had exhausted small talk about the restaurant, and we filled the time spreading the dip on the soft bread.

His body held less tension than mine, making me think he was okay with the lingering silence, which in turn, made me more tense. I could think of nothing to say.

He ended the protracted agony by launching into a new vein of conversation. "I went house hunting this afternoon with Eric Jameson.

Trace suggested him for my realtor. His partner works with Taylor, and Eric helped Taylor find her house."

"I know them. I've met them over at Taylor's place. Did you find a house?" I couldn't see Sam in a snug cottage surrounded by hollyhocks like Taylor's casita.

"Yeah. Now I just have to wait to see if the owner accepts my offer. There aren't a lot of choices for what I want, a place outside of town with a little land so I can have a shop for my wood working. I want privacy from my neighbors. I've lived in too many crowded barracks on base. Plus, Jasper needs some room to roam." He grinned. "That's not entirely true. What he really needs is his own flock of sheep to herd, but he's not getting them. Instead, I'm getting me a horse or two."

I could see this hunk of cowboy on a horse, but the woodworking image caught me by surprise. "What do you make in the shop?"

His face lit up, and he talked animatedly. "Custom furniture. I love the scent of a plank of freshly cut wood and turning it into a one-of-kind piece of furniture that will last through generations of family."

I smiled, grateful he enjoyed talking about his woodworking, which gave me more time to study him.

"I work whenever I get the urge, and my saws make a lot of noise, so I need to have some space between me and the neighbors." He took the last sip of his bourbon. "The place has a great shop out back with electricity and water already hooked up, and it sits on a couple of acres. Plenty for horses."

"What's the house like?"

"What?" he teased. "The house is more important than the shop and a place for a corral? It's an adobe in the Territorial style with tile floors, vigas, and a nice wood-burning fireplace, but it needs a little work."

"Can you see your neighbors' houses?"

"No, the lot is dense with pine. I'm gonna like the privacy, and they're going to like not hearing my saws."

The server stopped at the table. "Would you like another drink?"

I declined, but Sam asked for a second bourbon.

"Ready to order?" she asked me.

"I'll have the seared ahi tuna."

"The Wyatt Earp's Turf, rare please." When she disappeared, he said, "We could drive by the place this evening if you like."

I nodded over my drink.

"Have you lived in your apartment long?" he asked.

"Two years. It's my first home away from my childhood home. After a few years of paying back all my school loans, I might be able to think of buying a place." As soon as I told him I had been living with my parents through college, I mentally cringed at the image I had painted.

He cleared his throat. "That's a lot of years of schooling. I admire your grit. I graduated Window Rock High. I wasn't a stellar student and joined the Marines after a less than outstanding year at the U here in Flagstaff."

I fiddled with my drink, buying time, taking a sip. Here was the conversation Taylor had warned me of. "I don't value people based on their education. My parents never finished school and have worked on the Nation all their lives, and I'm proud of them. They haven't always understood what I was doing, or even approved, but they value me even though I became someone different from them."

His smile lighted his eyes, softening his angular face. "I also come from a family of traditionalists. My dad expected me to follow him in taking care of his sheep. Instead, I saw just enough of the larger world during one year at the U to want to see more, so I joined the Marines. Eventually, I came home on my own terms."

The foundation of the carefully tended wall surrounding my heart cracked just a little, but enough to let the warrior slip through.

He squeezed my hand. "I like it here in Flag. I liked my life in Window Rock, worked with some great kids, and I got some years under my belt with the tribal police. But my life in Flag has just taken a turn for the better."

I interlaced my fingers with his and sat gazing into his eyes, having narrowed my world to the breath hanging between us. His overpowering male presence held all my attention. My rational self hoisted a warning flag, but I ignored it.

The server broke the silence, asking if we needed anything.

Sam shook his head.

We unclasped our hands, and I picked up my glass. "Did you make your own furniture?"

"Yeah, all of it. At first, I sold to friends and then friends of friends, and then I got lucky. Michael Phelps, who owns that gallery on Leroux, is selling my work now."

Our entrees arrived. I enjoyed watching him. His incongruous, angular warrior face bracketed by romantic eyes and a full bottom lip, a perfect *V* notch in the top lip. I bet this guy could thoroughly kiss a woman.

"I'm sorry Trace and I left in such a rush the other night." His words pushed me back to the surface of reality where we talked to each other about our jobs, backgrounds, and interests so we could gather data on each other to mull over later and decide if we wanted to continue to see each other. Beneath the chitchat and first date scrutinizing ran a sexual undercurrent as tense as a high-wire walk above a sea of lust, leaving me to ponder the question—*Will this work*?

"No problem." I hoped my voice was normal. "What happened out at Texas Jack's?" The question was open-ended enough he would have to talk for a awhile, and I could slip back into watching his lips move, his eyes light, and him unconsciously smooth his hair with his long, deft fingers.

He became animated as he talked. "The Dragons showed up. Crazy Gal's is a Cobra-protected joint. Jack's a savvy businessman. He hired Big Man, a Navajo gang member, as the bouncer and he, the barkeep, and Jack all live out on the bar property. Jack's sorta a lone wolf except when the Dragons make a move on his bar. You know about the gangs?"

"Yeah, the grant I wrote for a gang intervention program for second through fourth graders just got funded. The elementary school counselor and I are working furiously to get the curriculum written."

His face hardened. "Gang membership is sweeping aside the Navajo way. That age group you're targeting is about the age the gangs take them in as peewees. Tell me about your grant."

"It wasn't too hard to write because I didn't have to invent the wheel. California has a program in their elementary schools called GAP, the gang alternatives program, and the Phoenix schools have the GIC, the gang intervention curriculum. We're all trying to do the same thing—develop a holistic program that combines social skills training, problem solving, and moral reasoning skills. I'll set it up using the CPS guidelines for case management, and we'll get their families involved. What I've learned is what doesn't work—adult-led lectures like the DARE program."

Sam had hung his jacket on the back of his chair, and when he rested his elbows on the table and leaned forward, his shirt tightened across his chest, teasing me with a glimpse of bare skin between the buttons. His cotton shirt tightened, relaxed, and tightened again as he shifted his weight on his arms, tantalizing me as he listened. "We're losing our traditional culture. The old ones passed our ways down for generations, but now we have Internet and cell phones. We're going to have to decide if keeping the old ways is important or not, and we're going to have to stop sending our kids away to boarding schools."

"I know that's a problem. Nearly fifty percent of the people on the Nation are under twenty-one, and a lot of them went away to boarding school, courtesy of the federal government, so they weren't raised on the Nation with their families."

"Providing a sense of community," he added. He gently slapped his palm on the table. His eyes were alight, and fine lines crinkled around his eyes and mouth. "One problem is there aren't enough jobs on the Nation." He leaned back in his chair. "I started a youth work program with the council in Window Rock for teens to get them part-time work with anyone who had a job for them. Even better, the elders agreed to meet with the teens to teach them the Navajo ways."

His passion for his work captured my interest, and the edges of the tough image I had of him softened. "Did it work?"

"You bet. The best social program is a job."

"Are you starting the program here?"

"Already working on it in my spare time." He smiled. "Maybe you can help me out if I have to apply for a grant. I don't want to do the writing."

I agreed.

He laughed and thanked me. "How's that little girl you found?"

"She's in the shelter and doing okay. I don't think it makes Montoya innocent that Sofia can't identify him, and Taylor doesn't either. We've been snooping around gathering info on Montoya and his wife."

"Find anything interesting?"

"Montoya married a much younger elementary school teacher who volunteers in schools."

"Doesn't sound like any woman Montoya would marry unless she came with a pot full of money."

I jerked back my head in surprise. Uh-oh. I'd missed that. "I'll find out."

"More snooping by you?" he teased.

"Um, yeah. I'm like a terrier with a sock monkey when it comes to working my cases." I cocked my head and looked at him. "You seem pretty happy working as cop."

He sipped the last of his bourbon and nodded."Yep, I am what I am, and I'm good with it." He fiddled, taking his time cutting a wedge from his steak, then carefully placed the knife and fork across the plate. "Something else. What you see is what you get with me. No games, no pretense. I've never been a dreamer. I'm an action guy, and I do what I think needs doing."

Did he mean professionally or personally? Or both?

I put my hand on his forearm. Heat seeped through his cotton shirt into my palm. "Sounds fine to me."

He threw back his head and laughed. "Good. You've looked hard enough. I have, too. I want to see you again, and I don't mean professionally."

Our server had been hovering, anxious to serve dessert or give us the check and turn the table. She zoomed in. "Would you care for dessert this evening?"

Sam arched an eyebrow at me.

"Not for me, thank you."

"I'll take the check when you're ready," he said to our server.

She had the check ready and tucked it beside Sam's plate.

"Still want to have a drink?" he asked.

"Definitely."

We headed for the stairs by the hotel desk that led up to the Grey. His hand stayed protectively in the small of my back as we climbed the two flights of stairs. My senses were hyper alert to his presence, the warm pressure of his hand, the smell of his cologne, the brush of his jacket across my arm, the soft thud of his boots on the stairs. The nearness of him towering behind me was intoxicating.

We found a small table in a shadowed corner of the balcony that overlooked the square and the lighted shops on Leroux Street.

He ordered a Cognac and I opted for decaf coffee.

When the server put the coffee in front of me, I threw up one hand a bit chagrined. "I'm a one drink woman."

"No problem with that."

We were sitting so close our knees touched under the tiny table. "I've had a great time. You're a beautiful woman, easy to talk to, and you certainly gave me a lot of time to talk tonight." He brought my hand up to his mouth and kissed it.

Shivers shot through me. I was acutely aware of his knee pressed against mine under the small table and my hand under his. As soon as I blurted out, "I was worried that you would think I was too young and inexperienced," I wished I could snatch it back. But it was true, and I wanted to hear his answer.

"I don't think that," he said shortly. "I don't have nearly the education you have, and I worried that would bother you." His gaze pierced me.

"It doesn't."

He slipped his arm around my shoulders and hugged me closer to him. Up close, his eyes were nearly black and his skin was burnished bronze. His breath warmed my cheek as he ducked his head, and his mouth hovered over mine. When he kissed me, old desires flamed, and buried needs roared to life with the sweetness of his kiss.

He pulled his head back. “Let’s get out of here,” he growled. “I’ll show you the house I’m buying.”

He grabbed my hand, and we walked out to his truck. When he opened the door for me, I slid in, realizing I was no longer dissecting his every word and movement for meaning. Our two planes of interacting and talking had intersected with our mutual interest in each other.

We drove to a graveled road off the highway, and when we rounded a bend, a rosy-beige adobe house with a big front porch sat in a clearing. A pole light lit the entire area. A shop angled back behind the house inside a large fenced yard.

He put the truck in park and searched my face. “What do you think?”

“I like it. What’s it like inside?”

“Two bedrooms and two baths with an office. The kitchen and baths have been remodeled, but it all needs painting, and my God, the carpet is nasty. I’ll pull it and put in hardwoods.”

“Why is the owner selling?”

“Same question I asked Eric. The guy lost his wife last year and has some health problems so he’s moving closer to his kids.” He waved his arm at the open pasture. “Jasper’s going to love all this open space. See that flat area over there? That’s where I’ll build the horse corral.”

A deer edged out from the trees. She lifted her head at the sound of the engine idling and bolted back into the safety of the dark forest.

“It’s going to be mine by the end of the week.” He put the truck in gear and we U-turned in the drive back to the county road.

When he parked in front of my apartment house, he got out and held the car door for me. As we neared the door, Chloe Jane alerted with a single, low woof.

Sam slipped his arm around my shoulders. “I’ll give you a call tomorrow. With me, that’s not a throwaway remark.” He moved closer, enough for me to feel his heat washing over me. He turned my face up to him with his forefinger, and when his lips covered my mouth, I parted mine for him to explore and take. I put my arms around his neck, ruffling his hair. I could have stood there forever, held in his arms, kissed by an expert. I could feel his arousal. What would he be like in bed? Certainly not hesitant.

“Do you know how hard it’s been all night to keep from doing that? I’ve thought of nothing but kissing you.” He rested his forehead on my mine, and the only sound was our soft breathing. He pressed his warm lips to mine again.

At last, he took my keys that were dangling from my hand and unlocked the front door. He stepped down into the darkness calling, “Goodnight, I’ll be thinking of you.”

Chapter 6

While dressing for work the next morning, I replayed tidbits of my evening with Sam, remembering his touch and his smile and kisses. I had awoken from a dream in the deep of the night, confused and longing, thinking I had felt Sam's weight on the mattress and the heat of his body curling around me, only to be disappointed at his absence. Last night had softened my first impression. Any man who started up social programs to help kids get jobs couldn't be as rigid as I had hastily branded him after our first meeting.

Chloe lay on the bathroom floor, patiently listening to me talk about him. I stepped over her to get my hair dryer from the bottom cabinet. When I bent over to dry my hair, my phone rang. I dropped the blow dryer and fumbled, reaching for my phone. "Hello?"

"O'Brien here. You at work?"

"Not quite. What's up?"

"Sofia is over at St. Vincent's. She was attacked last night in the shelter—"

"How is she?" I blurted.

"Terrified. A guy was holding a knife at her throat when one of the other girls woke up and started screaming. He jumped through a window."

"Did he cut her?"

"He nicked the side of her neck. She bled like a stuck pig, but it was a shallow cut. She's gonna have a scar, but she'll be fine."

"I want to see her."

"I knew you would. I'm giving you the chance to get over there before she's released from the hospital this afternoon and disappears into a safe house. I need this kid to be safe and able to testify when we bring Montoya to trial."

"I'm on my way to St. V's. And O'Brien, don't you mean *if* you bring Montoya to trial?"

"Yeah, whatever."

"Did you find out anything about the guy Sofia called the fat man?"

"Whadda you think I am? A magician?"

I hung up without answering and was out the door and on the way to the hospital in less than ten minutes. Sofia was the target of a guy who, if he couldn't sell her, would murder her to shut her up and save his own skin.

A uniformed cop loitered in the entryway of the hospital, and a second cop was in the waiting room on the fourth floor where Sofia was. A third was sitting in a chair outside her door watching the corridor. O'Brien had done a good job of providing protection. I flipped open my ID and at the same time I said, "Jordan Bia. O'Brien cleared it."

When the officer guarding Sofia's door nodded, I pushed open her door.

A thick white bandage was taped to her neck. Tears oozed out of her eyes, and she thrust out her skinny arm and grabbed my hand.

I brushed a kiss across her wan cheek. "How are you doing?"

"Scared," she whimpered. She jerked away from me as though her skin was on fire. "You say I be safe," she accused.

She was a forlorn waif, curled up in the bed. Her accusation broke my heart. I had promised too much, and she had paid in terror and pain. When I reached out to touch her again, she scuttled to the far side of the bed. I dragged the straight chair around to the side she huddled on and faced her. "I'm sorry you're scared. I didn't lie to you. I thought, we all thought, you would be safe in the shelter. When you leave the hospital, you're going to a secret place where some good people will take care of you. Even I won't know where you will be."

She rolled over, turned her head away from me, and stared out the window.

I walked around the bed and straight into her line of sight. "Sofia, listen to me. The man who bought you is still out there." I pointed out the window. "The only way you're safe from Montoya and the van driver is to be hidden so far away that even I can't find you."

"Wanna go home," she said.

Her cry to go home to a wretched village in Mexico, to an aunt who sold her into slavery, killed me. "You deserve better than that. Immigration isn't going to send you home to your aunt. You'll get to stay in America."

At least she didn't turn her head away from me, and she was still engaged. The abused kids turned silent because they had learned their cries remain unanswered.

My Spanish was stretched to the limit and peppered with Spanglish, but I sensed she got the gist of what I said and struggled on. "Sofia, here's how the world works. You got sucker punched, and you can cry about it, but if you do, you give people the chance to kick you like a tin can down a dirt road. So stand up and make your life like you want. You've been offered a new start in America, and I expect you to pick yourself up and kick some ass."

Her eyes rounded in surprise, and her little face scrunched up as she mulled this over silently.

A uniformed cop knocked softly and stuck his head in the door, interrupting us. "She's being moved right now."

I squeezed her hand, hoping to give her the courage she was going to need. I turned to leave and heard her whispery voice. "I kick ass." Her fisted right hand was thrust high, her hospital gown slipping off her thin shoulders.

When I left her, I felt like an unqualified Dr. Phil and hoped I had done her no harm. Certainly, the child was in a world of hurt, but the opportunity to live in America was one I wanted her to seize and run with. My grandmother used to rail at me to get up and out of any pity party and make something of myself, and I had just passed her wisdom along to Sofia.

I doubted I would ever see her again. I released her to the universe with a murmured prayer for her safety and peace. She was the nexus between Montoya, his accomplice, and their contemptible commerce. I would pull the web closely around them.

A casually dressed Hispanic man in jeans and a T-shirt sat it the waiting room on Sofia's floor. He glanced over his newspaper, nodded, and smiled at me as I passed him. After the elevator arrived and I stepped in, he folded his newspaper, thrust it under his arm, and walked quickly to the stairs. When I stepped out of the elevator into the lobby, the same man exited the stairwell. He turned left to a side exit as I walked straight out the front door heading for my Civic that was parked in the middle of the lot.

Wishing I had thought to ask O'Brien the details of the search for Juanita preoccupied me on the drive to work. My office was on the northern outskirts of town in a deserted strip mall that a developer had dropped a ton a cash on and abandoned before completing. Few businesses were around but a garage and a lumber yard. Traffic was light, and I distractedly came up too fast on an intersection. I braked hard when the traffic light flashed red. A black SUV stopped suddenly behind me, barely missing my bumper. I puffed a sigh of relief because his vehicle was so high profile, his bumper would have slammed through my small trunk into my backseat.

The SUV followed at a decent distance when I turned right. Only one heavily loaded lumber truck passed us. Two blocks farther up, I made a left turn onto the narrow street that fronted the strip mall. The SUV hugged my bumper. Suspicious, I turned into the office parking lot and swung parallel to the street. The SUV continued past me, and I caught a clear profile of the driver; he was the man who dashed down the hospital stairs and exited when I did. My sweat-slickened hands clenched the steering wheel when I pulled out behind him, following him more to let him know I was there, than to find out where he was headed. I knew was no expert at trailing anyone. He turned back on the main street toward downtown Flag. I headed for my office.

Moisture beaded in my hair, dripping down onto my white shirt. I had been too wrapped up with Sofia to pay attention to what was going on around me, which I doubted was a safe choice.

***

I dumped my briefcase on the single chair in my office and called O'Brien to report the SUV to him. His concern was touching, but he pointed out that without a license plate or identification of the driver, he couldn't do much. He made the usual noises about being careful, alert to my surroundings, and if I saw anything suspicious to call him, but to my relief, he also didn't think it was a coincidence I had picked up a tail right outside Sofia's room.

"The smugglers aren't stupid. They have snitches everywhere. Of course they know we got Sofia and she's in the hospital. They know everything that's happening between here and Nogales before I do. You're the only person to visit her who's not a cop in uniform, so they followed you and figured out you're a case worker. They aren't interested in you. You don't know anything that will make them money or keep them from making money and that keeps you safe. Sofia is in transit right now, and I can promise you my people will be careful there is no tail on them."

My stomach was still doing little flips. I hoped he was right about my safety. "Anything on the rest of the girls?"

"No, and that's not good. Juanita's been missing for over forty-eight hours, and you know the chances of finding her alive are close to nil. We may not even find her body. There's a lot of empty land out there."

He sounded as frustrated as me. No Juanita. No ID of the van driver or Montoya. Only an eleven-year-old girl's word. But someone thought she was important enough to kill.

When I hung up the phone, I wished my apartment house had gated access and I had a better, faster car. *Work with what you have, do your best with what you have*, I could hear my grandmother lecturing. To her words, I added *watch my own back*.

I pulled out a clean, lined pad and went to work, making a list of people connected to Sofia and Juanita, their backgrounds, and any tenuous links between them. Then I made a list of what I needed to know. I circled and doodled around the question *Was Carolyn Montoya from a rich family?*

When my antiquated, slow, state-issued machine finally connected to the Internet, I typed her married name into the Google search engine and trolled for an article announcing her marriage. The paper in Tucson was the first hit. Her maiden name was Holgersson, and her parents' first names were Lena and Clarence. That would make my research easier. Theirs couldn't be a common name. I hit pay dirt with my first search—Clarence Holgersson was the CEO of United Technologies Missile Systems with 15,000 employees in Central Arizona and over 100,000 employees worldwide in 180 countries. Further research turned up the Holgerssons owned a second home in Aspen. Then I found the obituary. Her parents had died in a private Cessna along with the pilot when he overshot the snowy runway at Aspen/Pitkin airport. Carolyn had just graduated from college. She was their only child.

Sam's gut instinct was right. Montoya had married into money, lots and lots of money. I had a niggle of fear about Carolyn's welfare.

I called the tribal office in Tuba City to tell Sam he had guessed right. Officer Jessica Akee answered on the first ring.

"Officer Tohee is working a case. He might be gone some time. Would you like to leave a message?"

I gave her my name and cell number.

"Will he know what this is about?"

"Tell him it is about a child who is a case of mine. I'm with Navajo CPS. Thank you."

"Sure. Will do."

I owed Taylor the same information.

"Hi, got a minute?" I asked when she answered.

"A few. Louis and I are on the way to the robbery over at the 7-Eleven in Tuba City."

"That may be where Sam is. You know about Sofia's attack?"

"Yeah, heard it on the scanner. Her story leads tonight."

"Off the record, she has been moved to a safe house. She's all we have, no other evidence linking Montoya but her word."

"This investigation is going nowhere without corroboration."

"Agreed, but I did find out that Carolyn's father was a wealthy CEO."

"Fan-frickin-tastic," she hooted. "Wait a minute—was?"

I told Taylor about the plane crash. "She was twenty-two, wealthy, and alone—for less than a year. Can you meet for a quick drink late today, say at the Irish Pub, and scheme with me?"

"Only if you're going to tell me everything about your date with Sam," she said.

\Chapter 7

Taylor waved at me from a booth in the back of the Irish Pub on Leroux Street. Two frosty mugs of dark ale were sweating in front of her. She pushed one across the table over to me. "Here's one of the microbrews we liked the last time we came here. So dish it up. What about Sam?"

An explosion of hops with an undercurrent of fruit kept me from answering immediately. "Umm, love this beer. We're not going to talk about business first?" I feigned surprise.

She smiled over the rim of her mug. "Later. Start dishing about the date."

I finger painted in the condensation on my mug. "There's a lot of physical attraction between us."

"And?" she prompted.

"We had a romantic dinner, and we didn't have sex on the first date."

"Downer," she teased. "How are you doing with dating again? You've been in a self-imposed drought of male companionship for what is it now, two years?"

"Yeah, about."

"So, it's got to have been exciting." She paused and cocked her head at me. "You're not comparing him to that jerk, Collin, are you?"

"No, but dating again reminds I have had dreadful taste in men." I fiddled with the damp cocktail napkin under my beer. "I did love Collin."

"I know that. That's why the bastard hurt you so badly. But Sam isn't like Collin, and you won't have to steal around to see him."

"Ouch. That hurt."

"Sorry, but it's true. You may have forgotten what it's like to go out and be seen with the guy you're with and be able to talk openly about him."

Discomfort crept over me.

"Forget Collin." She waved her hand. "Don't measure Sam or you by that experience. Note I'm not even calling what you had with Collin a relationship. So what's next?"

"Right now Sam's still working. He's going to get in touch when he's free."

"Yeah, I saw him working the robbery at the 7-Eleven." She shook her head in disgust. "I viewed the footage from the surveillance camera. Stupid kid looked right into the camera. At first I thought it was an accident until the idiot smiled and threw a gang sign at the camera."

"Were they Navajo?"

She nodded.

"There're so many of them now, the Bloods and Crips that spread from LA and Phoenix to here, and now they've made up new gangs."

"It was the Cobras who robbed the 7-Eleven in Dragon territory, so there will be retaliation. Sam and Trace are going to be busy."

"Me, too. I bought a ticket to a tea Carolyn's holding at her house to benefit her reading program."

"Are you going to tell her the hubby may be in the sex slave trade?"

"Hardly. I'm going to get to know her, suggest we have coffee together, and tell her I might be able to help her recruit volunteers... You know, work the opportunity."

"How?"

"I know women who volunteer as court-appointed advocates for children, and they'd be great volunteers in the schools."

"Uh-huh. What do you really want to do?"

"If she is as innocent and naive as I think she is, at some point I'm going to tell her that her husband is suspected of human trafficking."

Taylor was adroit. "She ain't gonna take that well."

We finished our beers, and I headed home hoping to hear from Sam.

***

Sam called that evening after I had showered and gone to bed.

"Is this too late for you?"

If I could have put my palm flat on his chest, I would have felt the vibrations from the deep timbre of his voice. "No, it's good to hear from you."

"I'm sorry to call you so late, and sorrier I only have a few minutes. The Dragons are raising hell. They did a drive-by in Cobra territory, shot up a vacant building, and sprayed graffiti all over the buildings on the north side of Cobra territory."

"Are they done?"

"Probably not." His voice became softer. "Let's have dinner tomorrow night around seven. You choose the place."

"Is the 1899 Bar and Grill good with you?"

"Sure. I'll pick you up."

"No, I'll meet you. You'll be busy at work."

"I like picking you up. And, Jordan, when a man is interested in a woman, no amount of busyness can keep him away. Good night."

I couldn't resist him, but I wasn't trying very hard. I was rolling with the flow, getting sucked into the promise of satisfying my needs, and besides, the tinny sounds of alarm bells were getting softer and softer as I got to know him.

***

Carolyn's tea was this morning and I was a tad uneasy about getting the look right, and worse, I didn't have the benefit of a mom who could offer advice.

I wore my navy dress that belted low around my hips, draped a scarf around my neck, and paired the look with strappy black sandals I remembered as being painful to walk in. No Indian jewelry today, just my watch and a pair of fake gold hoops in my ears. I pulled my hair back and tied it at the nape of my neck, pulling out a few tendrils to feather around my face.

The only parking was a block down the street from her house. My feet hurt before I got up the front steps where the door stood open and the sound of women's voices drifted out. Near the threshold, a guy bulked up like a body builder, dressed in black slacks and a black polo shirt stretching tight over his pecs and biceps, stood watch just inside the door by a Regency table with a guest book on it. I smiled and nodded in his direction and signed my name in the guest register by a crystal bowl filled with sweet-smelling potpourri. When I passed by the man in black, I tried to walk without limping in my sandals.

The foyer opened into a large living room with hardwood floors and beautiful Persian rugs. The back wall was all glass, the distant mountains a backdrop to an equally stunning garden. Cut flowers expertly arranged in crystal vases scented the room. Having no background in art, I assumed the paintings were all originals. I mingled with a group of women who were animatedly talking about a painting of the Dover cliffs and followed them when they headed down a hallway to the guest bedrooms. All the rooms were airy and furnished with what one woman called "warm Italian antiques." Another security guard stood with his hands clasped before him in the hallway.

The women chattered about the antiques and art and then circled back to the great room where they headed for the wing with the master bedroom. I spied Carolyn in the garden talking animatedly to a group of women. She bent down, plucked a flower, and held it out to them. They leaned in close to see it while she chatted. Another security guy stood protectively at her back, but far enough away to be unthreatening."My mom loved gardening, and I started helping her when I was a child. When I was in middle school, she gave me my own plot to grow whatever I wanted. Our gardener was so helpful."

My mom had struggled to grow vegetables in the sand around our home in the government housing community on the Nation. She eventually let it die, hauling water out to the struggling patch just one more hard task for her after a long day of work. I wasn't envious of Carolyn; I respected my own world and ways, but since I didn't mingle often with women out of my class, I sometimes lost sight of how differently children were brought up.

"Have you built other large gardens besides this one?" a tall blond woman asked Carolyn. "I'm Mallory, by the way."

"Oh, this is my first. I lived with my parents until shortly before I met Nathan."

Mallory jerked her head back in surprise.

I'd lived at home to save money, but Carolyn? Why had she lived at home while in college? Was that a reflection of her hesitancy to step into the world alone, or did she live with helicopter parents who couldn't let her go and risk her faltering?

Mallory followed up with another question. "And how did you and Nathan meet?"

Carolyn's face flushed. "Oh, we met at my parents' funeral. He was so kind. He said he and Dad had done some business together. He was just devastated about the death of my parents. He was so good to me in the weeks that followed, and then he asked me dinner, and the rest, as they say, is history." She laughed. "We were just fated to be together. He swept me away to Paris for our honeymoon."

Carolyn returned to yakking with the women about dividing rhizomes in her day lily garden and feeding a special blend of rose food to her hybrid roses. The women were engaged with her, attracted to her earnest, open face, and responding to her. Carolyn was not playing the part of the lady of manor lecturing her guests, but had come alive sharing with them, and they genuinely appeared to like her. The more I heard, the more I believed it was highly possible this naïve woman, eagerly trying to please her audience, had been targeted and had no idea what her husband might be up to. I didn't believe her dad, the CEO of a global company, had any business with Nathan Montoya.

As the first group moved on, I loitered behind them and spoke to her. “Hello I’m Jordan Bia. I don’t know anything about gardening, but I know this one is beautiful.”

“I love sharing it with others.”

“I read about your volunteer work in the schools.”

She beamed. “Have you worked with children?”

“Yes, I’m a social worker. I heard you say you lived at home when you went to college. I did, too. Where did you go to school?”

“University of Arizona. I loved staying at home,” she gushed. “It was always the three of us. No brothers and sisters. My Dad was so good at taking care of Mom and me.”

“I lived at home, too.”

“Where did you go to school?”

“Here in Flag. I’m still going to school.” I laughed, hoping she wouldn’t see a student as a threat. “Working on my master’s in social work.”

“Oh, how exciting. I just loved my time at UA.”

“I know some court-appointed advocates for children, and I think they would enjoy volunteering in your reading program.”

“Wonderful. Let’s meet and talk about it,” she said spontaneously.

“For coffee?”

“Sure. You call me, anytime. It’ll give me something to do,” she said wistfully.

I handed her one of my cards and jotted her number on the back of another one for me.

She turned away to speak to another group of women coming out of the house. I walked through her garden that had been divided into a cutting garden, a scent garden, and a small alpine garden of stunted, twisted trees. I nursed the nagging feeling she must feel isolated and had difficulty filling her time.

When I left the house, the man at the bottom of the porch stairs was speaking quietly and fingering his ear piece. He nodded respectfully when I passed him on the walkway.

I pulled out of the Montoya’s street and headed through Flag’s business district toward my office. Montoya had pulled out all the stops hiring a security team to keep his wife and possessions safe. The house had an elaborate security camera system. The front door, back garden and house had all been covered by small inconspicuous cameras. Until one tilted on its base to follow the motion of a guest moving through the room, I thought they were motion detectors connected to an alarm system. He could have been watching the guests from his computer in his office. I tagged him as assertive, perhaps subtly aggressive, for not using the small pinhole cameras that people couldn't see. Montoya wanted people to know they were watched. I grew uneasy thinking Montoya might manage access to his wealthy wife and monitor her guests. And it would be easy for him to have found out I investigated child abuse cases.

Before I left work, I put together the list of CASA volunteers I had promised Carolyn. I tucked it in my bag. I would use the list as another way of earning her trust.

Chapter 8

Sam called me as I drove home from work. "Are you the spontaneous kind of woman who can stand a change of plans?" he asked with a hint of humor in his voice.

"Sure. What are we going to do?"

"Wouldn't be a surprise if I told you. Just dress casually and be hungry."

He murmured to someone else, "No problem. I'm ready to go." To me, he said, "Sorry about that. Pick you up at the same time tonight. See you soon."

He hung up, and I parked at my place thinking I liked a guy with a sense of adventure and a hint of mystery. Jeans, boots, and a jacket would be perfect tonight.

When I opened the door to him, delight lighted his eyes. He swooped in and kissed me on the lips. "We're going to have fun."

"Where are we going?"

"Come on." He urged me to the door.

Chloe whined her unhappiness at the lack of attention from him. "I didn't forget you, girl," he told her. He pulled a rawhide bone out of his pocket. He wiggled it at me. "Can she have it?" Chloe was going nuts, pawing his leg, begging, and whimpering.

"Yeah, and now she's your friend for life."

Chloe jerked it out of his hand and ran into the small living room. She plopped down, sighing with happiness as she licked the beef broth from it.

When we got into his truck, I smelled food. "You already have the food. Where are we having dinner?"

"We're having a gourmet picnic in my new house."

"You got the house this fast? You couldn't have closed yet."

"Nope, but the old owner's moved out, and Eric gave me a key after I signed away my life today at the bank. When the bank finishes my wallet biopsy, I'm a first-time home owner." He grinned. "I've lived on base and in god-awful off-base housing, but now I'm almost a homeowner, and we're celebrating." He pulled up the drive to his new house and shoved the truck in park.

He carried two heavy bags to the door, handed me the key, and I turned the lock. When I walked into the foyer, the living room fireplace was blazing, and a blanket and two flat chair cushions were before the fire. A bottle of wine chilled in a tall bucket, and a large hammered aluminum vase of loose white daisies and pink freesias sat in the middle of the blanket.

"Oh..." I twirled around to him. "It's beautiful."

He put the bags down on the floor, stepped in front of me, and skimmed his hands down my arms. "You bring out the best in me."

The air between us crackled like desert lightning shooting white-hot fingers across the canyons before a torrent of rain erupted. I took his hands and laced my fingers between his, closing the distance between us until our heat mingled. His full lips slightly parted, and he took my mouth eagerly.

"In that kiss was the beginning of your tender yielding," he murmured. He rested his cheek on mine. "We won't drift apart. You feel it, too."

I wanted to believe him. All my life I had longed for the one person who would be all to me—lover, friend, supporter, and on whom I would lavish all that I had to give.

He grinned. "We're talking about loving, not buying a car. You don't have to over-think it."

If I didn't take this chance, I would kick myself every night before bed. "I think we're going to make some incredible memories."

"You bet we are—beginning with our picnic."

I followed him to the impromptu dining spot in front of the fireplace.

Sam unpacked the food."Baby greens, roast chicken, and pine nut salad, a fresh baguette, and a bowl of fresh strawberries and blueberries. And the best for last," he said with flourish. "Chocolate cake. Wine for you?" He popped the top on the bottle of Prosecco and poured two glasses. He held his up. "To new beginnings."

I touched his glass. "To new beginnings."

He reached over and cupped my chin. "With me, there will be many more new beginnings. My life is better with you in it," he whispered.

I smiled. "And mine."

His eyes widened. He lifted his wine and motioned me to pick up mine. "To us and the songs our hearts will sing." We toasted, and he kissed me gently.

I was flushed with delight at his attention. He finished unpacking the cake, and I passed him a plate. "You didn't make all this food, did you?"

When he laughed out loud, the sound filled my heart. "No, not my skill set. Now, if you need furniture made or a horse broken, or even a little cop work done..."

"Or a woman romanced," I added.

He grinned, pleased with himself. "Only with you."

He plated the salad, and I cut the baguette. "As soon as Taylor bought her house, she wanted to change a dozen things."

"I'm no different. I came back over here from signing the papers and walked through the house, scribbling a list of things I want to do besides get rid of this cat urine-stained carpet and lay hardwoods. New interior doors, a big deck in the back—oh, lots of things to keep me busy for years."

"What about the shop? Anything to change there?"

"No. Once I move in my tools, I'm ready to work. I 'm going to start replacing the floors before I move in."

"Show me what you plan to do."

He pulled me up, and we walked into the kitchen, his hand at the small of my back. "I'm not crazy about the white cabinets. I'd rather see the wood's grain, but I'm not going to strip and stain them. I'm just going to buy a fridge and a washer and dryer." We walked down the hall to the bedrooms. "I'll turn the guest room into an office and put a fold-out sofa there." He pointed to a long wall with no window.

The master bedroom was airy with tall ceilings and a row of clerestory windows letting in slivers of moonlight. "Oh, the fireplace is two-sided. I didn't see that from the living room. Lovely."

"Your room at home have a fireplace?"

"No." I laughed. "My grandmother's hogan had a wood stove."

The ensuite bath had a large walk-in tiled shower behind glass doors.

"Big enough for two." He held the shower door open and wiggled his eyebrows.

"Raincheck. Let's finish eating before you show me the shop. I bet that tour takes you awhile."

We headed back to the living room. Embers popped and crackled when he threw a log on the fireplace.

"So, I've talked your ear off. Tell me what you did today," he said. He tilted his head and squinted. "You're worrying about something."

I picked a lint pill on the blanket. "Sofia's been moved to a safe house. I got to see her at the hospital before they moved her."

"I heard she was attacked. You're worried about how she is going to handle all that's happened to her."

"Yes." I sighed."I don't care how much psychotherapy and love Sofia gets, dead parents and an aunt who sells you into sex slavery are going to keep coming back to bite her in the rear for a long time."

"Depends on how she chooses to deal with it." He stretched his long legs out. "Life dumped hard on the kid, but it's her job to pull herself out."

He sat down his plate of half-eaten cake and cupped his wine glass with both hands. "I don't believe life ever wipes out all of your options until you're dead."

"She's going to need a strong role model, and I won't get to be that for her."

"Someone else will provide that for her. You saved her from the streets and got her into child protective services. The kid gets to live in America, and she has to own up and run with the opportunity. She can do it." He encouraged me to believe him. "She's going to have good people around her."

"You're right. The other thing I did today was attend a charity tea."

He raised his eyebrows. "Any fun?"

"I was working. Carolyn Montoya opened her home and garden for a donation to her reading program. I managed to finagle a few moments alone with her. I think she's lonely."

He lay on his side, propping his head up on his elbow, and sipped his wine. "You know something you're pretty pleased about."

"She's the daughter of the former United Technologies Missile Systems exec, Clarence Holgersson."

His eyes widened and he made a come-on gesture.

"You were right about Montoya. He married into money. Oodles and gobs of it, and she is the single heir to the Holgersson fortune."

He stared into the fire, stroking his hand through my hair. "If you meet her again, be careful. He probably keeps close tabs on his investment in her—she's both a financial and a social asset."

"He turned up at her parents' funeral claiming he and her dad knew each other from business. I don't believe that."

He mulled my statement over. “I don’t see how their interests could have crossed, but I do think Montoya is capable of worming his way into a fortune.”

“You should have seen the security at the house. There were security men and cameras covering the whole place. Don’t you think that’s security overkill for a guy who owns a trucking business in Flagstaff? Especially cameras covering the grounds?”

“Not if he’s worried about what’s coming.”

“Hmmm. Human trafficking could earn you some enemies. Tell me more about the bag of heads you found. I have an aunt and uncle who ranch on the border near Nogales—the smugglers’ corridor runs through their land. My uncle found a severed head on his ranch.”

“The land southwest of Tuba City is under populated and riddled with deep ravines and tall sandstone walls that make perfect hiding places. The finger canyons are plentiful and most aren’t mapped. I try to mark the ones I’m in with my GPS when I patrol out there. To understand the problem of smuggling and criminal activity on the Nation, you have to see it.”

“Then take me to see it.”

The firelight bounced off the planes of his face, digging deep shadows below his high cheekbones. “Okay, but we do it my way, and once we’re off the main road, you do exactly as I say. Our lives may depend on it.”

Sam’s take-charge personality had popped out. Oddly, I was not put off by his demand; I would be walking in his world. “Did you find the heads out there?”

“Yeah, inside Honoo Ji near the one dirt road that meanders through the canyon and out to the paved county road. All of them were young Hispanic girls, some as young as Sofia.”

I shivered at the sound of Honoo Ji. Too many stories of witches had kept me far away from the area.

“Talk of Honoo Ji upsets you. You’re fingering your ghost beads.”

I stilled my hands in my lap. “You know the stories, the talk of what people have seen. Witches practicing their rituals, plus all kinds of other stuff, evil...”

“I do. Are you trying to connect human trafficking with the witches?”

“No, human trafficking is all about the money.”

“I agree, and I went into Honoo Ji to do my job. Let’s not talk of the Witchery Way. I don’t want to arouse the interest of evil and bring it close to us on this lovely night.”

He was right. Evil lurked around the innocent as well as those who dabbled in it, always searching to lure someone new off the razor edge of goodness into the pit of darkness. I tried to keep my mind and voice free of witches. "Did you find the girls' bodies?"

"No, only the bag with the girls' heads."

"Oh, my God, why? They were children."

"It's part of what they call their 'reign of terror.' Smugglers abandon mutilated bodies along the single trail through the canyon as a warning to the other girls to submit to their fate and not try to escape. We may never identify them. Mexico is different from the states, few dental records and fewer data bases, and we don't have their fingerprints."

I leaned my head on his shoulder, and he felt solid and strong. "Show me what happens in Honoo Ji."

"Better that you are with me than trying it alone."

We sat, holding tightly to each other, watching the fire. Desire flicked through me.

He wrapped his strapping arms around me and nibbled my bottom lip. When he deepened the kiss, I surrendered to my lust and his heat.

He nudged me onto my back and covered my body with his, burying his head in my neck, nuzzling me. "So soft, so incredibly smooth and perfect."

I lay beneath him, bearing his weight, enjoying his soft kisses. The air cooled my wet lips. He bent his head and kissed my breast through my sweater. Tightness seized my chest and my gut. He pushed between my open legs.

His phone buzzed, and he abruptly rolled off me. I opened my eyes, and he was lying on his side by me, fumbling his phone out of his jeans. "Tohee, here...yeah...yeah... I can be there—Nez just got there? So you don't need me? Okay. Tomorrow."

My desire shriveled and scuttled away into some far corner of my brain, and I realized the carpet I was lying on smelled terrible.

"Shh." He laid a finger on my lips. "I want you more than I want my heart to keep beating. But, years from now when we say, 'Do you member our first time?' I don't want our answer to be 'On our second date, in an empty house, on filthy carpet.'"

He pulled me to my feet as he rose and buried his face in my hair. "As the years pass and we remember our first time, our desire will flame again. It will be that good. I promise you."

Chapter 9

Near dusk the following evening, I pulled into the Tuba City Stop 'n Shop parking lot. Sam was waiting for me, idling in an old Jeep I'd never seen before. I locked my car and dropped my day pack in the back of the battered four-wheel drive. "This Jeep yours?"

"Yeah, I've had her since I was sixteen. I can't let her go. She's not real comfortable, but she's great off road."

The seats of the Jeep held the heat of the day, and my jeans stuck to the duct tape mending the cracks in the leather bench. I yanked the seatbelt tightly around me. The decrepit Jeep had no windows, leaving little protection between us and the thorny brush along the road. The sun slinked behind the bruised, angry clouds that crouched on the horizon. Sam eased onto a narrow two-track, bouncing over bone-jarring rocks, and headed south to the remote Honoo Ji Canyon. At milepost 337, Sam passed a windmill marking the north side of the track, crossed a cattle guard, and turned left, fighting the wheel to stay on the packed sand.

Brambles whipped across my arms, tearing my sleeve, leaving wavy red lines filled with blood on my right arm. A bruising seventeen miles later, we were on the upslope of the Moenkopi Plateau. Honoo Ji hugged the base of the plateau for fifteen miles. The Navajo named Honoo Ji after the jagged edges of the dark labyrinth of hoodoos, fins, and sandstone towers eroded by the wind and singed red by underground smoldering fires from the vein of black coal that rimmed the canyon and plunged deep below the canyon floor.

Dread tugged at my senses, and I fidgeted with tension. I clutched my medicine pouch, dangling from a leather cord around my neck, my talisman against evil that held fragments from the four mountains that sheltered my people: white shell from Blanca Peak, turquoise from Mt. Taylor, abalone from San Francisco Peak, and red stone from Hesperus Peak.

The Honoo Ji canyon was a barren land, no water for corn crops and no lush grass for the sheep. Honoo Ji was home to the *Ant iihnii* who practiced the Witchery Way among the weird rock formations, and because of the witches, Navajos avoided Honoo Ji, providing a tactical advantage for the smugglers.

The fifteen-mile length of the trail that snaked along the canyon floor out to the county road was negotiable only by foot or by horse. Shadows from the grotesque formations darkened the canyon floor and made the labyrinth the perfect hiding place for smugglers holding their cargo until transportation was in place on the county road that paralleled the canyon.

Sam parked the Jeep on the upslope of the back side of the plateau, effectively hiding the vehicle from anyone below. He slipped his arm around my shoulders and hugged me to him, talking quietly. "I don't want you to be afraid of going into Honoo Ji. I know the terrain. I'll keep you safe. Have you been here?"

I shook my head and gave him a shaky smile.

"Don't slam the doors when you get out."

I eased the door until I heard a soft click and hoped the sound hadn't carried into the canyon, bouncing through the hoodoos.

"Bend at the waist before we start uphill to lower your silhouette." Sam demonstrated.

We each slipped on a daypack, and I followed his hunched frame up the slope. "There are a couple of rounded sandstone knobs up here on the plateau, and we'll use them for cover," he called softly over his shoulder to me.

My calf muscles were burning from the straight uphill climb when we broke out to the top. We dropped to our knees and crawled behind a small outcrop of sandstone. I gulped water from the bottle in my pack.

"Ration it. We may be here a while, and we're barely carrying a gallon apiece. Hand me your spare bottle. I'll carry it."

Sweat streamed down my face from the exertion to get to the top of the plateau, and the dry air made my mouth feel like cotton, but I reluctantly capped the bottle and shoved it in my bag. I handed him my spare water bottle."Thanks."

He shoved it into his already bulging pack and pointed at the rising sliver of moon. "The moon is just beginning to wax toward a quarter crescent so we'll have a little light, but we won't be spotlighted by a full moon. Smugglers don't like a full moon either, so we might get lucky tonight. Are you doing okay?"

My mouth was so dry, my tongue stuck to the roof of my palate, but I wasn't going to admit it. "Okay, I..."

He put a finger to his lips. "Quieter. We want to make as little noise as possible."He tapped my necklace. "You're wearing your juniper berry necklace. Pretty with the turquoise and silver beads threaded between them. You think you'll need them?" He cocked an eyebrow.

I fingered my ghost bead necklace, reluctant to speak of the evil it protected me from. He made no comment about the leather string around my neck holding my medicine bag between my breasts.

He whispered in my ear. "It's okay to be afraid out here. When I was a kid, my family was over in Tuba City visiting my father's people. My little brother and I had heard the stories of Honoo Ji, and we came over here one evening, two dumb kids thrill-seeking. We got separated down there in the labyrinth. Our flashlights quit working soon after the sun set. I couldn't find my little brother, but I could hear him calling. I spent most of the night following his echoes and working my way through the fins and hoodoos to find him. Then he quit calling."

I instinctively reached up to my necklace. "What happened to your brother?"

He shook his head, and a mask of regret washed his face. "He was only eight years old. I found him at dawn, naked, smeared with mud and bone ash, and curled up under a greasewood bush. When I asked him what happened, he stared into the distance and didn't speak. My Dad found us as I was walking my brother out. Dad hired a Hataali who blessed him, but he's never spoken since we went into Honoo Ji."

"I'm sorry.

Sam's lips thinned. "Yeah, me too. He lives in an assisted living facility over in Window Rock and has never been right since it happened. I used to visit him every day. He never knew, never even turned his head in my direction."

I clutched his arm. "I'm so sorry for you," I repeated.

He was staring over my shoulder, reliving an old tragedy that was as real to him today as the night he walked his brother out.

"My parents are both gone. My mother's brother agreed to visit him when I left Window Rock. To tell you the truth, I felt relieved to leave. It's easier to live with my guilt when I don't see him every day."

"You were young. We do stupid things when we're kids."

"My stupid thing ruined a man's life and took away a normal family life for all of us."

Suddenly, Sam was vulnerable and hurt, more human and less perfect. I squirmed on my belly closer to him and kissed his cheek. He circled his arm over my back and we lay on the rock face that was cooling fast without the heat of the sun. A crescent of moon shone weakly through clouds that threatened to eclipse the remaining light in the canyon. The wind was dead still. No raven calls punctuated the silence; no animals squealed in the darkness.

"Do you hear that?" I whispered in his ear.

He rolled over on his back, a look of concentration on his face, his eyes intent on the horizon. "What? From which direction?"

"Nothing. There is no noise out here. That isn't natural."

"It is out here."

"Creeps me out."

He pulled a leather pouch from his shirt and held it up for me to see, waggling it and smiling. "We'll be fine." He dropped his medicine bag back in his shirt, rolled on his belly, and scanned the canyon floor through his night vision binoculars.

I used his plain Bushnell binocs and saw only dark shadows. Nothing moved. "Is that machinery down there?"

"Yeah, abandoned mining equipment. There's old mining shafts on the floor and up on the walls. They're dangerous as hell, could have caved in any minute until the smugglers shored them up. I can see one directly across from us, but I don't see anyone in it."

I pointed my binocs at the far canyon wall. "I can't find it."

"Take these." He handed me his night vision gear.

The night became green-hued day, and the other side of the canyon jumped into focus. I panned the glasses and found the old mine shaft. I tweaked the focus. Boxes littered the mouth of the opening. "There's stuff in there." I handed them back to Sam.

"Yeah, it's been used recently."

"Will someone come later? Should we stay here and wait?"

"The lookouts aren't coming if they're not in place now. It's not a technical climb up to that shaft, but no one in their right mind would do it in the dark, even with night vision glasses. And they would want to be in position long before the smugglers were ready to bring the goods through."

"Did you find the bag of heads near here?" I asked.

"Directly below us." He fumbled his pack open and shoved in his binoculars. "I think we need to pack up and go down the backside and work our way down the plateau. Try not to kick any rocks and send them skipping down below. We won't do any talking. Just follow right behind me and I'll signal to you if I need to."

Laying on the cold rock had tensed my aching muscles, but soon I was sweating from the effort of hiking at an angle across the sloping backside of Moenkopi Plateau. Thirty minutes of hard work of toiling at a slant, and Sam signaled me to get down. I dropped to my knees. Sam was hardly sweating and his breathing normal. I ached for a drink. He talked with no breathless gasps. "We're going to go back up to the top, so scrunch down and get on your belly when I do. We'll belly crawl the last few yards up."

The water bottle in my backpack banged among the loose stuff, wallet, keys, Garmin GPS, carabiners, the junk I carried when I hiked. The pack shifted on my back as I pulled myself forward, first right side, then left. Each time it moved, the keys and GPS tinkled together. Sam turned around, shook his head, and rolled his eyes. "Put your free hand on that pack and balance it while you crawl."

He was flat and belly down behind a small mound of rocks when I crawled up beside him. He studied the valley floor through his binoculars. "It's gonna happen here. Right here."

"What do you see?" The moon had slipped from behind the clouds, giving us more light. I pointed my glasses the same direction.

"See that rock that juts up and forks on the floor?"

"Yeah."

"Follow it up and along the right fork. Now look up. There's the spider hole."

"I see shadows moving. Are people in there?"

"Yup. Two guys sitting on overturned buckets eating beans from a can. No fire. So dinner is cold beans and probably tortillas washed down by beer that's not cold enough." He grinned at me.

"What are you going to do if a group comes through?"

"Radio Nez and his guys. They're waiting just inside the canyon to snatch them before they hook up with their transport."

"You got a tip, didn't you? We aren't out here just hoping to get lucky."

"Yup. I like a gal with an analytical mind." He pecked a kiss on my cheek. "Your cheek is cold. I have a shock blanket in my pack." He unzipped his pack and pulled out a small aluminum-colored rectangle, shook it out, and spread it over me. "It'll keep your body heat trapped under the blanket."

"Thanks. I'm freezing. It's probably too late for Sofia's group to be coming through, isn't?"

"Yes, I'm sorry."

"And Juanita?"

He tightened his grip on me."I'm sorry. I think she's dead."

"I know, but I can't give up hoping."

"S'kay to hope." He kissed the top of my head. "We need to go silent."

I wriggled around, trying to ease the pain in my back and butt, but no place on the cold rock was comfortable. I finally dozed off into a troubled sleep, twitching with violent dreams that looped and twisted, finally morphing into the vision of a mutilated body of a woman lying on the canyon floor. Cold mist twined through the fins and hoodoos, swirling around her body, creeping over my boots as I inched toward the woman's corpse. Fear had me quivering, but I was drawn to her body like a moth to a flame. I saw no one, heard nothing, smelled nothing, felt only the cold steal into my bones and the unseen force pull me ever closer to her.

Dim moonlight shimmered over the dead woman, glinting obscenely off her sightless eyes. One of her arms and part of one breast had been gnawed; dark blood stained the sand beneath her, and an arm bone gleamed white in a shaft of moonlight. I tried to scream, but no noise came out. A single omen of death, the owl feather, had been laid across her neck, and gray ash powder covered her nude body.

Clumsy with terror, I stumbled over an up-thrust rock and crashed backward, knocking my head on a boulder. She arose and drifted to me, hovering over me, reaching out to me with her mangled arm. Rotting flesh that hung in tattered strips from her arm brushed my sweater.

I awoke to Sam shaking me and hissing, "Shush, it's all right. You're having a bad dream."

I was disoriented, stiff with fear and trembling, and knew I had witnessed what the witches had wanted me to see, an emblem of their power and a taunt they could enter my dreams at their will.

"Shh. You've been asleep. You're fine," he soothed.

I wasn't fine. My head hurt, and I was scared to death. "Did you see anything?"

"AK-47s, the gun of choice."

Guns? There were no guns. What was he talking about?

He cocked his head at me. "You okay?" he asked.

No, I was stunned. The witches had revealed themselves only to me, and to speak of them to Sam would bring the evil close to him, and I would never put him in that danger. My pouch and my beads had protected me. Or, perhaps the revelation of the vision was unfinished and they would come again, but I would never provide them an opening to Sam.

"Guns?" I asked bewildered.

"They prefer the AK-47 because it weighs less than nine pounds, and you just hold down the trigger and spray in the area of the target. You're going to hit something."

He shrugged his shoulders up and down and stretched out his long arms, warming his muscles. "They've been drinking beer steadily for over an hour and tossing the empties into the back of the shaft. No telling how long those two guys have been there waiting for their relief. One time, Trace and I found a spider hole filled with cartons of Marlboros and cases of beer and beans. There were even packages of socks and underwear and new Levis with the tags still on them—and a Glock nine millimeter for close-up work."

Sam picked up his night vision glasses and tweaked the focus. He swept the ridge in front of us, and then tracked slowly back to the opening in the rocks.

I listened to him talk normally, describing the scene before him. He had shrugged my distress off as a bad dream, but my experience burned in my mind. I knew it was a display of raw power and unspeakable desecration by a dark force.

He moved closer to me, slipped his arm around me, and continued to talk. "Nothing moves down here that isn't under the watchful eye of smugglers. The guy who packs in the supplies, the lookouts, the coyotes—they don't operate without the smuggler's okay. Word is the man giving the okay is Nathan Montoya." He peered into my face. "You're spooked. You were just dreaming. I was watching you. You're fine." He squeezed me to him. "I won't let anything happen to you."

I picked up the binocs and adjusted the focal ring. I *was* spooked. I had a vision, and I had a lump the size of an egg on the back of my head that hurt like hell, but I would not be responsible for dragging Sam into evil. I pointed the binocs at the far wall. "I see a glint of light from the hole."

"Put the binocs down." He gently pushed them down to the rock face. "That sliver of moonlight is glinting off his lens. We don't want ours to do the same. The spotters use burner phones and two-way radios to let the smugglers know if they're walking into an ambush by a rival gang or if the cops are near.

He pointed off to our left. "There's movement to the south."

"Do you think the spotter saw us?"

"No. They wouldn't come through if the spotter reported us. Be still and no talking."

Flattened to the rock, making myself as small as possible, I inched my head up enough to focus the binoculars in the dim light. A straggling group of shadowed figures trudged beneath us.

"Women," Sam murmured. He picked up his two-way and cupped his hand over his mouth as he radioed the position of the group to Nez.

The caravan of people wound behind a hoodoo. When they popped out from behind the rock, they weaved through the maze, disappearing in and out of our sight. Their silhouettes dotted the ridge line on the far side of Honoo Ji as they crossed down behind the hills and disappeared.

Sam keyed his radio and alerted Nez that the group was leaving the canyon. He pointed to his watch and held up one finger. We were going to wait to see if more followed.

We lay still and silent in the cold desert night until the sliver of moonlight was smothered by thin clouds. By my watch, an hour had passed. I was exhausted. I tried to fight sleep, fearing what it would bring, but I drifted off.

Mist swirled through the rock formations on the canyon floor. Wafts of vapor moved on wind I could not feel. The mist crept up the hoodoos and fins, smothering them in white, prowling the canyon, stalking an unseen prey. A burst of knife-cold wind pushed the fog up the front side of the plateau and sent it rolling over the cusp and swirling around us. A high pitched keening whistled on the wind, blowing through my hair. The hairs on the back of my neck raised, and goose bumps pebbled my arms. I couldn't see Sam through the thick miasma, and when I reached for him, he was gone. I screamed his name in the whipping wind, but he didn't answer. I lay on the thin edge of the veil that separated me from the dead and the Witchery Way. Moans of anguish topped the keening, and the mist grew thicker and icy cold. I weakened, sapped of initiative, unable to hold my head up. Before me opened the vent to the Underworld, spewing torment and fear, building an atmosphere so heavy it pressed my face into jagged red sandstone rock, slitting my cheek. Warm blood trickled down to my necklace, slicking the beads I clung to. I closed my eyes and prayed to the Holy People for their protection.

Sam's voice hissed near my ear, "Jordan. Jordan!"

"Where have you been?" I cried.

One of his eyebrows shot up, and a line wrinkled between his eyes, "I've been here, beside you."

"Did you see it? The mist?" I cried.

He shook his head. "Mist?"

"Did you feel the cold? I couldn't find you."

"I've been here beside you. I didn't see anything."

"No, that can't be..."

"Yes it can." His hands smoothed my hair, tarrying on my shoulders. "You experienced it. I didn't. I'm getting you out of here."

"My cheek is bleeding—there's blood on my beads."

He shook his head, touched my face, and showed me his clean hand. "Follow me. We're getting the hell out of here." He wiggled around with his head facing down the plateau and his feet pointed toward me, motioning me to follow. My body howled in protest as I pulled myself down the slick rock. When we reached the bottom of the plateau, a sudden gust of wind shrieked around us, throwing stinging dust in my eyes and nose.

The wind died to stillness as suddenly as it wailed. "Did you see that?"

"Yeah. That crap is common out here."

I spit dirt out of my mouth and carefully scooped dirt over the saliva with my boot.

Sam was watching. "You think a witch will use your spit to cast a spell on you?"

I hesitated."I didn't imagine the mist or being alone up there. It happened."

He studied me and massaged the back of his neck with his hand. "The witches have revealed themselves to you, and they will taunt you with temptation."

"Why didn't you experience what I did?" I pressed.

"Don't dwell on them. If you stare into the dark void, the darkness also peers into you."

"But why didn't we both see it?" I persisted.

He shook his head vehemently. "Don't. It's not ours to know. I do know I'm a strong man, not a teenager this time, and I will not let what happened to my brother happen to you. I promise you."

His radio crackled to life. He listened to whoever was talking, and his only words were, "Yeah, got it. Damn it."

He shoved the radio on his utility belt. "Nobody has come out of the canyon to the county road. Either something spooked them, or they got word their transportation wasn't gonna make the rendezvous. Nez and his guys have been working their way through the fins, hoping to cut their trail since I radioed, but they can't find a sign of them. They're probably holed up in a shaft."

Chapter 10

On the way back to the Stop 'n Shop, bitter cold wind blew through the open Jeep. Sam pushed the old heater to the limit, but only a cough of warm air swirled round my feet. Icy wind poured through where windows had once blocked it. We pulled into the parking lot by my car. "I'll see you home before I meet Trace."

"I want to go with you. I was there, too. Maybe I could add something."

"You're bone tired and chilled. Let me follow you home."

"Please, I don't want to be alone."

He agreed, and I followed his taillights into the nearly deserted parking lot of the tribal police station.

Trace was waiting in his office. He leaned back in his chair and propped his feet on his messy desk. "You two look like something the cat dragged in. How about some coffee? Just made a fresh pot."

"Yes," I answered before Sam could speak.

"Have a seat. Be back in a sec."

He returned with three steaming mugs of coffee. I used my mug as a hand warmer.

"Is Nez back yet?" Sam asked.

"He's on his way."

The door banged shut and Nez came through the outer office and joined us.

Trace dragged his hand through his hair and pounded his fist on the top of his desk. "Christ, I feel like the little Dutch boy with his finger in the dike. I have no idea how many girls they're running through there, and its driving me crazy to miss them again tonight. Hell, we were so close. One of our best street sources gave us the tip a load of women were coming through."

"He couldn't know there would be a screw up. We'd need an army to march from one end of Honoo Ji to the other to flush them out," Sam said.

"Nez, what did you find on the canyon floor?"

"The usual trash and spent shells, and, uh...I found a fire pit and a rock altar." He looked uncomfortable. "There were animal bones burned in the pit. Looked like owl bones to me." He shifted in his chair and studied the far wall.

I shivered, fearful of an evil I had been taught since childhood to never speak of. Witches were initiated into the Witchery Way by killing and eating a relative, and what Nez had described was another dark rite, eating owls and saving the feathers for their curses.

"You sure it wasn't a natural outcrop of rock someone built a campfire by?" Sam asked.

"Yeah, it's a rock altar." Nez handed Sam his phone.

Sam thumbed through the pictures.

"It's not the work of smugglers," Sam said obliquely.

Sam handed me the phone. The first picture was of a traditional sand painting between two rock circles. In the middle of the painting was what seemed to be human waste. The edges of the painting were darkened.

"I was close enough to smell it. That's urine darkening the perimeter of the painting," Nez said.

I passed the phone back to Sam.

None of us had said the word "witch" aloud, nor had Sam shared that I had experienced something in the canyon he didn't see. I wasn't about to start talking. None of us wished to draw the evil any closer. I shivered when I thought of Nez out there alone at the site where witches had worshiped.

Sam handed the phone back to Trace and broke the uncomfortable silence, abruptly changing the subject. "I wish the feds would seal the border with Mexico. Sure as hell would make our jobs easier." He leaned forward and rested his elbows on his knees. "We gotta do some of that nation building we did in Iraq and Afghanistan down in Mexico if we want a secure border."

"You want to send in the Marines?" Trace asked.

"Hell no." Sam snorted. "But it's true." He leaned back in his chair and wiped his hand across his face. "The fed's policy of pushing smugglers out of urban areas forces them onto the Nation, and we're not equipped to deal with them."

Trace stood and stretched. "I agree. Brief me about what you found out there—the short version tonight, please. Follow up with a detailed report in the morning. I need some firsthand intel."

Sam briefed him, and I listened carefully. "I suggest we get a cadaver dog into that area where Nez was to look for Juanita's body."

"You think this was the group she and Sofia ran from?" Trace asked.

"Probably not. Timing's not right. But when Sofia's group was picked up for transport, they may have dumped Juanita there."

Trace ran a hand over his jaw. "Good call. I'll get a dog out there."

Sam nodded. "I need to get Jordan home. We can jaw about it more in the morning."

Sam followed me back to my apartment and parked beside the Civic. When I got out of the car, a stiff wind whipped leaves through the parking lot.

Sam stepped out of his car. "Storm's blowing in." He walked over to me and bent forward and kissed me on the mouth. "I'll stay if you like—on your sofa."

"I'll be okay."

"Call me if you need anything." He motioned to my door. "I'll wait here until you're inside."

Impetuously, I invited Sam to dinner at my place the next evening. His face crinkled with smile lines around his eyes and mouth. "Sounds good. Talk to you in the morning."

Chloe was miffed with me when I opened the door, averting her eyes to let me know she felt she had not received the attention she thought she was due. I went to the bathroom and stared at my reflection in the mirror. My cheek was fine, not even a red spot, and my beads weren't blotched with blood. Fear skittered through me as I relived the mist clinging around the corpse. I was happy that the witch had hidden himself from Sam, but terrified to be the witch's target.

Chloe danced in excitement when I clipped the leash on her and braved the cold again for her to do her business. I watched the shadows whip around us in the brisk wind. Nothing tickled my fear, but I was happy when we went inside. Chloe Jane listened closely as I told her about my evening. Just because she didn't talk didn't keep her from being the perfect sounding board. She stared balefully at me, sighing and hunching down on the floor by my bed.

I turned on the electric blanket and let the warmth chase away the night's cold winds. Sam had impressed me with his cool detachment from danger and his expertise at his job. He had taken care of me and walked us in and out of what had been a dangerous situation.

When Chloe was snoring softly and the apartment lay silent in the early morning hours, the witches came in my fitful dreams and drew me again to the top of the Moenkopi Plateau. Out of the cold night and under the sliver of light from a dark moon, two ghost dancers appeared on the floor of the canyon. One from out of the shimmering mist and the other from the gaping mouth of a mineshaft. Their long hair was matted and fell across their faces. Animal fur was draped like a cloak around their necks, and they were bare-chested and wore loin cloths. They grasped hands and danced in the darkness. One cackled and flung his hand up, pointing up at me on the rim of the plateau. A ring of fire exploded on the ground by his feet, and they danced wildly around the fire until it vanished and the maze below me was plunged into darkness. A foul odor wafted up and curled around me on the plateau.

I bolted upright in bed, sweating and taking in great gulps of air, terrified to be alone and a target of their evil attention.

***

When my alarm went off, I was exhausted from a restless night of poor sleep. I dragged myself through Chloe's morning care and my shower. My emotional gamut pinged between terror and sluggishness from the fatigue.

Benally wasn't even in yet, armed with a fresh round of demands for me. I prepared what would be the first of many pots of coffee and went to work, calling O'Brien.

He answered on the first ring. "I've heard from my female officer. Sofia is okay. Stop worrying. She's in a better house than she ever lived in, gets three meals a day, and they're springing for a psychologist. You can still call me, just stop worrying about the kid. Worry about Juanita. We haven't found a trace. You doing okay? Anyone following you?"

I assured him I was fine. As I put the phone down, Ms. Benally barged into my cubicle, her shoes clunking on the old vinyl floors. She sat down before I could say hello and tugged her long skirt demurely around her knobby knees. "I heard you were out at Honoo Ji last night. Doing exactly what?"

I tried to cover my surprise she had a network of informants. I knew she was friends with some of the cops on the Tuba City force, and her brother-in-law was a Captain, but maybe her network stretched further than the police. The Benally family had lived in Tuba City for generations.

"Ms. Benally, I'm not employed as a regular case worker in this office. I'm assigned as an investigator. Have you worked in that capacity?"

She tilted her head up, peering down her generous nose at me imperiously. "I have not, and we're not talking about my career."

"I was learning about the hiding places of human traffickers on our Nation. Juanita is still out there somewhere."

Ms. Benally sniffed. "You're a childish fool if you think she's still alive. You young girls with your ideas." She sighed dramatically as though I were an immense burden to her.

I stood to claim the high ground and look down at her. "I'm a professional and quite good at my job. If Juanita is alive, would you prefer me to just assume she's dead and do nothing?"

She jerked her head back, surprised at my push back. "I prefer you conduct yourself in a professional manner. Forget Juanita and carry on with your work with Sofia."

Which showed how out of touch she was with the changes in our system. Sofia was now out of their jurisdiction and in the hands of the legal system. Benally was walking out the door when I answered, "Certainly, Ms. Benally."

Most of the morning, I worked on developing the curriculum for the gang intervention program. The elementary school counselor and I had agreed to call the program GIP, keeping in line with the successful federally funded programs in California and Arizona, GAP and GIC.

When I took a break, I called Carolyn. "Could you meet for coffee? Say in an hour or so? I've talked to a couple of my volunteers, and they're interested in helping with the reading program. Some of them are retired professionals with plenty of time on their hands."

We agreed to meet at the Starbucks on the old Route 66 in an hour. I hoped to build a bridge to Carolyn, earn her trust, and learn more about her. I was consumed with curiosity of how she had gotten wrapped up with Montoya.

In college, going to Starbucks was a rare treat, and my friends and I referred to it as "Fourbucks." I was still in awe of the price of a grande skinny vanilla latte. Carolyn joined me at my table with her venti.

"I'm so glad you called me. I don't get out much with people unless it's someone Nathan knows from his work or some charity function we are hosting. I've found it hard to break in to social circles here since I don't work. I miss socializing with my old group of teachers."

Guilt slammed me. I was fond of her, and I knew in other circumstances we could be friends, but if I did my job well, I would frighten her away from her husband, out of Flagstaff, and to somewhere where she was safer. I stiffened my resolve.

"I'm glad you could come. I have a couple of names and e-mail addresses for you of women who have been volunteers for CPS." I passed her the list I had compiled.

She scanned the names. "I don't know any of them, but maybe there are some new friends for me on the list."

She spoke of her garden and her decorating project in her kitchen. I didn't have much to add, so I let her talk. She smiled often as she chattered.

At a lull in the conversation, I asked her about her wedding.

"We eloped, and it was so romantic, taking a private jet and flying to Paris to be married. I didn't even tell my best friend." Her face crumpled. "Nathan used to be such fun. He used to pay me so much attention, he just swept me away." She dabbed at her eyes. "We only dated a few months, and he was crazy insistent we get married. He claimed he couldn't bear to be away from me, and I knew he was the one. So strong like my Dad was. He made me happy, but now..." She hung her head and twisted her napkin. "I want a family. Nathan promised me babies before we married, but we've never..."

She surprised me by revealing her sadness. She had played the role of loving wife to the women touring her home. "That must be hard."

She bobbed her head. "Nathan uses protection every time. I've told him I'm ready. I'm responsible enough now to take care of a baby. I've grown up."

What an odd thing for a woman in her mid-twenties to say.

The dam burst and she cried. She told a story of virtual abandonment by Nathan except for public functions. Her story was one of two people in a big house who never shared a meal or the same bedroom, of late nights alone until the wee hours of the morning when she heard the beep-beep-beep of Nathan resetting the burglar alarm. "I can't tell him how I feel. He shrugs and leaves the room and tells me he doesn't want to hear it."

She daubed her eyes. "Could we go to dinner sometime? We can go after you get off work. Nathan and I rarely have dinner together. He'll never know I'm gone."

I agreed to have dinner the following week.

As we were leaving, she said, "I put you on the invitation list to our annual auction that benefits the university. Nate's secretary will get out the invitations."

Perfect. Another reason for me to be around her. We hugged goodbye beside her Mercedes.

On the drive back to the office, my cell rang.

"Hey, what are you doing?" Sam asked.

"Driving. When I get to the office, I have a Skype conference with a colleague who works in a California gang intervention program. Their program has an assessment tool for identifying at-risk kids, and she's going to share it with me."

"I have a meeting with the DA about the 7-Eleven robbery in a few minutes. I called to see if I can bring anything tonight? Wine?"

"Yes, that would be great. White would be perfect."

"White it will be. Umm, how are you doing?"

"Better, I think..."

"We'll make it even better tonight."

***

I raced home, wanting to spiff up my house before I started working on me. I showered and blew dry my hair, pulled it back, only to brush it out and let it tumble freely. Chloe Jane picked up on my nervousness and paced the small apartment. She stopped by the front door and woofed when Sam knocked at seven.

When I opened the door, I drank in the sight of him—his weight balanced slightly forward, his skin bronzed by the sun, and a warm smile just for me. He was holding a bottle of wine and a loose bouquet of tiny pink flowers.

"They're beautiful. Thank you. Come in."

"I could smell your cooking outside your door."

"All I have to do is cook the chicken in the sauce and add the chopped basil." The water for the fettuccine was bubbling away. Damn straight, I could cook.

Sam followed me into the kitchen and stood behind me with his arms around my waist while I put the flowers in a vase. He rested his head on my shoulder. "I'm impressed. Looks good and smells good."

"Nothing to it. By the time you set the table, we'll have chicken in a basil Alfredo sauce over pasta.

"On it." He took the glasses and silverware I handed him to my tiny table.

I lifted the lid on the sauce. Big curdled lumps simmered in a watery liquid. Panic rose in my throat, but I beat it down. Maybe it all came together when I added the basil and chopped chicken. I dumped the final ingredients in and whisked the lumps around, turned the burner down low, and hoped for magic.

The timer dinged on the fettuccine. I drained it in the colander and fluffed it with a little butter. "I think we're ready. Will you pour the wine?" The candlelight danced across the angles and planes of his face as he filled the wine glasses.

I piled two plates with the fettuccine, quietly thanking the cooking fairy that I hadn't overcooked it and made a gooey mess of the pasta. When I lifted the lid on the sauce, the lumps swam resiliently in the watery sauce. I used a whisk to try to break up the chunks of dough and thicken the sauce.

"You need any help, there?" Sam asked as he joined me in the kitchen.

My shoulders sagged. "The sauce doesn't look like the picture."

"Plate it up, sweetheart. I bet it tastes just fine. Here I'll put the sauce on the pasta."

He carried our plates to the table. "Looks good,"

I took a bite. "Oh, my God, the sauce is salty and the lumps are nasty tasting."

He tried to twirl a piece of pasta around his fork. I heard the crunch of undercooked pasta when he bit into it.

I cut a piece of my chicken in half and pink blood oozed out of the center. "Stop!" I screeched. "The chicken's raw." I jerked Sam's plate out from under him, his fork mid-air and dripping sauce onto the table. A frond of basil stuck on his lower lip.

I couldn't help it. I started laughing and finally collapsed back in my chair hooting with hilarity. A backlog of fear and tension roiled out of me in laughter.

I pointed at his lip. "You have basil hanging off your bottom lip."

He wiped his mouth and walked over to the stove. I had forgotten to turn the burner off. He clicked it off, dumped the sauce in the sink, and filled the pot with water to soak.

The laughter had evaporated my tension. "I'm sorry. I don't think this cooking thing is going to work out."

He came over, stood behind me, and rested his hands on my shoulders. "I'm here for you, not the food. I don't give a damn if you ever learn to cook. I do care if you're upset about this." His thumbs began kneading the kinks in my shoulders.

"I just wanted to fix dinner for us. Other women do it every night. I should be able to at least once."

"Your wanting to fix dinner for us is all I need. I don't give a damn what we eat. And, my darling girl, you aren't like any other woman I have ever known."

I stood and hugged him. "You're perfect. I have the pizza place on speed dial. What do you want?"

"I want to erase that haunted expression on your face. You've tried to game it, but you're tense and scared." He tucked a strand of my hair behind my ear. "Let me take you dancing at Crazy Gal's. Hold you tight and blow off a little steam." He grinned. "Besides, they have great bar food."

I returned to the kitchen and gave the rest of the dinner a decent burial in the trash. "I'm ready, cowboy."

He pulled the Tahoe out of the drive of my apartment house. "How are you feeling about last night?" He asked obliquely without naming the experience, careful to not give it power or call attention to us.

"I didn't sleep well," I admitted, "and I'm shaken up you didn't see anything. It was so real to me, and I was terrified when I couldn't find you."

He took my hand. "I was beside you. I would never leave you unprotected. Last night, I prayed the Shield Prayer for you, asking that the evil be turned back on the dark one."

"Thank you. When I was a child, my grandfather gave me my medicine pouch, and later he added gall medicine from a mountain lion. He is gone, but he still is my protector."

"As am I. I won't let anything happen to you."

When we parked in front of the bar, music throbbed through the walls of Crazy Gal's and boomed through the lot. "Busy for a Thursday night," Sam said. He clipped an arm around my waist as I stepped out of his truck.

We walked to the bar so close to each other, our legs brushed together. His arm never left my waist as we tread the well-worn steps onto a smooth wooden porch with a three-foot-high railing. Small tables were scattered across the floor, and several couples, cooled by the ceiling fans, enjoyed a little additional dance space or a dark corner for a little privacy.

The hobnail front door had a significant lock and metal plate. Standing beside the open door was a huge barrel-chested Navajo man. His arms were crossed over his chest, and his massive legs rooted him to the floor. He nodded as we stepped across the threshold and called, "Evening."

Sam acknowledged his greeting. We pushed through the screen door and let it bang closed behind us. Once inside, I whispered to Sam, "Big Man?"

He nodded and took my elbow, guiding me through the crowd. The band blasted out dance music from behind a chicken wire cage. No beer bottles were flying through the air, but the evening was young. A long bar edged with a brass step rail ran the length of the building. Padded faux leather bar stools with comfortable curved backs drew a crowd to the bar.

We claimed a tiny table in the corner of the room, and a waitress took our order for beer and nachos. She brought two frosty bottles of beer rimmed with lime and a platter of nachos steaming under a mound of melted cheese. We dived into the nachos. The band blasted out one great dance tune after another. The crowd roared approval at the end of the last song and clapped until another set begun. As many women as guys crowded the tables; no one was without company. The patrons were a mix of young professionals and cowboys and their women.

We polished off the nachos and Sam sipped his second beer. He nodded to the dancers circling the floor. "Dance with me. After last night, I just want to hold you close."

He pulled me to the floor, and we danced. Heat bloomed between our bodies. He kissed me as the band shifted into a slow, romantic favorite. Halfway through the number, lost in the sexy sway of his lead, a guy tapped Sam's shoulder. "May I?"

Sam broke away from me and nodded. As the man guided me into a turn, I caught a glimpse of Sam's face. Thunderclouds of irritation shaded his eyes. I didn't expect him to slink back to the table and wait for the guy to return me. Sam would stand his ground on the dance floor.

"Glad you came out. Name's Texas Jack." My new dance partner was fortyish with strong shoulders and a straight back. He had dirty blond hair and scrutinizing gray eyes, holding a hint of amusement. He wore well broken-in Levis and work boots. "This is my place, and I like dancing with the beautiful women and watching their guys squirm a little."

I cringed at his comment. *Weird guy!* When I pulled away, he tightened his grip. He did a quick turn on the dance floor, pulling me with him. He was light on his feet and graceful. He nodded to an overweight barkeep with a dramatic comb-over and an impressive set of man breasts behind the bar. "He doesn't look like much, but he's got a shotgun and a baseball bat behind that bar. Makes him a great bartender."

"I hope he doesn't need either one."

His smile was feral."I can tell you wanna get to know me, so I'll help you out. I like to win. Doesn't matter if it's money or gettin' a woman. I win. *Everything* I want, I get."

"I'd like to return to my table, please." I strained against his hand on my waist.

"Shortly, we haven't finished our time together." We danced around a couple entwined around each other. "Like what you see?" One side of his mouth quirked, lifting his upper lip to reveal straight white teeth. Without waiting for me to answer, Texas Jack pulled me closer to his body, holding my breasts tight to his shirt. He leaned down and spoke in my ear, "Babe, you and the cop need a little break. You need the right man by you."

"The right man was beside me before you came along," I huffed and tried to pull away from him.

He held his grip on me."I know your kind of woman. You need a man who can handle you. We got us a pull between us. You feel it. I see it on your face. You wanna pretend it doesn't exist, I'll respect that, but we'll deal with it eventually, and it will be the best you've ever had." He dropped his hands and stepped gracefully away from me.

Fuming with anger, I headed toward Sam. When a couple stopped to kiss in front of me, I had to work my way around them and through the crowded dance floor to the table where Sam took his seat only after I sat down. He picked his beer up, took a sip, and then waited for me to speak.

"I'm through dancing with the owner. Let's get out of here."

He grabbed my hand and pulled me toward the exit. As we passed the bar, Texas Jack was snuggled up behind it with a barmaid. He was feeling her butt and whispering in her ear. I tapped Sam's arm. When he looked back at me, I jerked my head in the direction of the bar.

He glanced at Jack and whispered to me, "Jackass."

The bouncer wasn't guarding the front door when we left the bar, and the patrons who had been on the front porch were standing at the rail gawking at something in the parking lot. They hooted and catcalled. "Fight! Fight!"

Sam and I elbowed our way through the throng. Under the pole light, a biker head-butted another, both snarling curses at each other. A leathered up, tattooed biker chick whined for her man to come inside and dance with her. Neither man was listening. The smaller biker darted in and swept the legs out from under the larger guy who tumbled awkwardly to the ground. The leather chick screeched as the men rolled in the gravel, grunting and flailing. The screen door banged open, and Texas Jack stalked out, yelling and brandishing a sawed off shotgun. Big Man hurried behind him, unarmed except for his substantial size.

"Stay here." Sam demanded and ran toward the bikers. When Jack fired a shot into the sky, the brawlers separated. Sam halted, forming a triangle with Jack and the bikers. Tatt chick rushed forward and hugged her favorite man.

"Get the hell outa here, all of you!" Texas Jack growled. The smaller guy kept his woman behind him until the larger man gunned his bike into the night.

When the screen door banged shut behind Texas Jack, Sam still stood with his feet apart, hands ready at his sides until the smaller biker roared out of the lot with his chick glued to his back. He and Texas Jack had never acknowledged the other's presence. Big Man stood at his post, telling the crowd to take their seats on the porch and everyone would get a drink on the house.

I had backed all the way to the edge of the parking lot into a stand of gray sage scrub and scratchy Santolina bushes that made my arms itch like crazy. The air stank of exhaust fumes from the big bike and cordite from the gun. Sam motioned me to him. When I joined him, he tugged me toward the car.

I didn't ask Sam why Jack hadn't acknowledged his presence. I knew Texas Jack was marking his territory.

Once in the front seat, Sam made a lazy trail up and down my leg with his hand. He still wasn't talking. I assumed he didn't like Texas Jack's possessive ways.

"The food was good, dancing with you was better, but the owner is a complete ass." I said.

When we got back to my apartment, he circled the living room, unable to sit still and evidently unable to start a conversation.

I studied him with renewed interest.

"The way you're studying at me, I feel like a bug pinned to a Styrofoam board in a grade school science fair," he said at last.

"Come here," I said softly. I took his hand and led him the few steps to my room. The bed springs squeaked with his weight.

My warrior man was all hard muscle and smooth bronze skin, and he had a distinct edge to him tonight. I slipped my hand in his shirt and finger-walked his chest, teasing his nipple until he took a sharp breath.

Lust clouded his eyes. "I've wanted you so long..."

"It'll be perfect, warrior man." I unbuttoned his shirt and brushed my hands across his bare chest to the thin ribbon of dark hair disappearing into his jeans. He slipped off my clothes, stopping only to kiss the hollow of my throat before he shrugged off his shirt and jeans.

My body shuddered with exquisite expectancy beneath his weight, aching for him to pleasure me with sweet release. He plunged into me, rode deep and fast, until we thundered to a tumultuous release.

I shimmered in the afterglow of our fierce coupling. The scent of our love would linger on our bodies all night.

Chapter 11

When I awoke in the morning light, I studied his face for remnants of last night's irritation at Texas Jack. His face was smooth and peaceful.

With him beside me, I had slept deeply and dreamlessly. I was stronger with him than without him.

He rolled on his side and swept me into his arms."Morning, darling girl," he said softly. "What time is it?"

"Early. Not yet six o'clock."

"Good. We have time for me to buy you some breakfast at Mike's Place."

"Never heard of it." I yawned.

"It's a greasy hole in the wall. Best breakfast you will ever eat." He slapped me on the rear playfully. "Up and at 'em, woman."

Sam and I breakfasted at Mike's Place surrounded by a noisy group of older men jawing about the weather and politics. I had coffee and toast; he had a working man's breakfast of bacon, eggs, and hash browns. His frame could support it, and I envied him as I put a little honey or my unbuttered toast.

"About last night..." he said.

A muddle of emotions painted his face, eyes round and soft, his brow furrowed. I quit spreading the honey, holding the toast and knife frozen in place, not waiting for him to continue. "Last night was wonderful. I hope you feel the same." I carefully lined the knife blade parallel to the edge of the plate and took a noisy bite of my toast.

He released his pent up breath, and his face softened. "Me, too. How about a romantic steak dinner at my house later in the week?"

He had pushed by happy button. I wanted him in my life. "Love to, nothing like a man who is a good lover and a cook."

He scooped some hash browns and a piece of crisp bacon onto my plate. "Here, eat some real food. I can see the longing in your eyes. I've got to go in a few minutes. Trace and I are meeting this morning to talk about finding some other lockup for Ketso."

"He's the Dragon who robbed the 7-Eleven?"

His mouth set in a grim line. "Yeah, and Ketso's been a pain in the butt since we picked him up."

"How?"

"He attacked his cell mate, so we moved him to solitary, only we don't have a separate space for solitary, which means we have to waste a whole cell housing only him, doubling up the rest of the prisoners. If they could get to him, they'd beat the crap out of him."

"How are the Dragons acting about Ketso in jail?"

"They're pumped up and strutting their territory, boasting Ketso's going to beat the charges, but no way that's happening."

"What about Juanita? Are you still hunting for her?"

He put his fork down and gave me his full attention. "The cadaver dogs didn't hit on a body out in Honoo Ji. O'Brien can't find a trace of her in Flag. No one has seen her on the Nation." He hesitated. "Sofia told us that story, but no one else has any corroboration that Juanita exists."

"But she was so upset, begging me..."

He touched my arm. "I know, Jordan, I've been fooled before."

"But you're not going to stop, are you?"

"No, of course not. I'm just saying we need some evidence Juanita ever existed." He gulped the rest of his coffee. "I have to go." He rose and put a few bills on the table, and I followed him out to the parking lot to my car.

***

As soon as I got to work, I pulled out my set of case notes on Sofia and the missing girls. I believed that Juanita was out there somewhere and Sofia wasn't a stone cold liar, but maybe my emotions had overruled my head. I had to assess the idea she might be lying. What evidence was there but her claim and the cops' knowledge girls had been smuggled out of Mexico onto the Nation? From what Trace had said last night, they were barely holding back the tidal flow of human trafficking with their few officers, but I might be wasting time and resources on a kid who didn't exist.

I searched the Internet and found the website for the local police in Banamichi, Mexico. Maybe, just maybe, Juanita's disappearance had been reported to the police in her village. But, first, I would have to get permission from Benally to make an international call from the state phone on my desk.

She was talking on the phone when I approached her open door. I waited until she hung up to knock on the door frame.

"Yes, what is it?"

"I'm working on Sofia's case, and I need permission to make a long distance call to Mexico to speak with the Banamichi police."

"Denied. Waste of state money and your time. She's here and well protected."

"But I'm searching for the other girl who got away with her."

"I hear you have no evidence she exists. The answer is still no. That's all." And she lowered her head to the papers on her desk, shuffling them noisily.

Her obstinate tone surprised me so much that I stood still in the doorway for a moment too long.

"Anything else? If you don't have plenty to do, I can assign you a routine case that came in last night..."

"No, nothing else." I fumed. Bessie Benally was the classic example of a mid-level manager gone bad—when promoted to a position of authority, her ego bloated and commandeered her judgment. Plus, the bitch had damn good informants.

I flopped down in my office. My cell phone had no international minutes. But I knew someone who could make the call. Taylor.

Her phone rang a couple of times before she answered, and I plunged right into what I needed. "Hey, it's me. I have a problem I hope you'll fix. I want to make a call to the Banamichi police department. Benally won't approve it on my state phone, and this working girl just has a dumb phone with no international service."

"No prob. Got you covered. I was just about to call you."

"What are you so excited about?"

"You're gonna love this. We've just been handed a new angle on Sofia's story. The FBI found a laptop in a known stash house in that area of Flag where you found her. The house hadn't been used for months, and the FBI was barely keeping an eye it, but they hit pay dirt when a group of girls were taken there," she finished in a rush.

"Did they arrest anyone?"

"Yep, the guys aren't talking and probably will remain silent all the way to prison. They have families in Mexico to protect who would be hanging from the village lamppost ten minutes after they talked. But here's the good part. The feds found a digital wallet and a Bitcoin account on the laptop. You know what this means?"

"The bad guys are moving money on the Internet?"

"Bingo. And there has to be a way to trace it. Gotta be digital tracks. Marty already called the FBI office and gave them my name, telling them I would be in touch to talk with anyone familiar with the stash house raid. I got us an appointment this afternoon. Gonna make a hell of a story. That's selfish, I know, but..."

"This could bust up the ring bringing girls into the Nation if we can track the money," I finished for her. "Can we make the call to Banamichi before we go?"

"Sure. Come to the station, and we'll call them now. Whatever you get from the Mexicans, we gotta take with a grain of salt. You know the federales and the local police in Mexico are corrupt."

***

I left the office through the back door, closing it softly behind me so I wouldn't alert Benally. As an investigator, I came and went at odd hours, but I didn't want to set myself up for more of Benally's snark.

When I arrived at the station, the staff were trading bits of news about the FBI raid.

"Back in here, Jordan," Taylor called from inside her little office. "How good is your Spanish?"

"Good enough to carry on a conversation with Sofia. Did Marty okay the phone call?"

She nodded. "We're a news business. We spend a lot of time on the phone chasing down info." She rummaged in her desk and pulled out a legal pad and a pen. She stood up saying, "Make yourself at home. I gotta voice-over a bit of video that Louis has edited for the story about the raid. Oh, and dial nine to get an outside line."

"Hola, Policia Sectoral, Banamichi," a professional female voice answered my call.

I asked to speak to the desk sergeant, and she and I laughed nervously when I didn't know what title to use for the person I wanted to speak to. Finally, she settled on connecting me to the Comandante del Fuero Comun, an impressive title for the head of the local police in a village of less than a thousand people. I drummed my fingers on the desk, waiting for him to pick up, thinking of Taylor's comment about corruption. Most Mexican police officers had less than four months of training and their pay was miniscule, making them easy targets for bribery.

After a long wait, a man answered in an imposing voice, "*Comandante*."

I identified myself in Spanish and explained my relationship with Sofia. "Sofia told me a village girl named Juanita went missing when she did."

"*Si*," he said cautiously.

"Did Juanita's family report her missing?"

"*Si*, the Salvatores gave us a picture of the girl. We have searched for her."

He spoke only in Spanish, taxing the limits of my conversational Spanish skills.

"Have you found her?"

"No, senorita, we do not know where she is."

Our conversation was becoming as productive as nailing Jell-O to trees. "Could you put me in touch with Juanita's parents?"

Taylor came back in and perched on the desk. When I pushed the speaker button on the phone, his voice flooded the little office.

"No, I can't do that."

"Why?"

There was a long pause."Comandante? Are you there?"

"*Si*... Her parents are dead."

"What?"

"Juanita's mother was beheaded, but before she died, she saw her husband tied to four posts pounded into the ground and a fire set between his legs. He died screaming in agony, and it took a long time for him to die. My wife and me, we took our children and hid in the fields by our house when the burning started. When the men left, they tossed the bodies in the street. That night, my family, we crept into the church and lighted a candle for them. The whole village stank of roasted meat. My children kept asking, 'Who is cooking meat? Who has the money for meat?'"

Taylor leaped from the desk shouting, "Oh, my God."

I put my finger to my lips. Taylor nodded, but paced the small office.

"Why didn't you and your men try to save her parents? How could you let that happen in your village?"

"You don't know how it is here. I must live to protect my family. Who will keep them safe if they kill me?"

"Who are you talking about?"

"Smugglers. If you cross them, you are dead."

His words echoed my aunt's and Evelyn's when they talked of Stuart's death.

"Will you fax a picture of Juanita?"

"*Si*, I will fax you the picture, but if you find her, she has no one here. Don't send her back to our village."

"What about Sofia's aunt?"

"She knows what will happen if she speaks. I beg of you, don't send either girl back, there is nothing here for them."

Taylor jotted down the fax number of the station and thrust the pad in front of me. I read the number to the Comandante and hung up.

Taylor's face was a study of misery and disgust. "You remember the story I did about the Mexican nationals working in the uranium mine on the Nation? That's when I first ran into the incredible violence going down in Mexico."

"Yeah, I do. I was the caseworker for some of the children of those mine workers. One mine worker had married a Navajo woman. They went back to Mexico to see his family and got caught up in a gang war. They were burned out of his parent's house, and she lost all her and the kids' identification papers. I had pictures of the children and case notes that helped establish ID for the kids, and the mom got a duplicate Arizona driver's license. The problem was the dad was in the US illegally. He's stuck in Mexico, and she won't take the kids and leave him behind, though he begged her to take the kids and go. Misery just rolls out of Mexico."

"I don't know any good stories coming out of Mexico." Taylor grabbed her gear bag. "Let's go see the feds and break this open."

"When that fax comes in, I need to get copies to O'Brien and Sam," I said.

"Louis will fax them copies and e-mail it to you so Benally won't find your copy in the fax machine tray."

"Thanks. I'm so done with her disrespect. One more snarkasm, and I'm calling her out."

"Way past time for you to do it. I'm calling O'Brien to get the update on what the feds know before we get to Aguirre's office. In the favors game between police and reporters, he owes me one. I could have excoriated one of his officers last year for racist behavior reported by the eyewitnesses at the scene of an accident, but I didn't. I waited, and sure enough, the Internal Affairs investigation cleared the officer. I'm telling you those witnesses were champing at the bit to get on camera. One of them tried to wrench the microphone out of my hand. They creeped me out. They were rabid, reminding me of the Dickens book with the harridan who sat and knitted before the guillotine, waiting for the head to roll in the bucket. If I'd given them airtime, they would have made Internet shaming look like a picnic for O'Brien's entire command. I protected O'Brien's butt, and he knows he owes me."

Taylor called O'Brien and put him on speaker phone."I'm leaving for the federal building in a few minutes. Get me up to speed before I walk in there."

"The FBI found the laptop in a broken down old house off the grid—no water or electricity that could be traced, standard for a stash house for human trafficking. You know what that is? A way station before they get them to the distribution spot on the Nation. They had a composting toilet, a bunch of stained mattresses, and crap everywhere. The goldmine is that laptop, and the FBI has had plenty of time to data mine it."

"What was the address of the stash house?" Taylor shot back. She scribbled an address on the pad in front of her.

"What else did they tell you? Any link to Montoya?" Taylor asked.

"I already told you what I know and don't attribute anything to me. I got to work with the feds, and they can make it damn hard if they don't get all the credit," he grumbled. "And you and me—we're even now."

My phone vibrated at my waist. An unknown number.

"Hello?"

"Jordan, it's Trace. Are you alone?"

"No. I'm with Taylor." His guarded tone told me something bad had happened. "What's the matter? What's happened?"

Taylor hung up with O'Brien. In an instant, she was alert to the alarm in my voice.

"There's been a shooting, and Sam has been shot. He's in an ambulance on his way to St. Vincent's. Get Taylor to drive you."

I swayed and balanced myself on the desk. The room shimmered and spun. I clung to the chair arm, my heart pounded in my ears, my vision tunneled to a small hole in the darkness. We were in a relationship. We were lovers. He cooked dinner for me; I just had breakfast with him. *It couldn't be true*, my heart screamed.

"Jordan, you there?" Trace said.

"Yes, on my way."

"What? What is it?" Taylor cried frantically.

"Sam's been shot." My high pitched voice ricocheted off the walls. I bolted, hitting the station's front door at a dead run. Taylor yelled to Louis, "I'll be on my cell."

From behind me, her heels clacked a staccato rhythm on the asphalt. "My car!" Taylor yelled. "Over here. I'll drive."

I grabbed the door handle of the Rav, jerked hard, but it was locked and I pounded my hands on the glass. *Oh my God, keep him safe. Don't let him die.*

Taylor popped the locks and threw her gear bag in the back seat. "Where to?"

"St. Vincent's ER."

She floored the Rav, and it whined in protest as it leapt out of the drive into the boulevard. "How bad is he?"

"I don't know. What if he *dies*!"

"Stop. Don't put yourself through that. St. V's is the best." She took my hand and held it all the way to hospital.

She pulled into the hospital lot, and I was out of the car before she turned off the motor. I hit the ER door at a full run. "I'm Jordan Bia. May I see Officer Tohee, please?"

The desk clerk peeked up at me over her cheaters, glanced over my shoulder at Taylor racing up to the desk, and then raked her gaze back to me. "She's a news reporter. I recognize her. The hospital press officer will make a statement to you media folks later." She went back to reading her papers.

"No. No," I anguished, "I'm..."

"Ms. Bia is Officer Tohee's significant other," Taylor said from behind me.

"You guys would lie about anything," the desk clerk retorted.

"I'm not lying. Please tell me how he is!" I begged.

She rose, and a pile of papers on the desk slipped to the floor. She let out a noisy sigh and tried to gather them, but a few escaped her grasp. "I'll see if he can see you. I better not be making a fool of myself," she grumbled as she walked off.

"I'll call and reschedule our appointment with the FBI," Taylor said to me.

I didn't understand for a moment, and then remembered we had been on our way to interview Agent Aguirre. It seemed a lifetime ago.

"Ma'am...ma'am." Texas Jack sauntered up to me. "I was with Officer Tohee when he was shot."

Now he had all my attention. I plucked at the sleeve of his plaid work shirt. "Where? Where was he shot?"

His dark eyes skimmed slowly over my face and to my feet before he answered. I felt as though he had run his hand down my body. He brought his eyes back to my face, impudence stamped on his handsome features. "Upper right arm. There was lots of blood, but it looked to me like it went clean through." An insouciant grin flitted across his face. "Happened out at my place."

My chest caved in, and my shoulders sagged with relief. Taylor slipped an arm around my waist, and I leaned on her. Sam couldn't die from an arm wound and St. V's *was* the best. I stuck out my hand. "I'm Jordan Bia."

"I remember you well." He grinned lazily. He held my hand a little too long. I wiggled my hand in his, and he let go.

"Thank you for coming in with him."

"I called the ambulance after the gangbangers backed off. Hell, what do they think? They're in LA prancing around with their baggy pants and pea shooters?" he growled.

I pounced on his words. "Pea shooter? Sam was shot with a small caliber weapon?" *Oh, please God, let this be true*. He needed full use of his right arm.

"Twenty-two handgun, and didn't look to me like the shooter used hollow point bullets. Small entry and exit wound, ma'am." One side of his mouth quirked up, and he leaned toward me. "He'll probably be out of here in no time."

His gaze lazily skimmed my body, lingering on my breasts. When his eyes met mine, a wolfish grin flitted across his striking face. I took a step back, rattled by his brazenness and repulsed by his timing.

The desk clerk shambled out and huffed, "Doc says you can come back. Just you Ms. Bia. You, Ms. Reporter"—she pointed at Taylor—"have a seat."

"I'll wait with her." Texas Jack nodded at Taylor.

The nurse led me to a curtain-shrouded cubicle labeled *Major Trauma Room 2*. Sam lay pale and shaking in a hospital gown covered in a little blue and white squiggly print. An IV line dangled from his left arm, and his right arm was heavily bandaged.

"Hey big guy, how are you feeling?" I leaned over and kissed him softly.

"Stupid. I got shot by a kid."

"Texas Jack is outside. He said—" I broke down. "I-I was so afraid of losing you."

Sam jerked his head up. "Hand me the basin, quick."

I thrust the stainless steel emesis basin under his chin.

"Hold it for me. I can't move either arm."

I cupped his neck and held the basin. He heaved and vomited until there was nothing left.

A nurse slipped into the cubicle, took the basin from me, and handed me a clean one. She pressed a damp cloth into my hand, and I dabbed at the sweat running off his forehead.

"God, I'm sorry. I didn't want to do that in front of you." His eyes beseeched me, searching for any sign of repulsion.

"Here's some water. Rinse your mouth. I'm fine, big guy. And you're going to be fine, too. When are we getting you out of here?"

A doctor stepped to Sam's bedside.

"You feeling nauseous?" she asked him.

"Yeah, better now."

"We'll put a little something in your IV to take care of the nausea, might make you a little sleepy. Nausea is a common reaction from the body when it has sustained a sudden trauma."

The doctor stuck her hand out to me. "Dr. Marcia Gilvers." She gave me a forced smile.

"Jordan Bia. How is he?"

"May I discuss your medical condition with Ms. Bia?" she asked Sam.

A weak grin creased his face."Sure. She just held the basin. She's entitled."

"He was shot with a twenty-two handgun through the flesh of the upper right arm." She launched into her spiel of doctor talk. "It missed the subclavian artery and the brachial plexus, a large nerve bundle that controls arm function, so I don't think he'll have any disability. The exit wound was clean, but we gave him a tetanus shot and are running some antibiotics through the IV. If he does well tonight, he can go home tomorrow."

The doctor turned to Sam. "You'll have to let that arm heal. I know that's your dominant hand, but you're going to have to go back on limited duty. We'll be getting you up to your room shortly." She nodded to me and left.

The nurse checked Sam's IV flow. "She ordered morphine for the pain. Going to make you a little sleepy." She pushed the drug in and thumped the IV line. Satisfied with the drip, she left us alone.

I stroked his cheek. "I was terrified."

"I'm lucky, very lucky." His thumb turned circles in my palm."Don't give up on me."

"Give up on you?"

"A lot of women wouldn't put up with their man putting them through this." His eyes searched my face for an answer.

"I'm not them. I'll never give up on you."

He grabbed my hand, kissed it, and lowered it to his chest.

His eyes closed, and his grip on my hand softened. His jaw relaxed as he fell asleep.

An orderly brushed back the curtains and wheeled in a gurney. A nurse was on his heels. "We're taking him up to his room now. He'll sleep a couple of hours. Why don't you come back this evening?"

I kissed his forehead before they wheeled him into the elevators. The aftermath of my adrenaline rush was stumble-bum lethargy, laced with gratitude that Sam was alive and with me.

Taylor was drinking coffee and pacing the ER waiting room.

"How is he?" Taylor demanded.

"He's going to be all right. Clean shot through his upper right arm. They admitted him for the night." Tears of relief tracked down my cheeks.

Taylor handed me a Kleenex as Texas Jack sidled up.

"Can we offer you a ride back to Crazy Gal's?" I asked Texas Jack.

"No, thank you ma'am. I got myself a ride."

When he stepped aside, a lithe, bleached blonde in a spandex micro skirt and tube top was sitting behind him thumbing a worn copy of a fashion magazine. She popped her gum, glanced at me, and said, "Hiya, I got his ride covered."

"Okay," I said to the top of her head as she noisily went back to flipping pages.

"Thank you for coming with him..."

"My pleasure ma'am. We'll be leaving now." He put a well worn Stetson on his head. "The body takes even a flesh wound seriously. There'll be a lot pain and stiffness until he can use that arm. I'd be obliged if you would pay us a visit out at Crazy Gal. I could answer any other questions you might have."

I shifted uncomfortably. His dark eyes had a hint of amusement, and one side of his generous mouth tilted up.

"Uh, thanks, okay," I mumbled.

He tipped his hat. He walked over to the blonde who stood waiting for him and put one hand on her butt as they walked out the door.

Taylor had been hovering at my elbow. "You ready?"

"Yes." I pushed the ER door open.

Chapter 12

All I did at the office was to worry over the bullet wound in Sam's arm. The hours crawled slowly toward evening. At six o'clock, I was back at the hospital. Sam had an empty broth bowl and a barely-touched plate of red Jell-O on his tray.

"You have a burger and fries in your purse?" he asked softly.

I bent over and pecked him a light kiss on the mouth. "I see you're feeling better."

"Much. Spring me, woman, and I'll be forever in your debt."

"Tomorrow, big guy, and you are already in my debt," I kidded.

"I need to go to work tomorrow." Sam turned his head to me. "Here's my house key. Will you go out to my place and bring me some clothes for in the morning? And I need a ride to work. Nez took my Tahoe back to the station from Crazy Gal's."

"Are you sure you're well enough to go work? What did the doctor say?" I asked suspiciously.

"Nothing yet. I'll talk her into it in the morning. I've got the use of my hand in this sling." He raised his bum arm and wiggled his fingers. "Now bend back down here and let me kiss you."

"You're just trying to take my mind off your hardheadedness."

"Partly. And partly, I am just so damn glad to be alive. I watched Mike Haskie raise that gun at me, and you know what I felt?"

I shook my head.

"Disbelief. I just couldn't accept he was going to kill my sorry ass. Then my training kicked in, and I quit feeling. I rolled, but not fast enough, and he winged me."

"Is Haskie an adult?"

"Yeah, he's booked for assault of an officer and attempted murder. He'll do time," he said grimly. "And the Cobras won't like seeing him go to prison."

"What happened out there?"

"The Dragons attacked the Cobras in retaliation for robbing the 7-Eleven in their territory. When Nez and I stepped out of the Tahoe, Haskie pulls a gun out of his pants and starts shooting. I knew what was coming when his hand disappeared in those baggy pants. Nez hit the dirt, and we drew our weapons, but I was too damn slow."

"Was the bouncer there?"

"Yeah, Haskie dropped his pistol when Big Man pointed his shotgun at him. The rest of the Cobras backed away with their hands up."

"Why?"

"He's literally the big man of the Cobras—the shot caller. He covered them with a shotgun until Nez cuffed the shooter."

"So a Cobra turned on his fellow Cobras?"

"No, the enforcer for the Cobras disciplined his underlings. Big Man doesn't want the Cobras shooting cops. Brings them under our scrutiny, and it's bad for his boss's business. "

"Hmm. How bad were you hurting?"

"Not much at first, but when the initial shock wore off, my whole arm was on fire, and I had the shakes."

His tone changed, and he became a cop again. "We've been treating them like bored kids who swagger and throw gang signs at each other and talk trash about their territories." He shook his head. "No more. The Cobras stepped their game up with attempted murder and a robbery. Haskie is joining Ketso in prison." His voice trailed off.

He was tired from the shock and from talking. His eyelids drooped. I hugged him as best I could with one of his arms tied to an IV and the other heavily bandaged. His breathing was slow and steady when I tiptoed out into the hallway to go home for some much needed sleep of my own.

***

Sleep eluded me. Sometime during the long night, I realized I had fallen in love with Sam. I hadn't planned it, hadn't created a blueprint and carefully constructed it. I fell into love, a dizzying, astonishing tumble into a tumult I eagerly surrendered to. If I got hurt, loving him was worth the risk because I couldn't imagine a morning without him in my life.

Sam had shaved and showered, but he was still stuck in the humiliating backless gown when I arrived at the hospital. I had his favorite breakfast burrito and a change of clothes for him.

He was unfettered from the IV. "Your stomach up to a burrito?" I handed it to him.

"Hell yes." He grabbed it from me. "I'm starving. Thanks."

While he wolfed it down, I laid his clean uniform, socks, and underwear on the bed. "You cleared to leave?"

"Yes." He threw the burrito paper in the trash.

"Get dressed, cowboy, and I'll take you to work. While I was at you place, I fed Jasper."

"Thanks. Help me with the shirt, will you?"

I tried, but the bandage was not going to fit through the short sleeve of his uniform shirt. I ripped the underarm seam up to the shoulder. "Sorry. I have some safety pins in the car."

"Just get me out of here."

"How much pain do you have?"

"It's okay as long as I don't move my arm much."

By the time I helped him get the arm back in the sling, a sheen of sweat glistened on his forehead.

"It's hurting now, isn't it?"

"Yeah, let's go." He was already striding to the door. "I may have a gang war on my hands."

Sam was a warrior, trained to accept pain as a naturally occurring part of life. I figured he'd never fill the prescription for Oxycodone he carried in his pocket as we left the hospital.

I parked by his Tahoe in front of the Navajo Police headquarters. He grimaced and braced his arm on the console.

"Don't overdo it and call me if you need anything. Are you cleared to drive?"

He opened the car door and called over his shoulder, "No, Nez'll drive me."

***

I picked up Taylor at the TV station for our appointment with the FBI. "Was Agent Aguirre mad about our cancelling on him?" I asked.

Taylor laughed. "He's FBI. He's not used to being ditched, but I think he understood. How was Sam this morning?"

"Much better. He's at work."

"And how are you?" Taylor probed.

I took one hand off the wheel and turned up my palm. "In love with him."

"So happy for you and him." She grinned. "Have you told the lucky guy?"

"Not a chance." I parked in front of the office and turned off the car engine.

"You'll find the right time. The man looks like he's in love with you, too."

"Come on." She pushed open the exterior door to the nondescript brick building with a single brass sign identifying it as a federal office. "We still have work to do."

We walked into the FBI office, and I asked for Agent Aguirre. He was sitting at a beat-up metal desk in a windowless office surrounded by top-notch computer equipment and techie gizmos I couldn't identity.

We shook hands. "Thanks for seeing us, Agent Aguirre. I'm sorry we had to cancel. I'm Jordan Bia, Navajo CPS."

He stood and shook my hand. "I heard about Officer Tohee. How is he?"

"Better, thank you. He's back at work."

Taylor and I settled into two chairs facing him across a large messy desk.

"Tell me about this case you're working," Agent Aguirre said.

I told him all I knew about Sofia and the Banamichi police.

He nodded. "I've been interviewed by Taylor before. Hope you won't chew my ass as hard as she did. Taylor told me you were interested in Montoya."

"I am. Does the laptop you found connect to him?"

He clasped his hands behind his head and leaned back in his chair. "You go for the guts and glory question first."

"Yeah, I don't beat around the bush well."

He addressed Taylor. "Before we go any further, I want you to know I'm going to structure what you tell your viewers. We agreed to that, remember?"

"Not exactly in those words, but I agreed to do nothing to impair your investigation," she answered.

"Yes to the question we believe this computer belongs to human traffickers. Off the record, no response to the question about links to Montoya."

Taylor laughed. "Awww, shucks. How can I whip up the viewers' interest in Montoya if you won't let me tell them you said 'no comment' to talking about him? A gal's got to make a living."

A tight smile flashed across his face, but he didn't answer.

He was at least suspicious of Montoya, if not trying to prove a case against him, or he wouldn't have declared talking about him verboten. I breathed in slowly and tried to appear nonchalant. "Can you tell us about what you found on the computer?" I asked.

"There's a digital wallet with a sizable amount of Bitcoins. You know how that works?" he asked.

I shook my head. "Tell me."

"A digital wallet is really software used for e-commerce purchases and Bitcoins are a virtual currency. The online wallet contains all your personal information and money, including your credit card information. You can even access your account from a mobile app."

"Doesn't sound illegal," Taylor said.

"It's not. You can buy a comforter from Overstocks with Bitcoins right now from your digital wallet and use your phone to do it," he said.

"Explain Bitcoins. I'm not getting it."

"They're nothing you can hold in your hand. Bitcoins are a crypto-currency that you exchange peer to peer for services or goods—and the value of a Bitcoin fluctuates daily. You store them in your digital wallet. That's where this laptop gets interesting."

I leaned forward in excitement. "Why?"

"Ever heard of Dark Wallet software?"

We both answered, "No."

"It's a free software, released earlier this year. When you run Dark Wallet software, you make all your electronic activity secret, just like money in a Swiss bank account."

I was puzzled. He explained, "Dark Wallet software uses high-end encryption technology to mask transactions."

"So no one can see what was bought or sold?" I asked

"Correct. But I can see the sites this laptop visited. Ever heard of the Dark Net? The web your common browsers like Explorer and Firefox can't go to?"

"No, but this is getting interesting. What's on the Dark Net?"

"Every nefarious good or service. It's the place to be if you are buying or selling drugs, weapons, including stolen military ordnance, people for the sex trade, or services like assassination or forgery. Hell, stolen credit cards go for ten bucks a pop. It's an encrypted, anonymous, electronic bazaar for criminals." He laughed grimly. "The two most common Dark Net sites are SilkRoad 2.0 and Black Market Reloaded, but new ones pop up each day. This laptop we took had visited SilkRoad 2.0."

"How do get you on the Dark Net?" I asked.

"First you have to download a new browser, developed for penetrating the Dark Net."

"Free, I assume," Taylor said.

He steepled his fingers and grinned. "Oh, absolutely—drives more buyers and sellers into the marketplace. The browser is Tor, stands for The Onion Router, which refers to Tor's software which bounces packets of data through services all over the globe, making it impossible to find where the server is that hosts a criminal website. We try to peel back the layers of the onion between the transaction and host servers."

"Where do you find Tor?" I asked.

"Google it. Click the link to Tor, open it, click the link to download, and in a moment you get a message, 'Congratulations! This computer is configured to use Tor.' Click the 'What Next?' box for directions and just type what you want to buy or sell in the search box, and you're up and running an encrypted browser cruising a Mecca of illegal stuff. But be wise about this kind of activity. No one downloads Tor who doesn't want anonymity, but your computer IP address can be seen downloading Tor."

"So you arrest people who download Tor?" I asked.

"If only law enforcement were that easy." He grinned. "There are legitimate users of the browser. The Electronic Frontier Foundation and other civil liberties groups claim it is useful for whistle blowers and human rights workers to communicate. Hell, the most famous recent user of Tor was Edwin Snowden. He used it to send comments to *The Washington Post* and *The Guardian*."

"After you download Tor, how do you find the Dark Net sites?"

"SilkRoad 2.0 and Black Market Reloaded are the two largest sites on the Dark Net. There'll be pop-up ads."

"Is the FBI trying to prevent access to SilkRoad 2.0?" Taylor asked.

"Much of what computer nerds like me are doing is off the record," Aguirre said.

He seemed to be enjoying himself. "I work with a complete alphabet soup. ICE, DEA, Treasury Department of Financial Crimes, Homeland Security, and the good old US Post Office."

"The post office?" I asked.

"Think about it. The exchange of illegal goods used to take place in dark alleys, but now much of it comes to you in the US mail. Except for the human cargo, and that's their weak point. I intend to push it."

"I can use that?" Taylor asked.

"Absolutely."

"How is the FBI monitoring users of the Dark Net?" I asked.

"I can give you some broad strokes. The Treasury Department developed the Financial Crimes Illicit Pathways Attack Strategy, and that's a mouthful. Their goal is to disrupt Dark Net sites that are involved in criminal activity. It's up, it's working, and that's all I have to say about that one."

"Meaning there is a second prong to your attack," I said.

"You know what a traffic correlation attack is?"

I shook my head no.

"Traffic correlation attacks can monitor the Tor network user's traffic as he enters and leaves the network and can reveal the user's identity."

"What's the success rate of correlation attacks?" Taylor asked.

"No comment, but I can tell you we can de-anonymize visitors to SilkRoad and Black Market Reloaded, and we're analyzing traffic entering and exiting Tor. If you're in there, I'll find your digital footprints."

"Do you have any names attached to an Internet address you've tracked? Like Montoya's?" I desperately wanted him to have found Montoya's tracks on the Dark Net.

"No comment. And that's all the time I have this morning."

"Thank you, Agent Aguirre," I said.

We hurried out of the building to my car. As soon as Taylor fastened her seat belt, she reviewed her interview notes, scribbling in the margins. "You know why he was so forthcoming?"

I shook my head.

"Because he's using me. He wants me to report everything he told us to put pressure on the smugglers. He hopes they'll make a mistake." She shrugged. "Of course, I get a great story out of it." She looked over at me. "Why are you just sitting there? We need to get back to work."

"I'm going to bait a digital trap and flush Montoya out on the Dark Net. I can hose this bastard out into the open."

She dropped her pen between the car seats. "Wh-what did you say?"

"I want to use your computer at work. You work for a news agency. I work for the State, and all hell would break loose if I downloaded Tor."

"And do what with Tor?"

"Go to SilkRoad 2.0 and buy an ad claiming I have a load of women for sale."

"Using what for money? Your credit card, the one with Jordan Bia on it?"

"No, the Bitcoins I buy with my credit card. That's not illegal. I might be getting a new comforter at Overstocks."

"Okay, but placing the ad is iffy."

"Yeah, it is," I admitted. "Better to beg forgiveness than ask permission."

"And what are we going to do if someone answers your ad. Then what?"

"We don't wait that long. We alert Sam and Trace to the ad after I place it."

"Humph."

"I'm not *selling* women. The advertisement is a fake," I cajoled. "And I don't think anyone looking to buy women will report me to the Federal Trade Commission for false advertising."

I could see her salivate for this story. "Crazy, but okay."

"When can we set up the ad?"

"Marty's got me on a deadline for the ten o'clock news. Meet me first thing in the morning."

"Done. And thank you."

I was headed home from the FBI offices ready for some quality time with Chloe and the quiet of my little house when my phone rang. I didn't recognize the number.

"I got something you might be interested in about your human trafficking case—you know, that little girl, Sofia."

The voice was familiar, but I couldn't place it. "Who is this?"

"Texas Jack, darlin'."

How did he know I worked Sofia's case? How did he get my private cell phone number? Did he know I had just left the FBI? I was paranoid, and maybe he was just a gossip who owned a dance hall, but I had no time to play games. "What do you want to talk about?"

"Oh, I got plenty I want to talk to you about," he said lazily.

"Let me rephrase that," I said, feeling my impatience rising. "What do you have that you think I might be interested in as it relates to human trafficking?"

"Plenty," he said.

"What?" I demanded.

"Settle down now."

"Hey, Mr.— What is your last name?"

"Don't know. Haven't used it in a long time," he drawled.

I hated being toyed with. "You said you had something relevant to tell me, so tell me."

"Sure, gal. I just don't see the need to get all riled up and pissy about it."

"I'm not riled up." I sounded defensive and immediately regretted taking his bait.

"You know Montoya used to own my bar. Back in those days, all those little shacks were full of beautiful women like you."

"Not like me," I corrected him.

"All in the eye of the beholder, darlin'. Anyway, as I was saying, Montoya used to live out here and run his women in the shacks. Dance hall was for dancin' like it still is. You come out, and I can show you around the place."

Drinking. He had to be drinking or nuts to think I would go out there alone and meet him.

"We could have a beer and get to know each other a little better," he added.

"Don't call me again. Email me the next time you think you know something."

"Sure, babe, but it would have been an evening you would always remember if you had chosen to spend it with me," he twanged.

Psycho? Or conceit? I didn't care which. "Good-bye."

What a waste of time. My phone rang.

"You sound like you're in the car," Sam said.

"I'm in the car on the way home," I blurted out. "Texas Jack just called and wanted me to come out to Crazy Gal's so he could give me a tour and show me how Montoya ran his business out there." Silence on Sam's end. "Are you there?" I heard crackling over his heavy sigh.

"Yeah, I'm here. You're going out to Jack's..." And then the phone either dropped the call or he hung up.

Oh yeah, right. Like I was going to dash out to canoodle at Crazy Gal's with Texas Jack. I slammed the phone in the console, then picked it up and called Sam back, but after five rings, his phone went to voice mail. I was lonely, angry, and misunderstood. A toxic mix.

Chapter 13

I awoke the next morning annoyed about never getting a call back from Sam. He should have given me an opportunity to talk with him about Jack, but I wasn't calling him again. I knew I was stubborn. My mother had nicknamed me Hard Headed when I was in grade school.

Benally called while I was still outside with Chloe. "A high school kid hung himself last night on the elementary school play ground," she said in a high pitched, strained voice.

"Why? Oh God, the school kids didn't find the body, did they?"

"No, the principal found him and cut him down before anyone else made it to campus."

"Did he leave a note?"

"Yeah, his parents found the note in his room," she said grimly. "He claimed he was bullied by the Cobras because he wouldn't join the gang. New Cobra graffiti is painted over at the high school and at Basha's grocery across the street."

"You want me out there?"

"Yes. Get out there and fly the flag of cooperation between the school and our agency. Tell them we'll provide support with our contract counselors for the kids."

"Who was the boy who died?"

"Jimmy Begay, fourteen years old. I already called Principal Mason Torres and told him you were on your way. You are ready for work, aren't you?" she sniped.

"Certainly. I'll keep you briefed on the situation."

I rushed Chloe into the house, grabbed my bag, and hurried out to my car and drove way too fast to the high school where I finally found place for my Civic in a dirt lot.

Taylor's Rav was parked in the high school lot and two police cars were angled near the grade school's playground. Sam and Nez were bent over, combing the ground inside the taped-off crime scene. Taylor was talking to them and Louis was shooting video. The coroner's van backed slowing out onto the street.

I hoisted my briefcase out of the car and hurried toward the high school's front door. Did the Begay boy kill himself on the school grounds to send a message? The last thing he saw in those choking moments was the empty, brown brick high school and the swing set for the grade school kids.

The hub of offices for the staff and principal were directly inside the front door. I waited until the harried secretary got off the phone, then identified myself and asked to see Mr. Torres. She ushered me into his office. I had not met the new principal, but I knew he was well thought of and had been recruited from a large high school in Albuquerque because of his success there in working with gangs. He was in his thirties, tall and reed-thin, built like a distance runner, and well turned out in dress pants and a neatly pressed button-down shirt. He was still obviously very upset, though he had control of his emotions. His hand trembled when he reached out to shake mine. His eyes were moist and red-rimmed.

"I'm Jordan Bia, and I represent Navajo CPS. I'm here to help. We can provide support staff to help your counselors."

He nodded. "I cut his body down." His voice wavered. "His face...his face was awful."

"I'm sorry you had to find him."

"Better me than a student." He pulled himself together and invited me to sit down. "We can use all the help we can get." He sat behind his desk and talked about the dead boy. "Jimmy was a good student. He wasn't involved in a lot of activities here, but he was well liked. He was a quiet, studious boy, and I wouldn't say that he would easily come to the attention of a group like the Cobras."

"Then what did happen?"

"I can't say. Not that I won't, I can't. I've spoken briefly to Jimmy's teachers, and none of them have any idea why the Cobras culled Jimmy out for bullying. All of that is supposition until the police finish their investigation, but the parents did find a suicide note in his bedroom and identified the handwriting as Jimmy's. He names the Cobras in it. "

"I'm so sorry for them and the school. How big is the gang problem in the school?"

"Big. There are two hundred gangs on the Nation, some with as few as two to three members." He sat up straight, assuming the role of the principal again. He had passed through the initial shock and was ready to talk of what to do. He took his glasses off and pinched the bridge of his nose. "The Cobras and the Dragons are the two biggest gangs on our campus. We do what we can. We try to steer students into sports, service clubs, social events—any school-sponsored activity we can get them interested in."

"Get your fuckin' hands off me." Someone exploded outside Torres's office.

Torres was on his feet and running for the door. He flung it open, cracking the doorknob back into the sheetrock of his office wall. "That's enough!" he roared in the face of a hulking male.

"Ain't no Dragon safe nowhere," the young man yelled.

"Bill! Bill Haskie. Get control of yourself right now!" Torres pushed into Bill's personal space and loomed over him.

Bill put out a hand to push Torres. The principal deftly grabbed his hand and bent it back until he screamed.

Torres's secretary ran in yelling, "I called the police."

Still wrenching the kid's arm up, Torres said, "Sit down. There!" Bill stood rigid with his knees locked until Torres knocked his legs out from under him. He fell onto the chair, Torres still clinging to his arm like a bull rider to the leather.

"What's this about?" Torres demanded.

"Dragons are fingering us Cobras for causing Jimmy's suicide. We ain't painted that graffiti out there." He pointed out the window to the spray painted wall. "Dragons done it, and if Jimmy was bullied, they did that, too, and they claiming it's us done it. Geek like Jimmy Begay wasn't ever going to be a Cobra." He puffed out his chest and sneered. "Lot of Dragons goin' die in this war, and I'm gettin' my share."

Sam's big frame filled the doorway of Torres's office.

Bill sneered at Torres. "You had to get the police in here to help you out? Man, how chicken shit is that. You cops don't want to mess with us Haskies. You know what that name means." He drew up taller and puffed out his chest. "Warrior. We're warriors."

Sam kicked a chair over by him and sat down, his knees touching Bill's. Sam jutted his face into his and growled, "You're an obnoxious little dickhead, and your big bro is going to prison."

Torres said, "Mr. Haskie threatened to kill Dragons."

"That right?" Sam asked the squirming Cobra.

"He didn't tell you why," Bill huffed.

"I don't care why. You threaten to kill someone?"

"Yeah. But the Dragons—"

"Mr. Haskie, stand up and turn around. It's a criminal offence to threaten someone."

"Ahh shit. You're the asshole that my big bro shot. Too bad he didn't kill you."

"Just your bad luck," Sam snapped.

Sam pulled the plastic cuffs tight on him, and Torres said quietly, "You can take him out the side door and fewer people will see him."

Sam nodded at Torres. He jerked Bill toward the side door. "Mr. Haskie, you won't be strutting the perp walk before the other Cobras today."

"Shit, man. Take me out the front."

"No way." Sam led him out the side door of Torres's office toward his patrol car. On the way past me, Sam grimaced in pain as Bill jerked and struggled to pull away.

Torres turned to me. "We're going to need your help. I'll have our counselors contact your office. I'm sorry I don't have anymore time to give you. The students need to see me in the hallways for the rest of the morning."

"I understand. Thank you for your time. We'll send out a contract counselor today to help your staff. Will you let me know if there is any truth to Bill's claim the Dragons bullied Jimmy?"

"I will. Though I can tell you right now, I don't think that's the case. Bill doesn't know we have Jimmy's suicide note, and that gang graffiti out there"—he paused and motioned out the window to the snake painted on the wall—"is a perfect Cobra's signature. Bill Haskie is just kicking dirt at the Dragons."

I handed him my card before I left his office.

I walked out to the little kids' playground. The only place tall enough for Jimmy to have hanged himself was the monkey bars. Nez walked concentric circles out from the bars, kicking at the weeds, occasionally bending over to pick something up in his gloved hands and shove it in a plastic evidence bag.

I found Taylor and Louis outside the crime scene tape, discussing what they still needed for the story. Taylor held up one finger for me to wait and asked Louis to get some footage of the graffiti on the building.

She sidled up to me. "Helluva deal. I've got to go over to the Begay's and talk to his family. I frickin' hate that part of the job—getting a reaction bite from the family." She cocked her head toward Nez. "You talked to Sam or Nez yet?"

"I saw Sam for a moment before he left with a Cobra in tow." I told her what Bill had threatened.

"So Mike Haskie's little brother Bill is threatening a gang war. I'll have to follow that up, too. Hell, I won't be back at the station for at least three hours. I have to go by the jail first. Can you wait a couple of hours to place the ad?"

"That'll work fine. I have to debrief my boss, write a report, and get some contract help out here."

She grinned conspiratorially. "See ya in a couple. Hey, Nez is still out there working the crime scene if you want to talk to him."

Nez was kicking at a small piece of metal embedded in the dirt inside the yellow taped off area.

"Hey there, are you working this case?" he asked me.

"Yeah, I'm the CPS liaison with the school. Bill Haskie denies the Cobras bullied the Begay kid. What do you think?" I asked.

"Don't believe his garbage. Jimmy called the Cobras out in the note."

"What's going on with the brother, Mike?"

"If he's smart, he'll take the deal the DA is offering. He shot Sam in front of me and his Cobra buddies, including the bouncer out there. Total waste of money to move to a trial."

"What's the DA offering him?"

"Reduced sentence, but he'll still do time in the prison over in Window Rock. Your guy, uh, you know Officer Tohee?"

"Yes," I said, alert to the personal turn of the conversation and Nez's hesitancy.

"I think he's not doing so well. Okay, he's still strong as an ox but..."

"What is it?"

"He's jumping at shadows, distracted, and irritable. That's not safe for an officer or his partner, *me*," he said while pointing at himself.

"What would you suggest?"

Nez dropped his gloved hands to his sides and lowered his voice. "He needs a Sing to restore his balance."

"Hmm. You want me to talk to him?"

"He won't take it as well from me."

"Let me think about it. I won't say you mentioned it."

He shook his head. "No ma'am, he wouldn't like that."

***

After two hours of tedium, some spent in Benally's office bringing her up to speed on the incident at the high school, the rest spent editing our GIC presentation, I headed for the KNAZ studios and Taylor's office, thinking about the best way to approach Sam, or even if I should after our truncated phone conversation. Taylor was close to Trace's grandmother,

Yanaha, who was a Shaman, and she would know the best Singer, but before I talked with Taylor, I had to decide if I should even broach the subject with Sam. And he had to agree to have a Sing.

Taylor was working at her desk when I knocked and entered. "I just spoke to Marty. He's on board with you using my computer for research. That's what he calls it, 'research,' but I explained it more thoroughly than that."

"He wants plausible deniability, right?" I asked.

She nodded. "Marty likes to keep his ass covered, but he wants this story, and he *really* wants another Emmy. Still no sign of Juanita?"

"None. Nothing from Flag PD or the Nation police."

She swung her chair around and stood up. " That's bad news. Sorry. Here you go."

I booted up her computer, and when her browser opened, I typed *Tor* into the search engine. I clicked the link, and the screen filled with the logo, a purple *T* and *r* surrounding the *o*, which was a picture of a transected golden onion showing the layers. "I got a digital wallet and a Bitcoin account last night on my home computer." I accepted the changes to Taylor's machine and the computer was configured to accept Tor. The site opened, headed with the purple and gold name. A search box popped up asking *Where would you like to go?*

I typed *SilkRoad 2.0*.

"Now it gets interesting," Taylor said from over my shoulder. "Whose name did you put the wallet in?"

"Janet T. Jones, not too original, huh? I had to use my card to buy the Bitcoins, but I put them in Janet's wallet."

The SilkRoad home page opened, revealing a picture of an Arab on a camel and the title, *SilkRoad, Anonymous Marketplace.* The graphic was surrounded with hot links, pictures of guns, drugs, credit cards, stolen art, and women. I hovered the cursor over the picture of a woman, clicked on her picture, and a new page opened. The caption was *Sweet & Sexy Erotic Girls*. On the left side of the screen were individual pictures of different ethnicities of women for sale, and when I scrolled to the bottom, there was a picture of a child.

Taylor stood behind me, shooting video of the screen over my shoulder. "Jeezus, look at that. Don't worry. I'll strip out our audio track."

I clicked a link for an ad and *Dirty Blond Bombshell for You* filled the screen. The Bitcoin hotlink blinked at the bottom of the page. I closed the page, returned to the home page for ads for women, and opened the link to the children's page. A picture of a child no older than twelve in a leather brassiere and thong was bent over jutting her bottom toward the camera. She held a dominatrix whip in one hand and peered over her shoulder into the lens. Her pouty mouth was painted a slash of red.

Louis had joined us. "Don't," Louis said to Taylor who had leaned closer to shoot the screen. "I can clean up the picture of the blonde in Photoshop, but not the child. Leave out the child."

Repulsion coiled through me as I imagined men trolling the site for dolled-up pouty-mouthed children. I returned to the SilkRoad home page and, on a whim, typed *assassin* in the search engine.

A site opened with a close-up picture of a large caliber handgun caressing the cheek of a beautiful woman. Her crimson lips pursed in a sexy '*oh*.' Beneath her picture were the details.

We are a two-person team operating in Europe, Canada, and the U.S. E-mail us here. The e-mail link flashed.

If we accept your job, it will be completed within four weeks after our acceptance. Payment rendered upon agreement. Only two rules:

No top ten politicos and no one under sixteen.

I blew out a hiss of air. My hand was shaking so much the cursor wobbled on the screen. "Oh, my God."

"Get video. I can put a Gaussian blur effect on the worst of it, and we can use it," Louis said grimly.

Taylor reached over me and tapped her finger on an ad on the sidebar of the assassin's page. "Go here."

A crowdfunding page opened, sourcing money to hire assassins to murder President Barack Obama, President of the European Commission, Jean-Claude Juncker, and U.S. Federal Reserve Chairman Janet Yellen. A running tally under each picture showed the money collected. Of the three, Janet Yellen was leading the pack in funding.

"Gal, I don't want to see this shit. I'm better off not knowing," Louis said.

"I thought crowdsourcing was for entrepreneurs. I didn't even know who the head of the Federal Reserve was."

"Too bad I can't forget I saw it. I guess you're thinking Montoya buys or sells his women here," Louis said.

"Yep, that's why I'm here, to get an e-mail account from SilkRoad and post an ad for hot Hispanic virgins."

"Holy shit, gal. How you gonna know if it's Montoya?" Louis asked.

"Let the FBI practice their traffic correlation and require the buyer to take possession on the Nation."

"Does FBI know what you're doing?"

"No," Taylor and I chorused together.

"This is a 'don't ask, don't tell' kind of situation. Well, at least don't tell until after the fact," I said.

"Been there, done that with you, Taylor," Louis said. "Can the FBI see the IP address of the guys that answer?"

"I'm guessing well enough that Agent Aguirre wouldn't give the success rate for fear of tipping his hand to the cyberpunks who have their own computer nerds. My ace in the hole is that I'm only agreeing to exchange the women on the Nation." I tried to placate Louis's fears. "We're telling Sam and Trace after we place the ad and, oh hell, should we give them the password, too?"

She nodded. "Well yeah, that's the first thing they're going to demand. We'll give it to Aguirre, too. Keep 'em all happy with us."

"I wouldn't bet on any of them being very happy with you two," Louis said.

I submitted my ad, closed SilkRoad, and clicked off Tor. "You'll have to check the ad. I can't do it from my state computer or my personal laptop." I pointed to a yellow pad of sticky notes. "I wrote the password on that post-it note."

"I'll call you if we get a hit. Let's go get a bite to eat. You too, Louis," Taylor said.

"Can't. You two go on." He rolled his eyes. "Marty has me following the intern around to shoot a charity golf event."

We took Taylor's Rav to lunch at the Galaxy, a red and chrome, neon-lit 1950s retro diner. We skipped the cheese fries and burgers, settling instead on salads and soup.

My phone rang. "Hello," I said hastily, swallowing hot chowder.

"You have time to talk?" Sam asked. "Sorry I lost your call last night. Once I left the high school, I was out on the Nation where cell reception is bad. I didn't get in until late, and I didn't want to disturb you."

"Everything all right?"

"Yeah."

"I'm having lunch with Taylor at the Galaxy."

"Call me when you and Taylor are finished, okay?"

When I hung up and explained to Taylor, she said, "Hey, I see an opportunity in your future to tell him you love him."

I toyed with my salad. "I'm not sure this is the opportunity. Sam thinks I'm attracted to Texas Jack."

She started laughing. "Yeah, right. What's going on?"

I bit my lower lip and gazed down at my salad. "That's not all. Nez thinks Sam is acting irritable and distracted, and he wants me to talk to him about having a Sing. I don't think I'm close enough to him right now to suggest that to him."

"You've met Yanaha. She'll help you set it up. Could be Sam thinks you and Jack have a thing, and that's causing part of his lack of *hozho.* I don't understand the Navajo concept of balance and the ritual of a Sing, but I do know you're in love with him, and I think it's your responsibility to talk with him about anything that will make him whole and living in harmony."

"Yeah, I know, and hey, Nez doesn't want Sam to know he said anything to me."

"Done. We're through talking about a Sing for Sam. Are you going to tell him you love him?"

"I guess. What's the worst he could do?" I toyed with my food. "Why did Sam really leave Window Rock?"

"Have you asked him?"

"No, I'm asking you. Is that a problem?"

"We'll see after I tell you. Sam left Window Rock because he was in a relationship with a woman that was going nowhere. She was a clinger and wouldn't stop pestering him. She has problems, real big problems. She's a single mom of two little boys, has a crappy job and an ex who is a drunken bastard who abuses her and gives her nothing for the kids."

"Sam abandoned her?" This didn't sound like Sam.

"No. He loaned her money, tried to get her to file charges on the ex, got her help for her alcohol problems. He did everything but adopt the whole group of them. But she couldn't, or wouldn't, pull herself together. She started hanging around Sam's apartment, claiming to be his wife to the manager, and one night she dropped the kids off at his door and did the knock-and-run, and then wouldn't answer her cell phone. She was out of control by then. The final straw was when she accused Sam of abusing her."

"Oh, my God. What happened?"

"A full-blown investigation. Internal Affairs nitpicked through all of Sam's life, talked to his friends, his cop buddies, his old officers in the Corps, and even combed through his financial records."

"He was cleared, wasn't he?"

"Of course, he was. That's when Sam decided to take the transfer Trace offered him. He should have had a Sing when he put her out of his life. Bad stuff has just piled up on him, most recently his getting shot," Taylor said.

"He told me once he got to know some little kids in Window Rock. Hers, I suppose?"

"Yes, he loved those kids."

"Does he have any contact with their mom?" I asked.

"None that I know of. Trace says Sam loved the woman, faults and all, and he still worries about her boys. I know he checks with their grandma to see how the kids are, and he sends them gifts for birthday and Christmas through the grandmother."

"Damn. I don't want to be the rebound woman."

Taylor's face softened. "We don't get to choose who we fall in love with or when we fall in love. It just happens, and we're along for the ride."

"But I don't want to be the woman that he goes to when he can't be with her."

"That's not what's happening. You two love each other. There is no evidence he is going between the two of you."

"I need to hear those three little words from Sam. Damn. That sounds so small, but I need to hear 'I love you.'"

"Give it time. Give yourselves a chance. Talk to him," she pleaded.

"I will, but I don't want to say 'I love you' first."

"Start off by clearing the air about Jack, suggest he have a Sing, then roll with telling him you love him." She stood up and checked the time. "I'm sorry. I've got to get back or Marty will kill me." She gave me hug. "Call if you want to talk more."

She left, and I called Sam. He sounded distracted. Damn, probably bad timing on my part to call him now. "You looked like you were hurting when you tightened those cuffs on Bill. Did you take the pain killers?"

"I'll be fine." He brushed aside my question. "Doc says the sooner I start using it, the less muscle loss I'll have. Can you come for dinner around seven? I'll cook. You just relax. Please, I want to talk."

"Sure." And maybe we would both talk.

Chapter 14

Sunset slipped toward darkness and painted the western sky a panoply of gold and red as I drove to Sam's house for dinner. He prized his property for the view of San Francisco peak, one of our four sacred mountains, and tonight her snowy top gleamed in the late light. Even though an Anglo had built Sam's home, the front door faced east and caught the first light of the new day, letting Sam receive the Ancient Ones' blessings when they assembled at dawn. I would need their help if I chose to talk to Sam about my love for him, his old love in Window Rock, his need for a Sing, Jack—oh, so many topics to broach—or I could just chicken out and enjoy the evening on a surface level.

Yellow circles of lamplight spilled out on his small yard from his bare windows. Sam wanted nothing to bar his view of his land and the peak, so he had ripped down all the curtains and rods, patched the holes, and repainted the walls. Jasper was barking like crazy from the front window when I stepped out of my car.

Sam flung open the front door before I could knock. "I'm glad you're here." He grabbed me in a bear hug and kissed me hello.

His face was etched in fatigue, and he was pale and drawn. Jasper nearly knocked me down when he jumped up to give me his kiss. I bent to pet his dog."Hey, big guy."

"Down!" Sam said. Jasper slunk to the floor. "Good boy." Jasper's tail thumped on the wood floor, watching Sam help me off with my coat and lay it on a chair.

"What breed is he besides border collie?"

"Who knows? He's a rez dog. His mom is a collie, and we don't know who the dad is. But he leads the life of a pampered lapdog. Come back this way." He took my hand and led me to the kitchen

A perfectly cooked prime rib roast rested in its juices on the countertop by a bagged salad and bakery bread. I relaxed at the bar with a glass of white wine and watched him toss the salad with bottled dressing, remembering my own disastrous home-cooked dinner.

The attention he paid me, his emotional friendship, and his hot lovemaking dimmed the image of him with his former love in Window Rock and my annoyance with his spurt of jealously about Texas Jack. He turned around and smiled at me. "Cooking is foreplay you know, like dancing."

"Yeah, but you do it so much better than me. Just look at all this." I slipped off the bar stool and joined him at the table where we had dinner by candlelight. He was an excellent cook and generous host.

"Let's have our coffee in the den by the fireplace." I took our plates to the kitchen sink and poured mugs of coffee.

I wrapped my hands around the steaming mug of dark roast and scooted close to him. The wood hissed and cracked in the brick firebox. I had mentally run through a dozen approaches in my head, and none seemed right. Finally I went with a direct approach. "I think a Sing would help restore your sense of balance. Your gunshot wound and Jimmy's suicide have taken a toll on you." After I had spoken, the words sounded cold and clinical, maybe even bossy.

He didn't turn away from staring into the fire. Finally, he exhaled a pent-up breath. "I agree. I can't accept what is and work with what life sends my way. Instead, I'm struggling trying to exert my will and control stuff." He turned his head to me, deep tired lines slashed around his eyes and mouth. "Trace's grandmother, Yanaha, is a Shaman, and he's contacted her. She's holding my Blessing Way out at her place in Kaih Canyon." He laughed quietly. "She's probably already got the women cooking."

He took my hand in his. "I need the Shaman to sing the sacred songs over me, and I want you there with me. You could use a blessing also."

"I could. I can't get the image out of my head of you with a gun pointed at you." I kissed his cheek.

He snugged me in close and kissed me. Relief flooded his face.

I took the plunge. "I, uh, have something else to talk with you about."

Eyeing me warily, he leaned back on the sofa. "Okay..."

I took a deep breath, not knowing how he would react. "I'm advertising virgins on SilkRoad with the caveat that the buyer has to take possession on the Nation."

"You *what*?"

"The FBI would screw around and waste time and mull over what might happen, could happen, and create scenarios for handling stuff that would never happen. I just bought the ad, and you'll monitor the ad." I handed my card to him. "On the back is my SilkRoad e-mail address and the password to the account. You need to configure your computer to Tor."

"Tell me you didn't do this on your state computer."

"Of course not. I used Taylor's computer in the newsroom, and her news director okayed setting up the account."

His face flushed hot with anger."Yeah right, you take the risk, and she gets a great story." "That's unfair to Taylor and just plain wrong," I shot back at him, mad at his accusation.

"It was my idea. The FBI announced to the media they had found a laptop with a digital wallet full of Bitcoins. We talked to the agent, and he told us the laptop showed activity on the Dark Net."

Sam abruptly jumped up and paced in stony silence in front of the fireplace like a marine who had lost control of his mission. He was angry at me for either acting without his knowledge or for taking a risk, or both. I remained silent and watched. He stopped pacing, whirled around, and faced me. Since I was sitting and he was standing, he held the dominant high ground. I stood and faced him as his equal.

His eyes locked on mine. He threw his hands in the air and then crossed them across his chest. "It's a helluva idea. I don't like that you took the risk. You're a civilian, and you'll turn it over to me now."

"Of course you have a part to play," I said to mollify him. "You provide protection, and you're there to snap the trap shut."

We stood toe to toe, neither budging.

Then he turned sharply away from me and exploded. "It's a dangerous gamble. I'll talk to Trace in the morning. Don't do anything and don't answer any damned replies." He turned back to me. "Promise me. Nothing more." Anger clouded his warrior face, and sharp angles and shadows shaded his eyes.

The scent of testosterone filled his den. I gathered my coffee cup and headed for the kitchen sink. "Okay, I promise. I think we both need to get some rest." I went to the front door, snagging my coat off the chair in the entryway.

He nodded, followed me to the door, and absently brushed my cheek with his lips. It certainly didn't qualify as a kiss.

When I backed down his drive, I could see him backlit and watching me out the front window. I hadn't explained about Jack or told him I loved him because I had taken the easy way out and talked about his Sing and work, staying rooted on safer ground, but he hadn't mentioned

Jack either. Maybe because it didn't matter to him if I was interested in Jack. Maybe I had put too much importance on what I thought we had, or maybe we didn't have anything. Maybe I misread everything, and maybe I was over-thinking something very real and very simple.

***

Sleep wouldn't come. I read, hoping to relax, but knowing it would be hard as I lay there hashing over the opportunity I had missed with Sam.

The book slipped from my fingers, and I dozed off. The dream began with me standing alone on the floor of Honoo Ji with a sliver of moon lighting the sky. I felt no fear as I sauntered through the weird rock formations. I knew I was dreaming, and I thought it was odd that I was so unafraid to be walking in Honoo Ji.

A large fin jutted out of a bed of red scrabble on the canyon floor in front of me. When I tilted my head toward the peak, I lost my balance, tripped, and fell on my rear. Before I could get up, an owl swooped down and tangled his talons in my hair, tearing at my scalp. He disappeared, taking the thin stream of moonlight with him. Warm blood ran down my face, and my head stung from the gashes.

The atmosphere became heavy with damp, and rank with the odor of putrid flesh. I gagged. Suddenly, the fin in front of me disappeared, and I was standing on hard-packed sand. A trail opened up through the rock formations in front of me, and a weak light flickered at the end. Mesmerized by the glow, I walked toward the shaft of light.

The path ran straight and smooth in front of me. I was gaining ground on the light when a large rounded hoodoo appeared in my path, blocking the light and plunging me into darkness. I scuttled around the side, squeezing between the hoodoo and the canyon wall, and broke free, running toward the glow.

The canyon walls on either side of me slowly moved in, narrowing the space, imprisoning me in a shoulder-width gash between the rock, then constricting into a tighter slash, so cramped I could only turn to my side to inch my way forward. Inside the passageway, the fog grew so thick I couldn't see ahead of me. I kept both my hands on the wall in front of me and sidestepped along the sandy floor, trying to keep from stumbling in the dark. A sliver of weak light hovered over the top of the tall walls. I slid my foot and touched something solid in front of me. I kept one hand on the wall, and with my other hand, I tapped along the wall, hunting for an opening. The canyon had dead-ended. The cleft was too tight for me to turn around. Frantic, I took two small steps and ran into a wall. The canyon had closed in on itself, trapping me in a small dark space surrounded by solid sandstone walls. A weak beam of light shone in the sky high above the walls. I heard harsh voices. One called my name; others spewed vile curses. I frantically felt the rough walls. There was no way out. What if the walls moved closer, crushing me between them?

I sucked in shallow rapid gulps of air, trying not to panic. The tight space and thick miasma disoriented me, and I beat the walls with my hands, screaming and screaming. Sinister, cackling laughter echoed off the walls. Soft feathers sifted over me. I caught one and held it up in the direction of the weak light. An owl feather forecasted my death.

Chloe barked and growled. How did she get in the canyon? But I knew she could lead me out. I groped in the tiny space, trying to grab her collar.

I awoke when she pulled the covers off me and put one big paw on my chest. In the gloom of my bedroom, her ears pricked forward and her head was down, staring at something. I snapped on the bedside light. Two owl feathers lay on my nightstand, crossed over one another at the tips forming a perfect V.

I shrank from them, and then bounded out of bed and ran to the front door. Chloe beat me there. The lock was bolted. I checked the windows; all were closed and locked. My hands were stinging and weeping from the abrasions. The bathroom mirror reflected a red, raw scrape on the left side of my face. The witches were toying with me, letting me know they were powerful enough to enter my world and take me into theirs at their will.

My mind raced through what I learned of witches from my grandmother. They used a bit of hair or a fingernail clipping to curse you. My nails were clipped short and my hairbrush clean from loose hair, but my clothes, *my skin cells clung to my clothes*. I ran to my dirty clothes hamper, rummaging through my things. The sweater I had worn yesterday was gone. I dumped the hamper and pawed through it, then searched the floor of the bedroom and on the sofa, knowing it was futile.

I took the prayer sticks and medicine bag and sank back on the bed, praying the Shield prayer until dawn brought the light of the Holy Ones, asking them in the rose-tinged dawn to purge the witches of their power.

I awoke to fierce sun streaming in the windows. I threw back the covers and hurried through my shower, hoping to escape Benally's ire for being late. Both my beads and pouch were hanging around my neck when I left home.

Since Benally's car was parked in the lot, I tried to circumvent her on my way to my office, only to run into her when she came out of the restroom. "You're late," she snapped. But Benally's ire at my tardiness paled in comparison to the night I had endured.

When she finally accepted my third apology and flounced off down the hall to her office, I tried to lose myself in work. If Aguirre wouldn't talk about Montoya, he must be under suspicion. I searched state and federal databases that I had access to as a state investigator and did the obligatory Google search. What I turned up other than press about his trial was trivial information: he sat on the YMCA board, he contributed a minimal amount to the Mayor's last election, and he was a supporter of the arts. He had a tussle with his Homeowners Association that landed him in small claims court. I sighed and shut off my computer.

I doodled ideas on the pad in front of me. If Montoya was buying and selling girls, he had to be moving money, and moving money left tracks. Plus he had to file taxes with the IRS, false returns perhaps, but enough to keep them off his back.

Sam would have to request the records. I picked up the phone and called him. After we exchanged the opening pleasantries but nothing personal, I said, "I need your help to get copies of Nathan Montoya's tax records to see if the income he is reporting supports the lifestyle and the charitable contributions he makes."

"I'm one step ahead of you. I've already called Maddie McGonagall. She's an investigator over at the IRS. I should get them from her in a couple of hours."

"Will you call me?"

"If Montoya's doing what we think he is, he's dangerous and well connected. You have to be careful. He could hire someone to make you disappear, and it would look like you took a hike in the desert and never returned."

"I know. Will you call me?"

"Yeah... and your ad just got an e-mail. The buyer was interested, but he wants the women delivered to the east coast."

"Damn. Waiting is driving me nuts."

"That we haven't snared his interest doesn't mean we won't. I'll call you," he promised. "Uh, I'm sorry about last night. The only excuse I can offer is lack of sleep."

"I understand, but I need better communication between us." I didn't want to sound accusatory, and I was at fault, too. "I didn't handle that well either."

"I agree, and I'm sorry."

A huge weight of angst lifted off my shoulders when I hung up the phone. Sam sounded much more rested and a bit more like the man I loved.

I went back to working the phone and called Principal Torres. Several of our contract counselors were working with the high school counselor to deal with the aftermath of the student suicide, as well as the ongoing feud between the Cobras and the Dragons. I told Torres I would be by this afternoon to talk with our contract workers.

Sam called again before lunch. "Aguirre has connected the digital wallet to Montoya. The FBI found his offshore account, and Montoya moved money by wire transfer into his digital wallet from his offshore account. He's bought Bitcoins with the cash, and he's holding them in the wallet."

"Maybe he saw the ad and transferred the funds to buy the women."

"Could be... I've got his tax records."

"Can I see them?"

"They can't leave this office."

"I'm coming your way to the high school. I could be at the station around three."

"I'll be here."

I gathered my laptop and cell and stuffed them in my briefcase. Benally caught me as I was leaving.

"Where are you going?"

"To the high school in Tuba City to check on our contract workers." That was enough information for Benally. I really only needed to have a few minutes of face time with our workers. They were all highly professional and needed no oversight to do their jobs well. What would take some time was studying Montoya's tax records.

"Where is that girl Juanita? Do you think she's alive? Recaptured and sold into the sex trade? Surely, you have some idea about the girl's fate," she bullied.

"The Navajo police are still searching. They used cadaver dogs out in Honoo Ji, but they didn't find her body."

Benally pulled herself up to her full height and smiled imperiously. "She probably never existed. I'm sure you agree with me. Anymore of your time spent on her case is a waste of state money." She turned and clomped down the hall to her office.

Flushed with anger at her sneak attack and worried about losing my temper and my job at her goading, I grabbed my bag and headed for my car.

***

Our contract staff at the high school seemed satisfied they had the resources they needed, and Principal Torres was happy with the additional help. I headed for the police station to meet Sam and see Montoya's tax records.

The police station was way too small, cluttered with too many desks, file cabinets, and chairs jammed into the small space. Sam was talking on the phone, jotting down notes. His face had a hint of healthy color.

He hung up the phone and stood to greet me, holding up a sheaf of papers. "You cannot share this information with Taylor. If she finds it on her own, we can't help that. But if Montoya sees his financial information on the nightly news, it'll screw our investigation."

"Understood." We were both in professional mode, and a fly on the wall would never know we had been together for dinner last night.

"The IRS is interested in him. Montoya paid income tax on a salary from the trucking company of a hundred and seventy-five thousand and capital gains on some stock for a total income of less than two hundred thousand a year. He took deductions on the generous charitable donations he made. But there is no way he's financing his high-flying lifestyle on the income he reports to the IRS."

"This sounds good. A digital wallet fattened from offshore accounts, a lifestyle well beyond his reported income, and named by Sofia as the man who bought her."

"But Sofia didn't identify him from his picture." Sam fidgeted with an envelope on his desk.

"What is it?" I asked.

"Nothing on this." He gestured to the computer screen. "I've got some business to tend to over in Window Rock. I'm leaving around noon tomorrow, and I'll be gone a day or two. Trace will stay in touch with you about the ad."

His eyes wavered from meeting mine.

"Are you okay?" I asked.

"Yeah, everything is fine." A stress crease divided his brows. "Just some stuff I need to do over in Window Rock."

My gut clenched. I waited for him to invite me to meet him for dinner tonight or for breakfast in the morning before he left, to offer an explanation for his unease, to throw me any lifeline to ease my fears. The crease between his slanting brows deepened, and his mouth tugged down in a sad half moon.

The silence was excruciating. Finally, tired from the mental machinations of trying to think of ways to reach him, I decided opening up was his responsibility for the sake of our relationship and not mine to tease out of him. I was at peace with that, but unhappy as I told him good-bye and left his office.

Driving back to Flag, I was hurt he hadn't asked me how I was or if I had any bad dreams. My suspicions were in overdrive. What was the something he had to do in Window Rock, and who was he going to do it with?

I called Taylor and told her the ad had no new answers. "Does Sam want to change anything?"

"Ask Trace. He's in charge now. Sam's going to Window Rock for a couple of days."

"Uh-oh. Did Sam say what he was doing?"

"Business to tend to."

"You want to stop by and have a drink? Talk a little?"

"No, thanks." I just wanted to go home and be alone.

Chloe met me at my door, whimpering and thumping her tail, piercing me with her soulful dark eyes.

"Let me change clothes, girl, and we'll go for a run." She whirled in delicious joy and barked madly.

Chloe loped beside me as I jogged the trail in the woods that ran behind the apartment house. Sam and I had talked very little in the past week. A cold wind blew through the desert of my heart. What had I done wrong? Was he returning to an old love? Did he believe I was two-timing him with a guy like Texas Jack?

What's the worst that could happen? *He doesn't come back, or he comes back and he wants out?* My demands were simple and non-negotiable. He must know and own his heart. I hoped running would take my mind off the searing fear he wouldn't return to me from Window Rock, but irrationally my mind kept playing over and over *I thought we had something, I thought he believed we had something.*

My face was flushed with heat and wet from angry tears. Chloe sat quietly at my feet, her big paw resting on my foot, and her presence reminding me I was not alone. She laid her head in my lap and nuzzled me until the emotional storm passed. I wiped my tears and begged the universe that if it wasn't meant to be, Sam would cowpoke on away and leave my heart to heal.

With the worst of the pain vented, I thought more clearly. "You know what I need? I need to stop waiting around for answers from someone who is controlling the conversation by not talking." For all the bravado of my words to Chloe, my forlorn heart ached. Lassitude engulfed me, and I sat, dejected. I didn't know how much time had passed, but the sun was low on the horizon when I headed for home. Chloe woofed in excitement as we jogged back to my apartment. When it came into view, it was dark. No welcoming lamplight spilled from the windows. I squared my shoulders; no more wallowing in misery, pining for a guy.

"I won't ask him to talk to me again. I won't give him the pleasure of leaving me begging."

Chloe's ears pricked forward, and she huffed her approval.

Bolstered by my plan to try to indemnify myself from pain, I felt better, unlocked the front door, snapped on some lights, and inserted an Eva Cassidy CD. No, Cassidy wouldn't work. Her mellow voice stirred deep thinking. I shut the CD player off. I flipped on the TV and tried but couldn't pay attention to the show. I snapped off the set and thought about Carolyn. It was still early enough for us to catch the dinner we had talked about.

Carolyn met me at the Tuuvi Cafe, located inside a combination gas station and truck stop. The place was packed with truckers, making it easy to find Carolyn, her blond head the only one not covered with a gimme cap. I slipped into the booth across from her.

"I didn't know this place existed..."

I laughed. "The double cheeseburger on fry bread is to die for."

When the burgers came, Carolyn picked at her fries, leaving the burger on the plate.

"Don't you like the food?"

"It's not that." Carolyn leaned across the narrow table. "I have to talk someone. I had thought about calling you and then, well, you called me..." She was distressed.

"What's going on?"

"I'm terrified Nathan will kill me if he finds out." Carolyn swiped at her runny nose.

She confused me. "Find out what?"

She hung her head and didn't answer.

"I don't understand what you're afraid of."

"I'm...I'm in love with someone else." When she raised her head, she was both defiant and radiant. "He's everything my husband isn't. He loves me, and he pays attention to me. He likes to talk to me and know what I think… I want to be with him," she finished in a rush.

Carolyn surprised me with her story of a lover. I was uneasy. We were in a truck stop full of men who might drive for Montoya Trucking. Or maybe Nathan came here to eat. I leaned over the table and said quietly, "You could leave your husband and file for divorce."

"Nathan would never agree to divorce. My guy is Nathan's business partner." She laid her hand on my arm. "Jack says to let him handle everything. He says he'll fix it with Nathan. He's wonderful."

Oh, my God, what was she thinking having an affair with Texas Jack? I disciplined my face into a neutral expression, forehead smooth, eyes wide with interest. "Until Jack fixes everything, how are you going to be safe?"

"Jack says I'm just a little worrywart and I'll be fine." She blew out a big sigh."But I don't know. I'm still scared. Jack wouldn't be proud of me if he knew I was afraid. He wants me to believe in him, and I do. Really, he's so good to me. He says we can have six children if I want." When she laughed, her face flushed with pleasure.

Her abrupt mood change startled me. "The safest place for you is away from here."

"I'm not moving away from Jack." She pushed her uneaten food toward the middle of the table. "I'm so glad I have you to talk to. We're girlfriends." She crossed her arms on the table and smiled at me.

"Carolyn, I'm happy to be there for you. These are some tough times, but you have to get out of here. If Jack loves you like he says, he wants you to be happy and safe. Tell him how you feel."

"He wants me to be brave. I couldn't disappoint him." Her expression changed from serious to giddy. "You know where our secret place is to meet?"

Before I could respond, she answered. "Out at Crazy Gal's. We have the whole place to ourselves in the early afternoons. We don't even answer our phones when we're together."

What rich irony. Screw your partner's wife in his former house of prostitution. "Aren't you worried about Nathan not being able to reach either one of you at the same time?"

She thrust her lower jaw forward and the corners of eyes pulled down in a moue of petulance. "I want to stay here and be with Jack."

I lost my patience. "Carolyn, you're screwing your husband's business partner. Don't you think—"

She jumped up from the table and she shouted, "We're not *screwing*. He loves me."

Gimme caps swiveled our way. One man raised his beer in a salute. "Atta girl."

Carolyn barged out the door, letting it bang behind her.

I waved a twenty at our waitress before I left it on the table and followed her out. I was just in time to see Carolyn gun the sweet little Mercedes coupe onto the road.

I phoned her, but it went to voice mail. I tried her twice more on the drive home. Each time I apologized for offending her and begged her to get away.

***

Carolyn's safety worried me during the night, and when I awoke, her welfare was the second thing I thought of, right after Sam. I checked my phone. No messages from Sam or Carolyn.

His side of the bed was empty and cold. No call from Sam inviting me to breakfast left my heart aching and my head pounding. My limbs felt too weary to crawl out of bed and make coffee, but I was cheered that I had not visited Honoo Ji during the night. Chloe stood by my bed, chirpy with her morning energy, swishing her tail and softly woofing.

"Yeah, girl. I'm getting up." I showered, fed her, and took her out. With a cup of coffee in the cup holder, I drove to work. *Aren't you going to contact him? See if he's all right?* The little voice in my head nagged. I reached for the phone and stopped. *Nope. He's a tribal cop. He can take care of himself.*

Chapter 15

Bessie Benally's car was not in the lot. In fact, no one was, and I was relieved to be alone. I unlocked the front door, turned on the lights, and made the first pot of coffee of the morning. Fresh cup of coffee in hand, I headed for my office. When I set my coffee on the desk, I gaped, sloshing hot coffee on my hand. Two owl feathers crossed at the tips lay on top of a crude doll made from a piece of my missing sweater.

Hozho nahasdlii dooleet, let peace prevail, I prayed to the Holy Ones to turn the evil back on the witches. I swept the whole mess into the trash can and took it out the back door. When I threw the can in the dumpster and it hit the metal bottom, it made a satisfying clunk. Back inside, I sifted corn pollen from my medicine pouch over the place it had rested on my desk.

I heard Benally slam the front door behind her. She passed my door and harrumphed, "Good morning." I slid into my chair and tried to concentrate on work. I kept my shaking hands in my lap and breathed in long slow breaths until my heart stilled, but all I wanted was to breathe the fresh, clean air outside my office.

I nearly ran to my car. I opened the car windows, letting the clean wind sing through my hair and blow away any evil that lingered around me. As I drove through the pine forest snugged at the base of San Francisco Peak, her snow-capped top sparkled in the blue sky. I parked in a pullout facing the peak and willed myself to envision a battle between the Holy Ones and the witches. In my vision, the witches cried curses into the keening wind, but the Holy Ones drove them back, step by step into the dark pit of the Underworld.

The witches had sought me out. *Why?* I wasn't an evil person for them to collect and take into the Underworld, nor was I dabbling in witchery. Why me? My grandmother's voice sung in the breeze, "Witches try to lure the good to the darkness of evil."

I whispered into the wind. "Then no one is safe."

Her wide, flat face shimmered before me, and I felt the pressure of her touch on my medicine bundle. "You are coddled in the safety of the Holy Ones." Her image faded into the sunlight morning. I prayed she was right.

I slipped through the back door, and when I walked into my office, I immediately sensed the dark energy evil leaves behind. I pried open the window and let the cleansing breeze sweep through my space, ruffling the papers on my desk and scenting the room with the tang of pines.

My phone rang. I checked the number, hoping it was Sam, but it was Texas Jack. I shrugged. "Jordan here."

"Good morning, Ms. Bia," he drawled.

"Hello," I said brusquely, "what do you have for me?" I immediately cringed at the way the words sounded.

He chuckled. "Oh, I got a lot for you Ms. Bia."

I braced myself, figuring Carolyn had told Jack that she had confided in me about their affair. "Why are you calling?"

"Why don't we meet at the Koffee Kup in an hour. You'll be interested, and you won't feel so alone and vulnerable at the Koffee Kup like you would coming out to my place."

"I was never vulnerable," I retorted.

"So you say. See you shortly."

I stared at the disconnected phone in my hand. He was cheeky as hell, but he might have useful information. I headed for the coffee shop.

Jack was in the back of the restaurant, sprawled out in a booth with a coffee in front of him. I slipped into the booth and faced him.

"Let's hear it," I said all business and in a rush.

"You always in such a hurry?"

"Yeah, maybe. I don't know." He flustered me, and maybe that was his plan, to get me off balance and then bust me for butting into his affair with Carolyn.

"Let's get you some java." He signaled to the waitress, who gave him a big smile.

"Watcha need, honey?" she asked him.

"Seems to be a popular question today." He smiled at me. To her he said, "I believe the lady would like some coffee." He raised his eyebrows at me.

"Yes, please, with cream and sugar."

He stretched his back and gave me an amused smile. "Do I make you nervous?"

"Of course not." I squirmed. Why did I always sound like a prim English teacher around this man?

"If I don't, I'd hate to be with you when you were nervous," he drawled.

"We're not talking about me. You said you had information."

"I do. How about a date with me?"

"A date?" I frowned. "You're asking me out on a date?"

"Sure. I don't think the cop will mind. He's not around much now, is he?"

What the hell was he doing? He was hot with Carolyn. I tried to read his face, but got nothing.

"The cop's distracted by his own needs. You need to take care of yourself," he goaded.

"It's not about whether or not Sam minds. *I mind.*" I rose to go.

"Sit down," he said quietly.

I stood and stared down at him.

"Sit down," he insisted. "I can get you in front of Montoya and his pretty wife. That's what you want, isn't it? An opportunity to ask him about stealing little girls?"

I sat down. "How do you know what I want?"

"I make it my business to know what's going on." A sardonic smile flitted across his face. "I'm very good at minding other people's business. I have an invite for me and a guest to his annual auction for charity. The guest invite is all yours. Put your hair up and put on your hottest dress."

Damn. I hadn't received the invitation Carolyn had promised was coming, and fat chance I would get one after last night's scene.

"Do we have to go together?"

"You are inquisitive. Haven't you ever gone with the flow? You think too much."

"I've heard that recently. So what's your answer?"

"I have the tickets, and I'll be keeping them. I'll pick you up at eight tonight at your place." He was amused at my discomfort. "I bet I'll have the best looking woman there on my arm."

"You don't know where I live."

"Yep, I do. I know a lot about you." He stood up and swaggered to the door.

"We're not having a date. I'm working," I called after him.

Without breaking his stride, he gave a wave over his shoulder.

He had left money on the table, and when the waitress appeared she said, "Hon, he don't seem like a bad sort."

My mind was whirling as I gave her a weak smile and nodded. Ohh, what would Carolyn think when I showed up with her lover?

Would she call us out? Make a scene? But this was an opportunity, and whatever happened would be worth the risk if I got a chance to gig Montoya and see what happened. But I wasn't dating Texas Jack no matter what he thought.

When I stepped out of the Koffee Kup, Sam's Tahoe was idling in front of the red light. He watched Texas Jack get in his pickup. As though my gaze burned him, Sam turned his head my way. His mouth was tight and his brow was lowered as he cranked the Tahoe into the parking spot Jack had vacated. I walked over to his truck, and he pushed open the passenger side door. I stepped up on the running board and got in.

"You have breakfast with him?" He jerked his head toward Jack's pickup retreating down the street.

"You didn't invite me."

His eyes narrowed, slashing angry lines around his nose. Red crawled up his neck, burning his face, and he was drumming a rhythm on his steering wheel. The air between us was tense as rebar.

"Sam, talk to me. It's not about breakfast. What's wrong?"

He didn't turn his head to me, just slid his eyes my way. His face paled, and his hands gripped the steering wheel so hard his knuckles turned white. Shadows of pain crossed his face, followed by resignation, then a flash of anger. "I'm sorry," he said.

"Me, too, buddy, and 'I'm sorry' gives me no information about how to make it better."

I was rebuffed by the scowl on his face, but pursued him into his man space. "What is it? Why are you upset?"

"I'm not upset," he said brusquely.

"Something's wrong, and I would appreciate you sharing with me beyond just scowling and snapping at me."

"Nothing's wrong. I'm fine," he answered in man-speak, directing me to back off.

I didn't want to open the car door and walk away from him, but he no longer inhabited a space I was allowed in. Not even a gossamer thread held us together over the chasm looming between us.

I jerked open the door, wanting out of the Tahoe before the tears came. "I thought we belonged to each other, had something between us." I wasn't going to exhaust myself, spending energy to keep the relationship going, nor was I going to beg for his companionship. I wanted it. I needed it. I deserved it, but I'd be damned if I *begged.* I was worth more than that.

I slammed the car door and stalked to my Civic.

Rational thinking helped cleanse the angry feelings I had about Sam. He could go to Window Rock and do whatever drew him there. He could tell me about it or not. I wasn't in charge of him, only my reaction to him, and I would take care of myself.

I picked up my phone and called Taylor.

"Hey what's up?"

I told her about Carolyn's love affair with Jack and her fear of Montoya catching them. I was careful to leave out Montoya's tax troubles.

"Jeez, what a sleaze ball that guy is. Remember him squeezing the butt of the spandex chick at the hospital?"

"Yep...and I'm going to the auction with him tonight."

"What? He asked you out?"

"He's getting me in front of Montoya. I just need his spare ticket."

We argued about how safe I would be. She reminded me Jack had a rep as a rake and Montoya was an ex-con. With more bravado than I felt and some arm twisting, she agreed I would probably be fine.

"Text me when you're home safe. And I have one other piece of news. Jimmy Begay's hanging was ruled a suicide. His family claimed his body, and they're burying him tomorrow."

"I'm so sorry for them. I can't imagine their loss, and while I'm glad he wasn't murdered in a gang war, his parents don't care. Their son is gone no matter how he died."

***

I raced home from work later than I had planned because Benally wanted to meet, droning on about nitpicking rules she wanted me to agree with her on. Once home, I headed for my closet and pulled my one all-purpose black dress off its hanger and tossed it on my bed. The image of my warrior man's naked body, inviting me to join him on the bed, teased me. What was he doing tonight? I sighed, went in the bathroom, did the minimum of makeup, and piled up my hair. I scrutinized my reflection in the mirror, turning this way and that. The dress was severe and plain. I reached for a strand of fat fake pearls. The black dress needed something other than the sad look on my face.

A check in the mirror convinced me I looked good enough. The doorbell rang.

Texas Jack had one arm slouched on the door frame and his leg cocked forward aggressively. Chloe rumbled low in her throat. Without a word, he took my keys out of my hand and guided me out with a firm, warm grip on my arm. He turned the lock and held my elbow on the way to a new Mercedes two-door sport coupe. He opened the car door for me.

"I figured you to be a truck-driving kind of man."

He closed the door softly and walked around to the driver's side. When he slipped into the driver's seat, he answered, "I'm a luxury car kind of guy when I take out a beautiful woman." His pale blue eyes were luminous in the interior light of the sedan. He leaned over and kissed my hair softly.

I jerked my head back. "Please, I'm working, and you know that." A knife of pain seared through me when I thought of Sam.

Jack smiled indulgently. "So you say."

"It's true. I don't even know your last name." I hoped to goad him into telling me.

Instead, he dug deep. "Your man is out partying tonight with friends in Window Rock."

I wouldn't give him the satisfaction of arguing. How could I? I didn't know how Sam was spending his time.

He smoothly handled the powerful car as we rode in silence to the Pepsi Concert Hall. He pulled into the drive, and a valet materialized outside his window. A second valet simultaneously opened my car door. Jack dropped the keys in the valet's outstretched hand, walked around the car, and offered me his arm. We walked into the brilliantly lighted hall, arm and arm.

All the beautiful people were there, sipping champagne and chatting as they cruised among the tables that showcased expensive items, brochures for fabulous trips and personal services, all to go to the highest bidder.

"Drink?"

"Yes, white wine. Thank you." I scanned the crowd as Jack walked away. A group of men surrounded Nathan Montoya. I got as close as I could without being conspicuous. His face was flushed, and he talked animatedly. The group hung on his every word and, on cue, they burst out laughing when he finished talking. One listener slapped Montoya on the back, and they fawned before him, looking like a group of minions currying favor.

I edged back into the crowd. Jack had picked up our drinks and was returning when Carolyn stepped away from a woman she had been talking to and touched his forearm. He turned to her, and a wide grin spread across his face. She kept her hand on his forearm and put her face close to his to murmur in his ear. He nodded and winked when she finished. When he jerked his head in my direction, she stared at me and frowned. Jack nodded to her, returned to my side, and handed me the wine.

I baited him. "I didn't know you knew Carolyn."

"Of course. I take the time to get to know every woman I'm attracted to." His eyes held a hint of amusement.

"I think I'll just circulate," I said.

He cocked an eyebrow at me and sipped his dirty martini. "You afraid I can't please two beautiful women in one evening?"

I kept walking. His laughter floated over me.

I worked my way through the crowd, not seeing anyone I knew but nodding and smiling at everyone. I broke through a throng of people crowding the largest display table. Carolyn stood alone at the edge of the crowd, fidgeting with a glass of wine. Absolutely no one was around her. Perfect for me, but odd behavior for the wife of our elegant and popular host.

I moved quickly toward Carolyn, hoping to reach her before someone else zeroed in on her, but I wasn't fast enough. Texas Jack rushed to her side. He kissed her on the cheek and kept his other hand at her waist. His face lit up as he talked to her, and when she responded to him, she was more animated than I had ever seen her. He stood close to her; so close their faces nearly touched. He pushed a wayward strand of hair behind her ear. There was something so intimate about his gesture that anyone who saw it would know they were lovers. Carolyn's face softened at his touch, and she reached up and cupped his cheek. He pulled her hand down to his side and leaned in and whispered something in her ear. Color washed over her face when she smiled at him.

Montoya stood with a group of men swapping stories, but he wasn't paying them any attention. His face was a mask of fury aimed at his wife and Texas Jack.

Jack stepped in closer to Carolyn, slipped his knee between her thighs, and kissed her cheek. When he melted away into the crowd, she watched him with a dreamy look in her eyes.

She risked a lot taking Texas Jack as a lover, and whether or not she knew of Montoya's other misdeeds, she shared the culpability of the IRS returns.

Her radiant face paled when I got near her. "Why are you here with Jack? You know I love him."

I took a deep breath and stepped closer to her. "He was kind enough to give me his spare ticket." I reminded her she didn't come through with the promised ticket. "Working girls can't afford such elegant events. Could we talk for a moment?"

"Why?"

"I don't have much time. I'm going to tell you something, and it won't be easy to listen to."

Her eyebrows rose.

"The IRS is looking into your tax returns." I was being rash, and I knew it. She could start screaming for her husband.

She peered at me."Nathan takes care of all that. He says we have a great accountant. How do you know anything about our taxes?"

I ignored her question. "Did you read all the pages or just sign the signatory page?"

"I just sign it. An accountant prepared them. I don't know anything about that stuff." Her voice had ratcheted up, and she was fidgeting. "Why are you telling me this?"

"Your returns are being investigated for tax fraud. *You're* being investigated for defrauding the government of tens of thousands of dollars on unclaimed income."

"What?" She jerked away from me. "I need to tell Nathan."

I grabbed her arm. "Don't. Think about it. Nathan knows."

"Let go of me." She gasped. "You're crazy. I don't believe you. How would you know? I'm going to tell Nathan." She craned her head, searching the crowd for him. "He'll have you thrown out of here."

"Why would I lie?" I hissed. "Why would I come to you to warn you, if not to help you?"

She hesitated. I watched her trying to click together the pieces so they made some sense. Sweat glistened on her forehead. Her body went limp, and she glanced around furtively.

"Don't accuse your husband." I pressed my small advantage. "He's a dangerous man. Get out of the house," I urged her.

Her mouth gaped open, and her eyes were wide with fear. "It can't be true," she begged me.

"It is true. I found out about it when I was investigating a different case. You need to get away from him for a lot of reasons."

"Wh—"

"Carolyn, my dear," boomed a voice close to us. Montoya was at her side. What had he heard? "Here you are monopolizing one of our guests." Nathan stepped closer into her space and hugged her to him. His face was a poorly concealed scowl, his lips tugging down in a sneer. "Come dear, we must mingle with these fine people who are going to make a lot of money for charity tonight." His bonhomie was forced as he took Carolyn's arm, kept her pulled close to him, and steered her into the crowd. His fingers bit into the soft skin of her upper arm.

Texas Jack held up his martini glass and waggled it at me as he waded through the crowd in my direction.

"Looks like you need a longer conversation with our host." The pointed toes of Jack's boots stopped inches from my bare toes in my sling back heels. He sucked the last drops from his martini glass. He was so close I could smell the gin-soaked olive he popped into his mouth. He dropped the toothpick in the glass and handed it to a hovering waiter.

"Another sir?" the server asked.

"Yes, please," he said to the waiter. He placed his hand in the small of my back. "C'mon. You need to get to know Montoya better."

He threaded his way through the elegant guests into the circle around Carolyn and Montoya. She was deathly pale and still, but standing by her man like a devoted wife. When her eyes tracked mine, I gave her an encouraging smile.

"Texas Jack!" Montoya jovially stepped back to allow us in the circle around him. "And who is this beautiful woman my wife knows and you wheedled into coming with you?"

I extended my hand, "Jordan Bia. Lovely event," I added smoothly.

His rough hand clasped mine too firmly for too long. My fingers were aching when I pulled my hand from his. What played across his lips was more of a rictus of a grimace than a smile. His eyes were dull, flat black tunnels. "I know you. You're an investigator with the Navajo CPS."

My heart raced, and fear clogged my throat. Had Jack told him? How did Montoya know? Carolyn blanched and didn't look at me.

"Human trafficking is such a nasty business. So bad for that kid, Sofia." He tut-tutted and shook his head. "And Ms. Bia, undue curiosity turns out so badly."

Carolyn inhaled sharply.

"Come my dear, we have an auction to host." He slapped Texas Jack on the back. "Glad you could make it. Bid large on something. Jack, my man, our business is makin' us rich. You can afford it for charity. This way, Carolyn dear. Good-bye Ms. Bia." Carolyn followed him meekly toward the dais.

I stared at her back, willing her to turn around and look at me. Ever the well-behaved wife, she didn't.

When the Montoya's had moved out of hearing, I provoked Jack, "So Montoya's your business partner?"

He nodded over his drink. "Yep, been real lucrative being in business with the Montoyas." He laughed. "I get fat checks and none of the day-to-day hassles of running a business."

"And you know his wife well too," I goaded.

"No law against lovin' beautiful women." He sipped his drink.

I pivoted toward the side exit door. "Thank you for invitation."

Texas Jack followed close on my heels. "You're gonna leave? Just because you quit working it doesn't mean you have to go. But that Montoya is a helluva scary guy, isn't he?"

"I think you set me up so he could threaten me."

"You're wrong. Watch your back. He doesn't like anyone meddling in his business."

"How about meddling with his wife? Does he like that?" I jerked open the door. "Watch your back. I'm leaving. I'll take a cab."

"I'll drive you."

"No," I argued, "I'll get home by myself."

I pushed the door open and walked into the night. He fell into step beside me. We walked in silence into the crystalline night, cooled with a west breeze scented with pines.

He hailed a waiting cab and held the door for me. As I got in, he handed the cab driver a wad of bills and his card. "Text me when you deliver her safely."

"I got this," I protested.

"You came with me, and you're my responsibility." He slammed the passenger seat door and stalked off.

"You two have a fight, lady?" the cabbie asked.

"No," I said, unwilling to strike up a conversation with the driver.

"Seems like a nice enough guy," he said.

He pulled up in front of my dark apartment. Damn, I wished I had left a lamp on. I fumbled with my key and opened the front door. Chloe rushed me, gleeful at my return. I clicked on some lights and walked to the bedroom. I couldn't bear the sight of the neatly made, empty bed. Chloe whimpered and nudged me.

"I know girl." While I changed into a sleep shirt, I heard her prowling the small space.

She came back and sat at my feet whimpering. "He's not here, fella." I stroked her big head, and she rolled over and offered me her belly.

God, I missed being with Sam, having his love quench the burn in me. I wanted him. Hurt and angry as I was, I would welcome him back into my life in a nanosecond. I wanted to hold his body, tingle with the excitement of knowing I would feel him inside me, but all I was left with was yearning for my warrior man in an empty bed.

Before I went to sleep I prayed for peace and safety for both us, *hozho nahasdlii dooleet*. And I remembered to text Taylor.

Chapter 16

I had my morning coffee while standing at the front window with Chloe huddled next to my leg. She sensed I was in a funk and wouldn't budge from my side. The sun broke the horizon, barely visible through the gray skies.

I moved into the kitchen and dumped the dregs of my coffee in the sink. "Come on. Let's get you fed." She perked up at the mention of food and raced to her bowl, eager with anticipation.

My phone was silent. No call and no text from Sam. Anger sparked at Sam for thinking I would two-time him with Texas Jack. I'd had a long miserable night worrying about what he was doing in Window Rock and with whom.

A deep cleansing breath let rational thinking edge out my emotions. I wasn't omniscient, and I didn't know what Sam was feeling or doing. But I wouldn't act like I needed rescuing because *I didn't*. From now on, when I ran into him as a part of my work life— which was inevitable—I would treat him as the professional he was. My rational brain coached me from the sidelines. If he chose to contact me, I'd be open; if not, he walked away from one helluva woman. I had run the entire gamut of emotions since our last conversation, but now my heart settled on pounding a staccato rhythm of painful determination to get over him.

I drove through the Coffee Hut on the way to work and bought their largest size with a double shot of espresso, hoping for an energy spike. Once again, I was first into work, and settled in to review all my case notes on Juanita and Sofia looking for anyone, anything, I might have missed. I shamelessly kept my phone in my pocket, just in case Sam called.

By midmorning, I had switched to adding some cute cartoon video clips to our gang initiative curriculum package to keep the second graders' attention. When I took a break, I called Aguirre and left him a voice mail about Montoya's warning to me, wanting someone to know of that conversation, and I wasn't calling Sam to share with him.

Within fifteen minutes my phone rang, and I recognized Aguirre's number.

"Sorry I missed your call. You said you saw Montoya?" he asked.

I told him about the interaction at the charity auction but left out my conversation with Carolyn.

"You feel threatened by his comment about curiosity and turning out badly?" he asked.

"Maybe," I said, thinking about it. "It may not be personal, just a throwaway comment showing he can chuck his weight around."

"When someone of Montoya's ilk links danger to something you're doing, sit up and take notice."

"I'll be careful, and I have a good dog."

I didn't tell him about warning Carolyn. I probably should have, but the FBI would see it as meddling, and I needed a good working relationship with everyone in our small community. I convinced myself I was just one woman trying to head off trouble for another woman. I called her cell number, hoping she was far away from her husband.

She answered on the first ring.

"It's Jordan. Can you talk?"

"Yes. I'm home. Nathan wants me to stay close to the house, and he's left a bodyguard here to keep me safe. He says he has some trouble brewing with the Teamsters Union. You know, nothing moves through Flag unless the union wants it to."

"Umm," I said, wanting to keep her talking. Surely, she didn't really believe her husband was keeping her away from anyone over union problems. The union wasn't going to bop his wife over the head and drag her off.

She whined, "I can't see Jack. The man Nathan left at the house doesn't let me out of his sight."

"You're probably safer not seeing Jack. Did you tell your husband anything we talked about?"

"No." She hesitated. "I don't want to think about it."

"Then maybe your bodyguard is there because your husband knows about your affair."

She hesitated, and I thought I'd lost the connection. "He couldn't. We were so careful, but I'll talk to Jack. He'll know what to do."

Before we hung up, I told her to make a plan to get herself to a safer place.

I quit work shortly before five, vowing to get my head screwed on straight before I came into the office tomorrow. When I got home, Chloe was waiting for me. "Let's run, big girl." She woofed and ran in tight circles, watching me change into running clothes. I tucked my phone in my pocket. Just in case.

The evening was perfect, cool from the cloud cover during the day. Now a fiery sun slid toward dusk through a cobalt blue sky. We hadn't had rain in weeks, and our feet kicked up little puffs of red dust. When we reached the big rock marking the north end of the trail, we stopped to rest before turning back. The park was falling into shadow as the sun sank from view, shooting its last fiery rays of red and orange into the dying light.

A marmot whistled loudly, and when I jumped, he froze in place. When Chloe gave him the hairy eyeball, it chittered and shook his tail at her from his safe viewpoint on top of a tall boulder. He gave a loud whistle, and the other marmots added their voices. They chattered, fluffed out their twitching tails, and scampered off together. They were enjoying each other's company—just like Sam and I used to do.

Don't go there. "Come on girl. It's dinner time when we get home." Chloe was up like a shot, bounding down the trail ahead of me. I kept pace with her, needing the surge of endorphins to sort through what was bugging me about this case.

Montoya was an older guy. How did he learn to troll the Dark Net? Hire someone? He would have to have unwavering faith in the guy who ran his web operations, or he would need something to hold over his head to threaten him and keep in line. Prisons had computers and basic computing classes. Maybe he met someone there. It was as good a place as any to start.

I was still dripping sweat from our run when I booted up my computer and searched the Arizona State Prison complex in Windsor. On the home page, I found the name of the warden and his contact information at the prison. I wrote his phone number on a pad.

***

At eight o'clock sharp the next morning I was on the phone with the warden of the state prison in Winslow. I identified myself as an investigator with Navajo CPS, wanting to talk with anyone who remembered Mr. Montoya.

"You're in luck. His old cell mate is back inside. He taught basic computing classes to the inmates in the prison computer lab in the library."

"Did Montoya take his classes?"

"Yeah, Montoya signed up for everything and anything to get out of sitting in his cell."

"Why is his cellmate back in?"

"He lied himself into a job with a cell phone company, hacked their data base, and sold the customers' credit card info. Old Alvin Byrd is a slow learner. He doesn't get any visitors but his old pal Montoya."

"I can be there in two hours."

The annoying mechanical voice on my GPS gave me perfect directions to the Arizona State Prison located on the outskirts of Winslow. Perimeter fences topped with rings of concertina wire surrounded the prison yard. The only spots of color on the brown territorial-style buildings were the red tile roofs on the guard towers.

I thrust my ID through the slot to the guard at the first gate. He scrutinized it and returned it back to me. The fence gate screeched open. I walked thirty paces and repeated the process. Then a brusque woman guard searched me. She buzzed me through the door to the prison. The hallway was flushed in bright florescent light, the smell of antiseptic cleaners not quite killing the rank smell of bodies who didn't shower every day. A third guard motioned me into the visiting room. I took a rickety chair facing the Plexiglas barrier.

Alvin Byrd's appearance shocked me when the guard led him in. He was only in his late fifties, but he was thin and stooped. He shuffled with an odd gait to his chair on the other side of the glass. The guard waited with him until he was seated, then he nodded at me and backed away. Byrd clumsily sat in the chair across from me. He reminded me of a shriveled gray crane with his gangly thin arms propped on the table. He cocked his grizzled head at the phone on the wall. I picked up the phone, the earpiece rimmed with oily grime, and held it gingerly away from my head.

His eyes were hooded. "What's a broad like you want with me?" he finally said into his phone.

"Hello, Mr. Byrd. I'm Jordan Bia with Navajo CPS, and I'm interested in your old cellmate Nathan Montoya."

"Long time ago. I don't remember much," he said with an air of apathy.

I studied his face. His cheek bones were sunken, and his face had an unhealthy pallor.

"Let's see if I can jog your memory. You worked in the prison library teaching basic computer skills to the inmates. He was one of your students."

Byrd worried a broken, dirty fingernail. "Yeah, I might remember."

"I think you taught him many useful things."

"I set his books up on QuickBooks—got all his accounts on spread sheets."

"What else?"

"Like what? Nah, scratch that. What's in it for me?"

"I'm an investigator with—"

"You think I give a shit what you do?"

"You should. What message would you like me to take out of here?"

"I don't talk unless I get something."

I decided to try to different tack. "Are you ill Mr. Byrd?"

"What do you think? You got eyes." He jeered. "Hell yes, I got diabetes, and I got to take that insulin every day."

"I'm sorry."

"Sure you are. Let me tell your sweet ass what it's like living in this hellhole with these animals. Last week an inmate bit the ear off a guard, and in the spring, we were on lockdown because two inmates beat the living hell out of a woman guard who is still in the hospital getting her face rebuilt. I'm not a violent offender. I don't belong in a cage with these brutes. The stress of prison life makes my diabetes worse."

I was cynical enough to think he had studied his disease and gathered his talking points to try to persuade anyone on the outside. My experience with convicts was that nobody conned like a con.

"I'm sure that's awful for you," I soothed.

"I want a different prison job."

"What's your job now?"

"I work in the kitchen. You know what that means? I work around all that food I can't eat. It's cruel and unusual punishment." He used the legal phrase deftly. "I gotta eat a special diet for my diabetes."

"Anything else you want?"

"Yeah, I want access to the computers in the library. I'm an expert. I could teach these animals something useful."

"I bet you could. Why don't you tell me what you taught Mr. Montoya?"

"I want something in return." He stuck to his demand. "I'm an old man. The diabetes is killing me. My eye sight is going, and I got neuropathy in my feet. I ain't no threat to society."

"You don't look healthy, Mr. Byrd, and I think you're right. Prison life makes your condition worse."

He leaned back with a satisfied smile.

Time for me to reel him in. "I read the newspaper stories of your trial. The prosecution offered you a deal if you gave up information about your dealings with Mr. Montoya. You chose silence and loyalty to him, and you're here in prison. Do you get the newspapers here?"

"Yeah." He squirmed.

"Then you've seen Mr. Montoya and his beautiful young wife at society parties. You know what else? He's very wealthy and owns a trucking business and a big spacious mansion, high up on the ridgeline backing up to the Coconino forest. You think he remembers his old pal Alvin dying in here?"

"What are you authorized to give me?"

"Nothing. You had your chance to deal directly with the prosecutor, and you turned it down to stay loyal to your old friend."

He grimaced.

"But I'll tell you what I can do. The feds are interested in anything you know of his business. You agree to talk, and I'll pass it on to the FBI and even hint you have more to share. Picture yourself living the rest of your days somewhere else. Peaceful sounding, isn't it Alvin?"

His eyes were darting around the squalid room, and he was twitching in his chair.

"Quit protecting him if you ever want to get out of the prison kitchen," I urged.

He leaned forward, wiping his lower face with his free hand. "What do you want to know?"

"Did you teach Montoya about the Dark Net?"

He sat back and stared at me. "I'm not sayin' nothing that incriminates me."

"I just asked if you let him know the Dark Net existed."

He nodded. "A lot of people were using it for business. Hell, that guy, what's his name, the blond guy—Texas Jack was his name. He and Montoya were in business together. He claimed he had some bullshit degree from some place out in California. Bragged he knew about computers."

"What is his last name?"

He shrugged. "He never said. I didn't like the bastard. Too smooth." He shook his head. "That guy hovered around Montoya like a vulture waiting for death. Jack put up the money for the trucking company. Montoya sure as hell didn't have enough. From then on, they were thicker than thieves. When Montoya got indicted, Jack pounced on buying the bar. You know about Crazy Gal's?"

I nodded.

"Jack paid Montoya a fifty-percent premium for the bar. Montoya was so greedy for the cash to pay his legal bills, he wasn't thinkin' straight."

"What are you saying?"

"That oily bastard wormed his way into owning most of Montoya's assets—he got the bar, he has a majority interest in the trucking company, and he 'helped' his ol' buddy out when Montoya was in the joint by buying another big chunk of the trucking company—at a huge deduction so Montoya could finish paying off his crappy lawyer. Jack made the poor fool think he was his best friend, but Montoya let a snake in the chicken house."

"Did Jack set Montoya's business up on the Dark Net?"

"I don't think Jack knew shit," he boasted. I told Montoya how the Dark Net works, how to get a digital wallet. But I didn't know what kind of business he was wanting to start."

I let that pass. He knew it was nothing legal. Montoya wasn't going to advertise his trucking business on the Dark Net.

"Did you help him use the SilkRoad site to place some advertising?"

"Can't do that from in the joint," he scoffed.

I shrugged. "So you consulted with him after he got out?"

"Maybe I saw him some."

"The warden tells me Montoya is a regular visitor of yours. You're still his consultant, and when you were out of prison before your problem with the cell phone company, you set his business up on SilkRoad."

"Maybe," he boasted. "You can't prove it."

"And you're still helping him out, giving him a little advice."

He gave an exaggerated shrug.

"What does he pay you for your expert advice?"

He grew still.

"I think the FBI won't look favorably at you if you're still Montoya's computer consultant."

He clenched his wiry hair with his hands and shook his head back and forth. "I gotta get out of here. I don't want to die in prison."

I hung up the phone and pushed back my chair. His mouth opened. He was screaming behind the Plexiglas. He kept motioning me to sit and mouthing, 'Please.'

I sat down and picked up the phone.

"You gotta help me. I'll talk to the feds. I won't see Montoya no more. I'll tell the warden I don't wanna see him," he pleaded.

"I'll tell the FBI you're willing to talk."

"When I am going to hear from you again?"

"It won't be me." I hung up the phone and walked out of the visitors' room, wondering what Montoya's reaction would be when he found out his computer consultant wasn't going to help him anymore, and more importantly, how soon he would know that I had come to see Byrd.

The two sets of guards checked me back through the mechanical gates to the visitor's parking lot. I had my hand on the car door when I felt a tickle on the back of my neck. An old, beat-up pickup missing a back windshield was parked a couple of cars down from mine, and a guy was slumped over the steering wheel. He turned his head my way, staring, but he made no move to get out of the truck. I jumped in the car and put it in reverse. He sat up, still staring at me, but he didn't crank over the motor of his truck. I squealed out of the parking lot, paranoid he was a spy for Montoya and scoffing at myself because he could just as easily be a guy waiting to give a ride to someone.

Chapter 17

I called Taylor and told her about Byrd and the guy in the old truck in the prison parking lot.

"Are you sure no one is following you? I don't like the guy was watching you leave the prison."

The highway was a long straightaway, and no one was behind me. "He's not following me. Hey, someone's texted me. I'll get back to you. There's more."

I pulled to the side of the road. Sam had texted, telling me he was on the road home from Window Rock. He asked me to meet him at the station at five to ride with him to his Blessing Way tonight. My fingers hovered over the keys. Being around my guy now made me feel edgy, unable to relax and be myself. I was so uptight, I couldn't remember how we used to act around each other or what we used to talk about. It used to be so easy. Now I felt stonewalled when I asked him what was wrong. I pushed my resentment away and texted him I would be there as I had agreed, hoping the Sing would restore his sense of harmony. Maybe he was only asking me because earlier he had said we would go together and he was simply following through, one last obligation.

Benally was in her office, but she was working with her head down and didn't see me pass by. A minute later she poked her head my door and started yakking. I closed my phone before I finished dialing Aguirre's number and gave her my full attention.

"You went to the prison in Winslow on state time. Tell me how that connects to your case load." She smirked. "I have cousin who works at the prison. He called me to see if I needed help with anything."

Damn. This crone had eyes everywhere.

"I talked with a prisoner who is important to Sofia and Juanita's case."

"You're not thinking. Juanita is dead and Sofia is safe. Who was this person and what did you get? No obfuscating. I'm your immediate superior." She crossed her arms across her ample middle-aged thickness. We were in a staring contest.

I stood up to even the playing field. "His name is Alvin Byrd, and he's in prison for computer fraud. I believe human traffickers might be using the web to buy and sell women."

Her eyes narrowed to slits. She spluttered, "Preposterous. Look around you. You think these lowlifes can use a computer? You're acting like a geeky college kid. No idea what the real world is like."

Was she jealous? Felt her job was threatened? Didn't matter. She *was* the boss. In a soothing tone, I tried to placate her. "He was just an old man suffering from diabetes. I know I need substantial evidence to prove anyone is using the web to sell women."

"Don't waste state time doing it. I know you'll do the right thing," she challenged. She turned on her heel and marched back to her office.

One thing I reluctantly agreed with her on, Juanita was probably dead. When her office door shut, I left by the side door for the short drive to KNAZ to check on my SilkRoad ad.

I called Aguirre en route to the station to tell him what Byrd wanted.

"Hello, Jordan. Before you ask, there are no new answers to your ad."

"Thank you, but I'm calling you because Montoya's old cell mate Alvin Byrd wants to deal for information."

"How the hell do you know?"

"I went to see him. An old guy like Montoya needed some high tech help."

"Why would Byrd want to help the feds?"

"He has diabetes, and I don't think he believes he has long to live. He's willing to testify he's working with Montoya and that he taught him about the Dark Net. He also claims Texas Jack has computer skills, but Montoya is the regular on the visitor's list for Byrd."

"You better hope he doesn't tell Montoya you were there. We'll have a nice chat with Byrd, and I'll be in touch."

I dropped my phone in the console, relieved to turn Byrd over to the FBI, and headed for KNAZ. When I got to her office, she was bursting to know what happened.

I explained that Byrd claimed he had taught Montoya how to set up a business on the Dark Net. "And Aguirre is going to talk to Byrd."

"You worried about Montoya finding out you visited Byrd?"

I shrugged my shoulders. "What's to say, but be careful?"

"You could stay with me."

"Thanks, but I'll be fine at home. Besides, I'm out on the road visiting clients. Montoya could take me out during the day."

Her horrified face had me placating, "I'm not saying he would. I'll be fine."

She mumbled her disbelief. "Is that all the 'more' information you promised me?"

"Carolyn's under guard in her home—she thinks her husband is trying to keep her safe."

"I hope she wakes up and leaves him."

I pulled over a chair and sat down beside her. "I think we should take out ads on other sites. We could word each one a little differently."

"You've been researching again."

I rolled my chair closer to her and nudged her hand off the mouse. "Look at all these other sites I found." I clicked on the Evolution website.

Taylor scooted closer to me. The Evolution page hawked stolen credit and debit card numbers, medical information, drugs, guns, fake IDs, and university diplomas.

"I don't see any human trafficking ads," Taylor said.

I thumbed through my notes. "I found some other sites." I typed in *Agora*. The page opened to ads for fully automatic weapons, heroin, videos, and women.

"Click that disclaimer under videos," Taylor said. The disclaimer popped up. *No live snuff images*.

"What are snuff images?" I asked.

"Video or still pictures of a killing. The Mexican cartels post that crap—sometimes even on Facebook."

"I guess excluding snuff images makes Agora feel all warm and fuzzy about their video business."

"Do you have enough Bitcoins to advertise here?"

"Barely." I clicked open the page for women and filled out the form for an ad, paid, and closed out of Agora. "I'll get the info on this new ad over to Trace and Aguirre. Guess what else I found out from Byrd? He says Jack bankrolled the trucking business. Byrd thinks Jack snookered Montoya out of his assets."

"Does he know Jack snookered Montoya out of his wife's affections?"

"I doubt it. But Byrd doesn't have anything good to say about Jack—though it could be jealously."

"We need his last name. Hmm, wait a minute. Move over and let me sit there. He had to provide a full legal name when he bought the bar. The transaction generated a deed." She opened a database.

"What are you searching?"

"Real estate records. The county records the names of buyers and sellers, and the deed is in here somewhere." Taylor scrolled through several pages of real estate records. "Here it is. John Henry Jacobson. That's his name."

"Byrd said he lived in California."

She closed the county records site and typed in the URL *searchsystems.net*. "This site will link me to over five thousand databases." She discovered Jack had graduated from Stanford, but not what he studied. She found his parents' names on his birth certificate. A search of them turned up that his dad owned orange groves in the valley and a shipping company. "He came from money. Montoya likes people with money—he married a rich wife and has a rich partner."

"So who is using whom?"

She shrugged one shoulder. "Anyone of the three of them. All of them? I'll tell Trace what we found, and the guys can run Jack through criminal databases." She closed out the browser.

"Will you and Trace be at Sam's Sing tonight?"

"Yeah, you need a ride?"

"No thanks, I'm riding with Sam. I'll see you there."

"Things better?"

"No, I think he's honoring his prior invitation that we ride together."

Her face was a moue of sadness. "Sorry."

***

Sam was waiting for me beside his Tahoe when I pulled into the police parking lot at five o'clock. I locked my car and joined him.

"Thanks for meeting me. You ready?" he asked.

I was wary about approaching him for a kiss so I hung back. My hesitancy spiraled into an awkward moment that he ended by opening the car door for me.

I belted myself into the passenger seat, and when he took the wheel I said, "Sam, tell me what's going on with you."

"Jordan," he said gently, "I'm too tired and wrung out to talk right now."

"Soon then. I won't live on this lonely piece of real estate."

"I know." He sighed. "I'm glad you're coming with me." He squeezed my hand, but didn't hold it or take it up to his mouth for a kiss. He put both his hands back on the wheel.

The sound of his turn signal blinking accentuated the silence in the car as we turned off the county road onto the dirt track that meandered through Kaih Canyon to Yanaha's home. Sam parked by the stream that fed a stand of willow trees shading Yanaha's hogan and Airstream trailer.

Yanaha met us as we got out of the truck and folded her thin arms around Sam's bulk.

He hugged her saying, "Thank you for everything."

She tilted her head to look up at him towering over her. "You're running late," she admonished Sam. "The Singer wants to see you before we get started." Sam turned and walked toward Trace who was talking with a hunched, elderly Navajo man.

Sam had left me with Yanaha. She reached out her hand to me, and I took that as my cue to go with her and see how I could help. She stopped before her hogan. It was empty of her belongings and had been swept clean with a new broom for the ceremony. She motioned to the open doorway. "Sam will find his peace here tonight."

She turned toward her old trailer, holding fast to my hand. The trailer door was propped open with a cinderblock to catch the evening breeze, and the chatter of excited women wafted out as I followed her up the metal steps.

The galley kitchen was cramped by two rows of women working on the countertops that ran parallel to each other. Their backsides brushed as they set up trays of food for the meal after the Sing. Taylor called a hello to me from the tiny kitchen.

"Come back to the bedroom," Yanaha said quietly. She led me to the back of the trailer and held back the curtains that separated her bedroom from the living area.

She spoke directly. "Child, I know your man, and I have grown to love him like my grandson. You and Sam are having difficulty."

I poured out my feelings of rejection and my growing anger with Sam for cutting his companionship off as easily as turning a spigot. "We've grown so far apart."

She took my hands in hers. "You will lose each other if you quit reaching out. After the Sing, things will be better. You'll see. You must believe he can find his balance tonight."

The deep boom of the drums rattled off the trailer walls and signaled the guests to assemble. She stood slowly, steadying herself on the back of the chair. "It's time for us to go. Being a couple is a process. Walk the journey of your heart, not your head." She shuffled close to me and feathered a dry kiss on my cheek. "Allow yourself to be led by what you feel during the Blessing Way and let it restore you. Wait for the Holy Ones to take their place in the sand painting and surrender to them, and receive their blessing."

The women from the kitchen clattered down the metal trailer stairs before us. I stayed close behind Yanaha as she held fast to the railing.

As we neared the hogan, Yanaha stopped beside the opening and clutched my arm. "Jordan, you will see. He will be restored, and the things between you will be eased." She urged me to believe, and I wanted to her to be right. I hoped the Sing would restore my warrior man's peace, and he would find a place for me in this heart.

People crowded into Yanaha's summer hogan and surrounded the Singer, who deftly sifted a thin ribbon of ochre sand around three sides of his sand painting on the hogan floor, careful to leave the east side open to accept the presence of the deities. Outside, the drums were silent, and the only sound was the rustling and settling of the crowd and the swish of the Singer's buckskin shoes across the sand. He placed bundles of twigs and herbs by the open east side of the sand painting to repel evil from the opening.

I sat cross legged between Taylor and Yanaha in the front row. The warm smells of wool and aftershave mixed with the wood smoke from Yanaha's stove into a sweet potpourri of human smells. Everyone waited expectantly for the Singer and the divine ones to help Sam experience harmony in all his actions and thoughts.

Sam was the last to enter the hogan. He didn't make eye contact with anyone as he sprinkled white cornmeal from south to north and across the west side of the sand painting. When he was finished, he sat in the center of the painting facing east to the open door of the hogan, protected from evil, and ready to receive the power of the Holy Ones.

The Singer raised his arms and chanted the ancient words seeking the attention of the gods. Murmurs of assent wove through the crowd. The Singer sifted colored sand, forming the stick figures of the spiritual Yeii. He prayed for the divine ones to enter the sand painting and transfer the powers of the painting to his patient.

Sam repeated the Singer's words in his rich baritone. The Singer's right hand was smudged yellow from corn pollen, and in his left, he held the Mountain Earth bundle of sweet sage above Sam's head. The murmur of the crowd's soft voices and the warmth from the wood smoke lulled me to a tranquil place.

The Singer prayed to break the power of evil. "Shatter the power of all witchcraft and sorcery, their curses and spells. Bind them in the power of the Holy Ones." From a leather bag slung over his shoulder, he pulled out a handful of dried plants and flung them in the fire. The pungent aroma of burning mountain dandelion and rosy pussy toes filled the hogan.

I drifted into a quiet space in my head, listening to the Singer and smelling the pungent herbs. Time slipped away. Yanaha shifted beside me as a fresh cool breeze swept over my face from the open door. When I opened my eyes, I was refreshed as though I had slept, but I knew I hadn't. I was in tune with the life force in my body, feeling each breath leave my lungs, each beat of my heart, and the blood pulsing through my body. A transformative energy swept through on the cool breeze, wrapping me in its life force as we prayed together:

Peace and light within us

Peace and light within our loved ones

Let all around us be in peace and light

"The Holy Ones ride on the winds," Yanaha said softly. The breath of the Holy Ones circled inside the hogan, wrapping our clothes tightly to us. The Singer took sand from the figures he had drawn and rubbed it into Sam's arms and legs. He sprinkled more sand from the Yeii figures over Sam's head. Red and gold dust shimmered in his dark hair.

When he stepped away from Sam, the wind stilled and those closest to the painting dipped their fingers into the sand and sifted it over themselves and their families. Yanaha dusted sand over my head and rubbed it on my arms.

Everyone grew quiet, and the crowd was deep in private prayer. I lowered my head, closed my eyes, and this time my vision wasn't terrifying. A thin, translucent veil of light separated me from the woman's mutilated corpse I had seen on the canyon floor. The cold mist slinked over her, and she reached out her disfigured arm to touch me. I shrunk away from her bony fingers. The mist raced to the veil between us, probing, rising, falling, but unable to penetrate the barrier and reach me. The sky cracked open and fierce sunlight burned away the mist, leaving her exposed to the heat and light. She shriveled to dust, and a gust of wind carried her away.

The crowd around me stirred from their meditations. I opened my eyes, infused with a vibrant energy and emboldened by the regenerative power I had received from the Holy Ones.

Taylor and I helped Yanaha to her feet, and everyone waited, allowing Sam to be the first to leave the hogan. He stood in the doorway facing east with his hands outstretched to receive the last touch of wind from the Holy Ones.

Yanaha whispered to me, "He is restored. And you, my child, you had a vision. The authority of the Holy Ones is written on your face."

The Singer and the elders carefully swept the leftover sand from the painting into a basket. They carried it outside and mixed it with the earth on the east side of the hogan. The drums throbbed, and the crowd joyously surged to greet Sam.

Sam was relaxed and animated as he talked with his family and greeted his friends. His body posture was less rigid, and his arms were open to the people around him. He hugged Yanaha to him. Trace grabbed him in a bear hug. When I joined them, Sam awkwardly draped his arm around me, but I felt no connection with my warrior man.

I stepped out of his arms. "Beautiful Sing. I'll be with Taylor and Yanaha when you're ready to leave."

"In many ways, I am at peace," he said to me. I wasn't going to spoil his pleasure with his friends and family as they celebrated his restoration, one that didn't seem to include a place for me in his heart.

I helped the women carry the food from the trailer to the cloth-covered picnic tables by the stream. The scent of fresh bread and mutton did little to pique my appetite. People wasted no time eating. Most of us wanted to catch a few hours of sleep before going to work.

I took a cup of coffee and sat alone on the hitch of the trailer, toying with the idea that Sam and I had a good run. Perhaps the relationship was over, but I still clung to the hope that I was catastrophizing.

I heard Sam ask one of the women where I was. I rounded the trailer to join him. "Ready?" I asked.

He took my hand, and we walked to his truck, but we didn't talk on the ride back to my car.

When we parked by my car in the station lot, he stared out the driver's side windshield. He turned off the engine and dropped the keys in the well between the seats. "Your car has a flat."

He inspected the sidewalls and the tire. "You got a little nail in it." He stood. "I'll change it for you."

I popped the trunk and unscrewed the spare from the well, grateful he was here and I wasn't standing alone on a road, trying to change the tire.

Sam got the car jacked up and wrestled off the flat. I rolled the spare toward him. He showed me the head of a small nail embedded in the tread. "Take it over to Walmart. They'll fix it for you."

"I will and thank you. I must have picked up the nail in the construction zone I drove through by the prison in Winslow."

He jerked his head back in surprise. "You went to Winslow?"

I nodded and told him Byrd's story.

"I suppose you've already told Aguirre?"

"You were in Window Rock. I didn't want to bother you."

He raked a hand through his hair. "It would have been fine to call me in Window Rock. Let me get these lug nuts tight so you can get home. We're going to talk about Window Rock later."

Chapter 18

A day passed, and I heard nothing from Sam. It was only six-thirty and a long evening loomed before me. Chloe was snoozing comfortably by my feet. The phone rang, and I snatched it up when I saw Sam's name. I was tired of being shut out and was close to saying, "Speak up buddy or let's take a break."

"Jordan, it's me."

"H-h-hi," I stammered. I'd turned monosyllabic, chagrined that I couldn't do any better than that.

He drew in a ragged breath. "I need to talk with you. I'd like to come by tonight if you're comfortable with that."

"Yes, I think we both have a little tidying up of loose ends with each other."

He didn't agree or disagree. He said, "I can be there in less than an hour, if that's okay. I need to clean up. I've been to the sweat lodge."

"I'll see you then." I put the phone down. I wanted this man, but I didn't want more pain, and I wasn't going to be ambivalent. I would hear him out, make a decision, and not look back.

I washed my face and combed my wild hair, and changed out of my ratty sweats into a long pull-on skirt, topped it with a T-shirt. For the next twenty minutes, I anxiously paced the small living room, thinking about what might happen, could happen, and all the unintended consequences I could dream up.

Chloe was on her feet charging the door as soon as he knocked. Sam was casually standing in the threshold. His jet black hair was still damp and falling down his forehead. Stepping aside, I said, "Come in." When he brushed by me, I caught the scent of his shampoo.

He bent down and petted Chloe, who was squirming with excitement. I was, too, but damned if I would show it. I gestured to the sofa, but instead he chose the overstuffed chair. He perched on the edge of the chair, his posture alert, and studied my face.

I took my place across from him on the sofa, waiting for him to speak, too proud to start this conversation and hoping I wasn't going to regret it. The space between us filled with the potential of pain. Chloe whined and bumped my hand, and I threw my arm around her neck. She was warm and solid.

Sam gently cleared his throat. "I've failed you," he said softly. "I haven't been fair with you. I didn't talk with you, and I shut you out because I thought I'd make a mess of explaining it to you and might lose you."

My hopes rose, but I stayed quiet, giving him space. He was a man who needed to talk.

"I have a lot on the line tonight." He cleared his throat and hesitated. "Did you and Texas Jack go out? Are you seeing him?"

"No." I didn't see any reason to fluff the fact up and start babbling. The man wanted a straight answer.

He leaned over closer to me. "I am a one-woman man."

One at time? Is that what he meant?

"I won't accept your bouncing back and forth between me and someone else. I don't want the chaos in my life," he said.

I arched my brows. "Me either, and why are we talking about me? Weren't you the one in Window Rock?"

"Did Jack pick you up the night of auction?"

"Yes. He wouldn't give me his spare ticket so I couldn't meet him there. I was working the night of the auction."

"Did he take you home?"

"I took a cab home. Alone. Jack's *not* the problem. What were you doing in Window Rock?"

Sam abruptly stood and paced off his energy. "I loved a woman in Window Rock. She was messed up bad. She had two little kids, and I loved them, too, but she couldn't get off the drink, and she and her ex were on again off again. I couldn't take it. I left, and I felt guilty as hell leaving those two little kids with her." He brushed back the hank of damp hair off his forehead. Anguish tightened his eyes."Every time she turned to her ex to console her, she swore it would be the last," he said bitterly, "but it never was."

Fear chocked my throat. I had a mental image of a rope tied to his ankle and a pile of baggage dragging behind him. It had always been so easy to see Sam here with me and not think about anyone in his past. I had been naive to be so out of touch with his deep well of sorrow. Doubt skittered up my spine. Was it possible he still loved her? Even a little?

I gritted my teeth. "Do you still love her?"

"No. Her betrayal killed any love I may have ever had for her."

"Did you see her in Window Rock? Is that why you went over there?"

"Yes..."

Pain knifed through my heart.

"I was subpoenaed to testify in the kids' custody case. The grandmother wants the kids. She's the closest thing they have ever had to a mom. Their dad left the Nation, and no one knows where he is, and their mom is awaiting sentencing for her third drunk driving arrest."

"But you saw her?" I walked over to him, facing him over a tense eighteen inches of space.

"Yes, I went to the jail and told her I was testifying on behalf of her mother at the custody trial. I owed her that. She wants her kids, but she's unfit to raise them."

"Does she still love you?"

"I don't think she loves herself, so she can't love anyone. She was angry as hell. She's got her pride, and she doesn't want to lose her kids."

"But you went to her..."

He tentatively put his hand on my shoulder. "It's over. I don't love her." His eyes searched my face. His haggard visage softened. "My mom said I was the kind of man who, if he ever completely loved a woman, he would turn his whole life upset down to make it work. She's right. I love you. You loved me once. I screwed up, and I'm sorry. I'm begging you to open your heart to me, to love me again."

"How could I quit loving you? We share one soul."

He pulled me to him, ducking his head, and caught my lips in a sweet kiss. "I love you," he said huskily, "and oh my God, I've missed you. I didn't think I could make you understand until Mother Earth softened my heart and gave me the words." He held me close.

"I was so lonely when you were gone," I murmured.

"I'll never leave you."

His words chipped the ice around my heart. My warrior was my soft refuge, where our hearts became one, our souls intertwined, and his beautiful face desired only my gaze.

He pulled my hand to his mouth, turning it palm up, nibbling slowly, making my palm tingle and my lust sizzle. His lips touched mine, and his gentle kiss turned fierce, burning my lips.

I led him into my bedroom and then excused myself to the bathroom. I took off my bra and panties and pulled back on the skirt and shirt. My breasts swung gently when I stepped out of the bathroom and into his unsuspecting arms.

He ran his hands up my arms to my face. He nibbled my neck gently using his teeth, sending shivers up my spine. When he cupped my breasts and ran his thumbs over my nipples, he abruptly stopped. "You're not wearing a bra."

His hands caught the bottom of my skirt and pushed it above my waist. His eyes widened when he grasped my bare bottom.

He picked me up and lay me across the bed. He kissed the inside of my thighs, licking and nibbling to my center. Only when I was gasping and stunned with pleasure did he undress.

He stood at the edge of the bed, his face flushed with desire, and bent over, placing his arms on either side of me. My need trembled on the edge of release until he came in a pounding fury, taking me with him.

He collapsed on top of me and kissed me. "Wear underwear anytime you don't want me."

I laughed, and it felt so good to laugh with him again. "I'll get rid of all of it tomorrow."

***

That afternoon Sam called me at work. "Got some info, or you can just watch Taylor on the news tonight. She's as excited as a kid at Christmas."

"I want to hear it from you."

"We caught two smugglers out at Honoo Ji. We've been watching that load-out point where we thought that group of women were going to leave the night you and I were up there. Been damn quiet in there until today."

"Were they moving women?"

"No, they were gun runners moving out a load of AK-47s and body armor. We arrested both of them. Both guys have priors, and they've cut a deal with the DA."

"What did they say?"

"They claim two rivals have been battling for control of the route from the border through Honoo Ji, slowing traffic. But the war's over and they're back in business. After we talked to the smugglers, we went into the canyon with a canine unit and found a guy's body. He'd been shot in the head—and within the last couple of days. His body had tumbled out of the spider hole into the ravine. Without the dogs, we would have never found him in the thick brush. Somebody else had set up shop in his spider hole, and we arrested him."

"This must be why I haven't had many answers to my ads."

"Ads?"

"I put one up on Agora, too..."

"Did you tell Aguirre you put an ad on Agora, because you sure as hell didn't tell me."

"I'm telling you now. There was a while in there when we weren't doing much talking."

He cleared his throat. "Yeah, okay. You gonna give me the password?"

I gave him the web address and password. "Are these two guys giving up names?"

"Not yet—they're afraid of retribution.

"Have you or Trace had time to run Jack through the criminal database?"

"Yeah." I could hear him shuffling papers. "I got it here somewhere... Here it is. He has no criminal record. I couldn't turn up much on him. He's nearly a clean slate until he turns up in Flag and rents an apartment, but there's no evidence he had a job when he got here. After he bought the bar, he moved out on the property."

"Trust fund baby, you think?"

"Maybe. I know Montoya has a long criminal record going back to when he was a juvenile. His family was in the sex trade when he was a kid. Jack—he's either clean or left damn few tracks."

"There's something... I don't know. Something planned or maybe sinister about how Jack insinuated himself into Montoya's financial life and then bedded his wife. It's just creepy."

"But nothing illegal. Interesting though. If Montoya isn't the heavy partner in the trucking business, then where is he getting his money?"

"He has a very rich wife."

"Yup, and I bet he got his fingers into her money."

"There's more. Carolyn and Jack are having an affair."

"Did she tell you that?"

"Yeah, and she's afraid her husband will find out."

Sam frowned. "That could put her in a bad position if he finds out. He could see her as a liability. Let's jaw about it tonight at my place. I think I'm going to be home at a decent time. We need some time together."

Chapter 19

Sam's "Love ya" still echoed in my head as I called Taylor to congratulate her on her story, but as soon as I said hello, she interrupted.

"Hey, you heard about the bust on the Nation?" Taylor asked.

"Sam just told me..."

"I'm on my way over to the university to interview a professor who is an expert on the Mexican economy. I need one final sound bite for the story tonight."

Before I could say anything, she fired, "I'll call you when I'm back at the station so we can take a look at the ads."

An hour later, I walked into Taylor's office. She was fast-forwarding through the video from her interview.

"Get some good stuff?" I asked.

"Yes, thank God. Soon as I got here this morning, Marty yelled at me, 'Get your butt in here.'"

"Uh-oh, what's he jammed up about?"

"He told me I was sitting on my ass too much peering into my computer monitor." She rolled her eyes. "It's been awhile since Marty was in the field. He doesn't realize we don't just walk up and down the street trolling for man-on-the-street interviews."

"So what's his real problem?"

"Who knows? He just vents his pressure down to the boiling point and, today, I was his target. Look at this video clip. The expert corroborated the turf war in the corridor."

She started the video. A middle-aged guy with wispy gray hair and little, round metal spectacles seated in a cluttered academic office said, "The Mexican economy is held at gun point by organized groups of smugglers who are willing to kill each other to control the spider holes from Nogales through the Nation."

She clicked off the video. "I have a source down in Nogales with the Border Patrol, and he verifies the professor's statement. He claims millions of dollars of goods pass through the corridor to the Nation, but they'll never know exactly how much or what is coming into the country since only a fraction of it is caught."

"I can come back if you have to get this story done right now."

"Nah, I got time." She clicked off the video screen and brought up the web.

She stood up and turned the computer over to me, and I typed in Agora's address. The home page had a large black X over it. "There aren't any ads here."

"Hacked," Taylor said. "Get out of there and check your digital wallet. You left a trail from Agora back to your wallet."

I typed in my digital wallet address. "Damn. It's empty." I laughed sourly. "Who do I report my stolen Bitcoins to?"

"How much did you lose?"

"Ten bucks, but whoever hacked Agora customers' wallets might have my card info." I called and cancelled the credit card I'd bought the coins with.

"Did you tell Sam about the Agora ad?"

"I did, and I'll tell him tonight about the hack."

She started to talk, but I held up my hand. "We cleared the air last night. It's all good."

"You look pretty pleased with yourself."

"I am." I typed in the web address of SilkRoad. "Might as well see what we have here. Two answers. Umm, the first one's a dud. He wants me to deliver the women to Phoenix. The second one…hmmm, this is more interesting, and he just now replied. He didn't balk at taking possession in Honoo Ji, but he wants to negotiate the price."

"What do you think?"

"I don't know. The going rate is between twenty-five and fifty thousand per girl. We priced the girls at thirty-five thousand each. This guy has to know the market price. He'll still have room for profit on his end. It's not as cheap as driving into Mexico and buying them there, but he thinks we did all the hard work of getting them through the corridor and into Honoo Ji."

She laughed. "You talk like you actually did move the women. Write him back and tell him you had to pay bribes to get them through the corridor, and it's a prime load of girls. Then, let's see what he says."

"You're forgetting we aren't in charge. The FBI is." I picked up my phone and called Aguirre.

Aguirre wanted to stick with the original price. "Make it short and to the point. The more you write, the more he has to read between the lines. In fact, don't write it at all. I will."

I said to Taylor, "Well that's that. They're writing the answer. Let me know when he finishes writing my response."

"Sure."

I slipped in the rear door of the building like a teenager past curfew. Benally's loud voice carried down the hall. I was grateful she was distracted, but tired of sneaking into the back of the building to avoid her.

Taylor didn't call me with any answers to my ad, and I fumed that maybe the whole idea of trolling the Dark Net had been a bad idea, and now probably dangerous, since my Bitcoins were stolen. A good hacker could follow the footprint to me.

***

When I pulled in Sam's long driveway, dusk was swallowing the last light of the sun. Red blooming skullcap plants marched up the sidewalk and clustered under the front windows. Jasper was doing his happy dance as I walked up the driveway.

Sam opened the door. "Jasper didn't know if it was you or the pizza guy." He swept me in his arms, angled his head, and kissed me. "Only been a day, and I've missed you," he said hoarsely.

All eighty pounds of Jasper edged between our legs, whimpering and moaning for attention. Sam bent down and petted his big head. "Ears," he said. Jasper wailed in protest and slunk away. Sam pecked a light kiss on my lips. "I'll feed him and take care of his ears. He's got that mite thing going on, and he hates the medication. He's not too crazy about his vet either."

While Sam had Jasper pinned, the pizza guy rang the bell. I took the two steaming boxes into the kitchen and set them on the counter. "Dinner's ready. I love saying that when no cooking is involved."

Sam opened the cabinet doors, rummaging for plates, and handed me two.

I set them and extra napkins on the table and plated up the pizza. "I haven't heard from Taylor about the ads. Do you know anything?"

"Just that Aguirre firmed up the price. No response from the buyer yet."

"Do you think the buyer's bolted?"

"No way to know. We just sit tight." He shrugged and helped himself to another slice. "For all we know, we're talking to some eleven-year-old kid who is just jacking us around."

"I hope not. The Agora site was hacked, the ads pulled down, and someone stole the rest of the Bitcoins out of my wallet. Wait a minute. Did the Feds close down Agora?"

"Not that I know of, but they're famous for not sharing information. It could have been a rival hacker. You did cancel the credit card you bought the Bitcoins with, didn't you?"

"Yes..."

"Good. Can't be too careful. Speaking of which, I think this case is going to go down fast. Traffic is up in the corridor, you have a promising answer to your ad, and Aguirre is assembling a team for the exchange. This is no time for either of us to get sloppy."

"So Aguirre thinks the buyer is for real?"

"He's playing it that way, and it won't take him long to set up the exchange."

"Who is the 'we' who will be there for the exchange?"

"Navajo PD and the FBI."

"You'll have to have some women to show the buyer."

"We will, and they'll be police officers or agents. At this point in a case, everyone is tense, things move fast, and we react to a changing battle plan. I want you to be at work or locked in your house or with me. That's the only way I'm going to feel good about you."

I kept my face neutral. "Okay."

"I mean it." He ticked the reasons off his fingers. "You may have had your web address hacked when you were on the Dark Net, and you piqued Montoya's interest when you befriended his wife, and especially when you went to talk to Byrd." He cocked his head at me. "Are you still plagued by those visions?"

I told him of my revelation of the Holy Ones defeating the witches during his Sing.

"I prayed you would be blessed." He reached over and cupped my face. "I want the chaos out of your life."

"I don't know that the witches are through with me, but nothing has happened since the Sing when the Holy Ones pushed them back into the darkness."

"Then we'll pray they stay there." His voice was like steel. A quirky little grin tugged at the edges of his mouth. "I'm ready for dessert. What did you make? Shall I get it out of your car?"

I screwed up my face, surprised, and then momentarily perplexed. Was I supposed to have brought a dessert?

He laughed. "Gotcha, gorgeous, I bought a cheesecake. It's in the fridge. I know my woman."

"Mean, Officer Tohee. You'll have to be punished for that later."

He arched a brow. "Hold you to it." Micro expressions of lust and excitement flashed across his face.

"Come in here," I said in a low voice. I tugged him into his bedroom. His handcuffs were balanced on the night stand on top of a messy pile of papers and loose change. "Sit." I pointed at the bed. He sat down and held his hand out to me to join him. I snatched up the cuffs and twirled them on my forefinger.

"You or me?" he said throatily.

I snapped the cuff shut on his hand and before he could react, I clamped the other cuff to the post of the headboard. "Oh, absolutely, you. Lay down on the bed."

I stepped out of my skirt. His breath hitched, and his eyes dilated. "Nice," he whispered. He beckoned me closer. I danced away, peeling off my shirt. "Come here," he demanded.

"Not on a bet." I stood out of his reach, unhooked my bra, and my breasts tumbled free.

He groaned as I stepped out of my panties and kept out of his reach. He was awkwardly fumbling with his buckle. He unzipped his pants. "Give me some help here."

Standing at the foot of the bed, well out of his reach, I pulled his boots off, grabbed the hem edges of his pants, and yanked them off.

When I unbuttoned his uniform shirt, he lifted his head, kissed me hard, and plunged his tongue possessively into my mouth. I broke the kiss and tongued my way to the thick patch of dark hair below his navel.

"You're killing me, woman."

I mounted him, and he arched his hips, trying to reposition me. "Not yet." He slipped his hand around my neck and pulled my face to his. His kiss was urgent and when I nipped his delicious full bottom lip, his took my mouth, demanding my submission. He raised his hips and thrust deeply into me. My vision tunneled to his face, time suspended, and all that mattered was the sea of sensation building. We shattered in a release that racked our bodies with tremors.

I nestled my head on his shoulder, smelling the faded scent of his cologne. He nuzzled my neck, and when he raised his head, he grinned. "You think you could uncuff me now?"

"For the time being." I found the key in a pile of coins and unlocked him.

He chafed his hand, and I got back in bed and spooned him.

He whispered, "All I have to offer you is my love."

"You're love fills my heart perfectly."

Sated with the pleasure of his lovemaking, I fell into a deep sleep. Sometime during the night I stood again atop Moenkopi Plateau surveying the labyrinth of Honoo Ji below me. I felt no fear, keeping watch as a silent sentinel to the strong wind blowing my hair freely around my shoulders. I viewed my body from outside myself, knowing the witches had drawn me into their world since I was unable to leave the ridgeline.

The wind cooled, and low moaning cries and fetid air floated out of the maze. A sweet, rotting stink I couldn't identify wafted around me.

On the canyon floor below me, dim firelight filtered from behind the hoodoos, beckoning me. I fought against the pull to descend into the canyon. I looked away, prayed for strength, but I failed. I effortlessly negotiated the dangerous slick rock in the dark—down, spiraling down to the canyon floor. The keening wind picked up, whistling a grinding whine, tearing at my clothes, and shrieking through my hair.

Goose bumps popped out on my arms. I was not alone. Three menacing figures coated in white ash and wearing only buckskin loincloths to ward of the frigid wind slithered along the canyon floor toward me. They floated around me, circling endlessly outside my reach. I tried to break free and dodge between them, but they tightened the circle, keeping me imprisoned. The cold mist thickened until it was hard to draw a breath from the wet. From out of the mist, one witch snapped fire from his fingers and a ring of fire burned wild and hot around me. I screamed as tongues of fire licked at my clothes and singed my hair. Another witch bent the wind to his will, forming a funnel, kicking up dirt and dousing the fire. Embers and sand rained down on me, stinging my skin. Grit clogged my mouth and eyes. A yellow-eyed owl perched on the forearm of the third. He swiveled his head to keep his eyes on me while the three surrounded me, shaking gourd rattles and chanting "Hey-ya, Hey-ya." Their guttural voices bounced off the slick rock until it seemed a choir of witches drowned out the night sounds.

I ran. I hid. I searched for a way out, diving between slashes in the rock, ducking behind fins. I kicked up a storm of red dust, digging my heels into soft dirt of the canyon floor. I zigzagged around pinnacles of rock, ran so fast I stumbled and caught myself on a sharp outcrop and slashed open my hand. I ran until I thought my lungs would explode and the pain in my side made me dizzy. I breathed a sigh of relief when I saw a huge outcrop of rock. I dived to the safety behind it, and they were already there waiting for me. I was so tired of running, and my side throbbed with pain. I dropped to the ground and curled up in a ball, making myself as small as a target as I could.

A witch darted in, snatched hair from my head, and raced back to the others. Another triumphantly dangled a piece from my missing sweater before me. I mewled, powerless to stop their curses.

One pointed his finger at the floor and the canyon opened to the bowels of the earth. They flung my sweater scrap and the strand of my hair into the opening. They stood in a ring and urinated into the void. The smell of rotting corpses rose on the steam boiling from the earth. The fissure closed over the curse.

The witches howled their unholy prayers, and the sounds of their curses chased light and hope from my soul. I scrambled back like a terrified animal until my back hit solid rock. I cowered and shouted I would kill them. They cackled in glee. "Kill ten of us, and a hundred more will spring from the Underworld." They circled closer. I caught the flicker of movement in the shadows behind them.

A woman carrying an infant emerged from the mist, walking toward them. I cried out to warn her to flee, but she paid me no heed and acted as though she didn't see the evil before her. When she came closer to their circle, I screamed at her to run and save her child. The witches turned on her in a fury and snatched the mewling infant from her. I shouted at her to grab the baby and run, but she didn't fight for her baby or beg for mercy.

A mighty river appeared in the dry canyon, tumbling over rocks, roaring toward the thunder of an unseen falls. Holding the wailing baby by his legs above the torrent of water, the three chanted and laughed maniacally. The mute mother stood still, transfixed by the sight of the witches holding her crying child. I lunged and screamed, but I was too slow, too late, and the witch dropped the squirming infant into the foaming water. He bobbed once as I helplessly crouched by the river and watched him swept away.

The river vanished as quickly as it formed, and the mother morphed into the fourth ash-coated figure in the mist. Their power of three had grown to four.

My knees were skinned, and my bloody hand throbbed. I leaned on the rock to pull myself up and face the four of them, terrified by the display of power and the evil they had conjured.

They spread out around me, inching closer, beckoning me to come to them, join them. They promised me power, the potency of curses and spells, the world bowing in fear at my feet, and more riches than I knew existed. "You know this is what you always wanted," they chanted.

"You're a poor girl from the Nation. Come to us, and the people will know your name. You will have everything you ever dreamed of having."

I covered my ears to blot out their promises. I shouted over their cajoling, but my left foot slid forward, one tiny step toward them and then another tentative step followed. Their hands thrust out to me, summoning me, encouraging me in melodic voices. *"Come, come..."*

I lifted my arm, reached out my hand, and stretched my fingertips to accept their bond. I opened my mouth to speak, but the bright, white light of the Holy Ones poured from my body, grew in intensity, surged toward the witches, and flung them back, deep into the maze, far from me. They cast spells, shrieked, and shot fire from their fingertips into the flow of light, but the pure white light relentlessly pushed them into the pit of darkness.

***

I awoke in the quiet before day with Sam sleeping beside me. A deep sense of peace replaced my terror. I slipped quietly out of bed to let him sleep.

Dawn had not broken when I crept out of the house and followed the gurgling sound of water tumbling over rocks to the creek behind his shop. The morning grass was cool and damp and the soft rustle of the wind blew through the pines. Tucking the blanket around me, I warded off the morning chill and sat cross-legged in the meadow grass, waiting for the dawn to bring the Holy Ones.

The eastern sky glowed, shimmering in a haze of gold, before it burst into a fiery morning. The tree leaves quivered in the luminous morning light, and the rays raced across the prairie grass, lighting the thin space between The Earth People and The Holy Ones. Last night I had been tempted, and I had stumbled and nearly failed. I waited now for The Holy Ones who had snatched me back and spewed the witches to the Underworld. Quiet seeped into my soul. Sunlight bathed my face and danced over the blanket, shrouding me in clear light. I lifted up my prayers of gratitude.

I didn't know how long I sat sending prayers of thankfulness to the Holy Ones before I noticed the long shadow cast on the ground beside me.

Sam sat down by me and slipped his arm over my shoulders, closed his eyes, and lifted his face to the east sun, chanting softly, "May beauty always surround me." Light reflected off the gold flecks in his dark eyes. "The Holy Ones have come with the dawn."

"We're standing on the edge of eternity, surrounded by them. Do you feel it?"

"Yes..."

"The calling to a purpose beyond this moment?"

"Yes," he repeated softly.

I held my hand out and let the sun chase up my arm and settle on my shoulders. I wanted to lift the veil and glimpse the magnificent presence of the Holy Ones, but the gift was not given. "When my prayers become rote, I'll remember this morning."

We sat together and watched the sun rise and burn off the morning mist. Wild things moved through the meadow. Blue jays chattered and cawed at a red fox dashing across the grass. Sam nudged me and pointed at a doe elk and her trembling fawn stepping tenuously from the tree line. Full morning light warmed the meadow, and the thin space between us and eternity vanished in the strong sun.

"The witches came to you last night. I held you and prayed for peace for you."

"I didn't know I made any noise. Your prayers helped keep me safe. They know I'm not theirs."

"What happened?"

"They tempted me with wealth and wisdom, and I nearly failed. Their power was greater than mine. They would have taken my soul if the Holy Ones had not come and chased them into the darkness."

Sam's face creased in pain, and his eyes were tightly closed.

I put my hand on his arm. "I'm okay. Your prayers were with me."

When he opened his eyes, they were twin dark pools of pain. "My little brother was only eight when the witches took his soul. I should have never taken him into Honoo Ji. When the witches caught him, I wasn't there to protect him."

"You were young. It was fate that he wandered off and the witches found him."

"There's no healing for him. He's just an empty husk, lying on a bed. He doesn't even know I'm in the room with him."

"The fates are cruel and amoral. They make no distinction between good and evil. Your brother's fate was cruel, but you couldn't protect him from what life had written for him. You're not responsible for what was fated to happen."

"I've nursed my guilt—"

"For too long. You have to let it go. You've provided good care for him. You're a good man."

"I don't want to live in remorse anymore. I know I need to let it go, but I don't know how to do it."

"You have to forgive yourself first."

"I hear the words, but I don't know how to forgive myself, and my brother can't forgive me."

"You can't change what happened to your brother. You can't restore him to who he was before he walked into the canyon with you, but you can silence your inner critic. Forgiving yourself means owning your mistakes *and* acknowledging the good in you."

"How will I know when I have forgiven myself?"

"You won't beat yourself up anymore."

Chapter 20

Once at the office, I drank coffee and tried to concentrate on writing a progress report to our grantor, only to have my attention diverted to worrying about Sam and the guilt he had held close for too many years. I hoped he could finally let it go.

My cell interrupted my ruminations. "That buyer you've been haggling with has come back with a second offer," Agent Aguirre said.

"How much is he offering?"

"Thirty thousand, and he says it's his final offer. We're going to take it. They're worth fifty thousand apiece as sex workers, so I doubt he turns tail and bails. He hasn't balked at taking delivery in Honoo Ji either. If we don't agree, we can't be sure its Montoya."

"Do you think it's him?"

"Won't be certain until we see him in the canyon taking the women. He's leaving the same digital tracks, tracking back to the IP address at his home."

"Maybe he did learn all of Byrd's lessons."

"You can't share any information. He thinks the women are in transit so we have the liberty of setting the date for pickup and we'll be ready soon. I don't want to do anything that panics him and makes him bolt."

Taylor was calling in when I hung up with Aguirre.

"Have you heard? The guy came back with a price for the girls," she said. "When are they going to make the exchange?"

"He told me he's getting the mission together."

She sighed. "Fed time. They work on a different clock than us mortals."

"Did I get any other answers to the ad?"

"No such luck. Wait a minute. Something's coming across the scanner."

I heard static and a garbled voice from the police scanner in the background.

Taylor said in rush, "I gotta go. There's a fatal wreck out on East Route 66. Call you later."

The half finished progress report demanded my attention. After twenty minutes of revisions and rewrites, my phone rang and Taylor's number came up. She couldn't have finished at the accident scene. "Hey..."

"Jordan. It's about Carolyn... She died in that wreck over on 66."

"What? Ohhh..." Suspicion churned through me. "It *was* an accident, wasn't it?"

"It sure looks like it, and that's what the police are calling it. She crashed into a concrete abutment where East Route 66 meets Enterprise Avenue—you know, the most dangerous intersection in town."

"Was anyone else hurt?"

"That's the odd thing. No one hit her car and pushed her into the concrete barrier. Witnesses say she just drove into the wall without even slowing down."

"I don't like it. That intersection is known for car wrecks, but with *other* vehicles. Was the trunk popped open?"

"I don't know. Why?"

"Maybe her bags are in there, and she was leaving Montoya."

"You think he killed her..." She paused. "I've got a cop buddy who will tell me if impound finds anything in the trunk."

"I made her a target."

"She made herself a target," Taylor corrected. "She married an ex-con and took a lover. You can't beat yourself up about this. You told her to get away."

Is an autopsy required?"

"Maybe not, I didn't see her, but the patrolman said she had a bad head injury. The ME has been here, and they're moving her body now." Taylor placated me, "Hey, I think she had an accident. I gotta run. I'll call you if I hear anything else."

Carolyn had been prey among raptors. Young and inexperienced, wealthy and grieving, she had been the perfect foil to Montoya's greed, and an opportunity for Jack to notch another win and humiliate Montoya. I couldn't concentrate, and the office seemed close and stuffy. I shoved away from my desk and decided to go for a ride. I felt like a like a voyeur when I parked in front of Montoya's house. No cars were in the drive, and no lights shone out the windows. I had no evidence it wasn't an accident. She was certainly distracted enough with Montoya's tax problems and her affair with Jack to drive into a concrete barrier. Oh no, could she have committed suicide? No, no way. Women didn't kill themselves in messy ways, and she was in love with Jack. She wanted out of the marriage, but she *wanted* to be with Jack.

I headed back to work, treating myself to coffee from Starbucks, but the unsettled feelings about Carolyn's death wouldn't go away. Damned if Benally wasn't lying in wait for me, standing in the doorway of my cubicle. She arched her brow as though expecting me to account for my absence. I disappointed her. "Did you need something?" I asked as sweetly as I could muster and slipped past her to my desk.

"One of our contract counselors called from over at the high school in Tuba City. The Navajo police are making arrests."

I marveled at her ability to leave out what happened and to whom it happened. "What's going on?"

"The Cobras and Dragons had a knife fight on the athletic fields."

"How bad are the injuries?"

Her mouth slacked open showing big, yellowed front teeth. Squint lines formed around her small eyes. "I don't have all the details. Do your job, get out there, and provide support to our contract workers."

I rose to go.

"I want a full report on my desk in the morning. And I certainly hope that grant you and the school counselor are spending so much time on is going to keep the little kids from becoming pee wees." She marched off, pumped up with her power to dictate to others.

***

The blue and red flashers of police cars threw garish light on the playing fields behind the high school, reminding me of the last time I had been here, Jimmy Begay's suicide. An ambulance pulled onto the highway and hit its siren when it passed me. I left the Civic in a parking lot well away from the scene. Taylor was talking on camera, and Louis was shooting video.

Sam, Trace, and a young female officer were talking separately to small groups of young men, who milled around burning off their adrenaline. Trace and Sam began to load some of the students into a police van parked on the side of the field.

I headed toward one of our counselors, Sarah Cervantes, who stood among a group of boys who were yelling and thrusting their fists into the sky. She attempted to cajole them to reason, but they weren't having any of it. Sam peeled off from Trace and took control of the group in front of Sarah.

Sarah pushed her wild hair out of her eyes and turned on me when I joined the group. "They're too many of them for me." Her shrill voice shimmied down my spine as she leaned into me aggressively. "I needed more help out here. They nearly started a riot."

I took her elbow and steered her away from Sam and the boys. “Are you okay?”

“Of course not.” She tugged a hand through her hair. “That’s the second ambulance to pull out of here. The first guy they took out was knifed right in front of me. There was blood everywhere.” She wrung her hands. “I didn’t sign on to work a gang war...” Her voice was frantic.

She was interrupted by Mason Torres joining us. “Ms. Cervantes, I know that was difficult. I appreciate your good work.”

Sarah stopped talking, but her hands were still shaking and her mouth was drawn down. She wasn’t taking any solace from Torres’s soothing talk.

A female officer hurried up behind Torres and joined us, stuck her hand out to me, and said, “I’m Officer Jessica Akee with Navajo PD.” We all exchanged names and associations with her.

“Principal Torres,” she spoke over the din, “please keep the rest of the students in lockdown while we finish out here with these guys.”

Torres nodded and answered, “Let me know when you’re done. I’m closing the school and will release the students who ride the buses first and then dismiss the walkers by family groups. I want these kids scattered, and I want a police presence here early in the morning.”

She nodded, and he excused himself to head back to the school.

Sarah turned to me and said, “I quit, today, as of right now. I don’t want to work juvie gangs and knife fights.”

“I think—”

“I don’t care what you think. You weren’t here.” She headed for her car.

She made a harried retreat to her car, leaving me unhappy to be the one who had to tell Benally she had quit.

Sam walked up to me. “She quit, huh?”

“How did you guess?”

“She was pretty shook up.” He waved his hand at the police van. “This is going to be an all nighter for me. Trace has made me the lead investigator.”

I shrugged. “I have to go tell Benally we lost a contract counselor and write yet another report. How about dinner tomorrow night?”

“Works for me.”

***

By the time I left the high school, it was close to five o’clock. I could avoid seeing Benally by writing the report tonight at home. Just to cover my ass, I waited until after five and left a voice message on her work phone that Sarah Cervantes had quit and offered to help her with the search for her replacement.

Chloe and was ready for her and walk and I wanted to clear my head. I didn't think Montoya would push for an autopsy. Carolyn's death was an all-around financial win for him, and there would be no more embarrassing affair. I wondered what Jack's reaction was to her death.

When Chloe and I got home, I called him.

"Hi-ya sweetheart. Been thinkin' of me? I've been thinking about you—on your back."

I ignored his comment. "I called to see how you were doing. I know you and Carolyn were...um, close."

"We were finished. I lost interest in doin' another man's wife."

"Was she unhappy about that?"

He snorted laughter."Of course she was. She'd had the best. How 'bout you and me having breakfast again?"

"I don't think so..."

"Let me satisfy your curiosity. You called to see if I killed her. I didn't. Her old man did."

"Why?"

"He'd nearly drained her dry of that big pile of cash she had..."

"Any cash she had was a premarital asset. It wasn't his."

"*Riiight*. But she was such a sweetie, she just kept forking it over to her old man. She inherited a pile from her granny when she turned twenty-one and a bigger pile when her parents died. Between shoring up his part of the trucking company and keeping up their lifestyle, she damn near gave it all to him."

"That doesn't make any sense..."

"Don't gimme that. She was a dumb kid. Her husband told her he just needed a little loan. He'd pay her back in ninety days. When that passed, he was in a rough patch and maybe it would be six months before he had the money—and she's still writin' the checks to him. She believed him, the good little wife. Six months down the road, she's crying on my shoulder. By then, I own his bar and most of his trucking company—and I'm doin' his wife, but I didn't kill her. I win. I don't kill. I'm always the winner. Think about it. Her putting her family cash into the business kept me from having to bail him out, *again*."

"So he killed her because she had no more money? If he's indicted, he can't get the life insurance money, and he can't collect on the insurance policy if it's ruled a suicide."

"You're thinking with your brain. He was thinking with his cock. She was fuckin' me. How do you think he took that news?"

***

In the morning, Taylor's phone call woke me. "The ME is doing a full autopsy."

"Why? I thought you said—"

"Her arms and back were covered in bruises. Montoya fought the decision, saying he wanted to lay his wife to rest—that her poor body had been through enough in the wreck, but he was overruled. You were right. Her bags were in the trunk."

"Hmm. Montoya knows his wife talked to me, and he knows I was Sofia's case worker."

"Yeesh. As his wife, Carolyn couldn't be made to testify against him, and she ended up dead. You *could* testify against him. He doesn't know you don't have a lot of evidence."

"I know, I know. Carolyn's bruising doesn't explain her driving into the barrier."

"Yep, we'll know more when the autopsy is done."

"When will that be?"

"She moved to the head of the list. She's the first case this morning."

"Call me. I'll be in the office all day. Sarah Cervantes, the contract counselor out at the high school, quit on the spot yesterday."

"I'm not surprised. They probably heard her screaming all the way over in Flag."

"Sam said the same thing. Anyway, call me. I'll be sitting by Benally doing interviews all day for Sarah's replacement."

"That's a safe place for you to be. I'll let you know when I hear something."

Chapter 21

I took Chloe with me to work, unwilling to leave her home. I packed her water dish and a chew toy and parked in the lot under the one shade tree, leaving all the windows open a couple of inches. She slurped water and stretched out, covering most of the back seat, and was asleep before I locked the car.

When I walked in her office, Bessie Benally had the application files strewn across her desk "You're late." Her one continuous eyebrow arched slightly on the left side.

"I'm not late. It's three minutes past eight and I made a pot of coffee." I sat a fresh cup down beside her.

"Thanks." She sniffed. "Now, you know I like to cast a wide net and study all the options when we have an opportunity like this."

Yes, I did *know*. Hers was a tedious, time-wasting process. We had at least four good application files. We didn't need to look again at all the files spread over her desk that we had already reviewed and rejected during previous searches.

"I've been here since six this morning reviewing these files." She swept one arm dramatically across the desk, waiting for my reaction.

"I suggest we reduce the files to those who live in the area and have completed the bachelor's degree. We need someone on the job immediately. There are at least four applications right there that meet that standard. Let's see if they are available, and then start calling references. We could interview someone this afternoon or early tomorrow."

"That's impossible, Jordan. We must look again at all twenty files, cast our net far."

Benally was a paper pusher and my boss, so I didn't let her see my exasperation. I picked up a file. "With whom would you like to start?"

By three in the afternoon, we had culled the stack to the four I had suggested at three minutes past eight in the morning and a fifth applicant who met the criteria, but whose address on the application placed him in Provo, Utah, making it hard for him start at the same time the local applicants could. I also found nothing particularly outstanding about his application.

"You go start calling references." Benally dismissed me. I went out the back door to check on Chloe. She was snoozing until I awoke her when I filled her water bowl.

I was back in my office checking refs when Taylor called. "Got the autopsy results. You're never gonna guess. She was loaded up with Valium."

"Valium?"

"Yeah, ten milligrams of valium can cause the same impairment as having a blood alcohol concentration of 0.10 percent."

"How much did she have in her system?"

"Twelve hundred milligrams. Would have probably killed her if she hadn't had the car wreck," Taylor said.

"Did she have a prescription?"

"O'Brien says neither she nor her husband had a prescription. They're tossing the house now. He's also got a warrant for Montoya's car and the business."

"Montoya doped her up with Valium and put her in the car, hoping an autopsy wouldn't be needed. The bruises may explain how he got the pills down her."

"Carolyn's has scratch marks *inside* her throat. The ME says that's consistent with someone shoving stuff down her throat."

"Have you talked to Montoya?"

"He's made a public statement through his lawyer, claiming his wife was despondent and seeking treatment. He's asking people to support him and his need for privacy during this difficult time."

"Yeah, right. What's his alibi?"

"He was at the office and had been there for hours before she died."

Benally was clomping down the hall. I hurriedly said, "Keep me posted. Benally's coming."

"Jordan. I hope that's a reference you're talking to. It's nearly five. How many did you get to talk to?" Benally harrumphed.

"I talked to references for both my applicants. All got glowing refs. How about you?"

"Good refs for both of mine."

"Then we can't go wrong. Let's hire the first one who says, 'Yes, I can start this week.' They'll be eager, Ms. Benally. Most of them are hungry grad students."

"I'll have to sleep on it. Tomorrow..." She stroked her index finger across her incipient mustache. "Tomorrow I think I'll make the decision. Yes. That's what I'll do."

She drove me nuts. I could hardly wait to get out of the office. Sam was coming for dinner, but cooking was still a conundrum in my life. When I finally admitted to Sam that the cooking fairy passed me by, he had bought me a cookbook, *365 Easy Meals*, but that was false advertising. Nothing about the whole sauté this caramelize that was *easy*. My forte was picking out desserts at the bakery, which I planned to do on the way home. That and a bagged salad with bottled dressing and a fresh baguette, and I was fairly sure there was no way I could screw this up. The whole plan hinged on Sam being a man who could and would grill the steaks, and I was betting he was hungry enough to do it.

***

While the coals in my new grill smoldered, I rinsed the salad greens, arranged the flowers, and finished fifteen minutes before Sam would arrive, allowing me to indulge in thinking about him. Warm appreciation of my guy bloomed in my chest. There was no one I would rather be with than my warrior, the man who loved me as I was. Life unfolded in unlikely ways, and I was a young social worker in love with a Navajo cop. It was wonderful, more than wonderful. I was ready for some action with my guy.

When Sam rang the doorbell, Chloe barreled past me, wriggling with excitement over his arrival. She fawned on him and followed us to the kitchen where Sam set the wine on the countertop and admired the steaks. He put the meat on the grill, and when he returned, Chloe was beside herself. He rubbed her head, and she presented him with her belly, wanting the full Monty of hedonism.

"Can I have a turn?" I asked.

"Absolutely." He opened his arms. He was still in his uniform, his collar open and his black tie yanked down in a messy knot. When he stepped toward me, I grabbed his tie and pulled him in close. I ran my tongue around the curve of his bottom lip while unbuttoning his shirt to slip in my fingers.

His reaction was swift. He took a step forward, forcing the kitchen table into the back of my legs.

"I can handle it from here." He hoisted me up on the table, skimmed down my pants and thong, kissing his way to my foot. He paused long enough to unbuckle his uniform pants, and then pulled them and his silky black boxers to the floor.

I wrapped my legs around his waist. His first thrust had me lost in pleasure. My body coiled in sweet expectation. In a rush of wet and reckless release, I came, carrying him with me into a warm pool of lassitude.

Above me, he was breathing heavily. "Nice touch, not setting the table," he murmured.

"I try to stay one step ahead of you."

He pushed Chloe down. "Chloe has been driving me crazy licking my leg and moaning."

I laughed. "But that's my job."

Sam grabbed his pants and tossed me mine. He swooped down for a kiss. "You're a ferociously good lover, and you always surprise me. But—and this is hard—I have to go out and see if the fire is still burning." He thrust one leg in his uniform pants. "It was damn well worth the risk if it's not."

"I'll feed Chloe. She's tired of waiting for her supper."

"Next time we make love on the table, she goes into another room," he called from the balcony.

Sam brought the steaks in while I set the table. When I opened the bottle of Okanogan Valley Riesling, it smelled of sweet apples.

I handed him a glass. "Cheers." I tapped my glass on his. "I can't tell you how happy I am to be home with you."

"If you were any happier, I'd be in traction." He chortled. "I like cooking with you. It's foreplay, as you know."

"Breathing around you is foreplay, big guy, and you did all the cooking."

He put a steak on my plate.

"Perfect, I love mine medium rare."

"I aim to please," he said, sitting down. "You're antsy to ask me what I know about Carolyn's death."

"Taylor told me about Montoya's alibi."

"Everyone who provided his alibi works for him." He shrugged. "But it doesn't rule out that he didn't hire someone to kill her. We reviewed all the footage from the traffic cameras, and a camera on the north side of town caught her heading south into town in that little Mercedes of hers."

"Where was she coming from?"

"South on Arizona Boulevard."

"Hmm. I don't know of much out north of there..."

"We got a clear picture of her at the traffic light on Arizona and Chaparral Road—the first traffic camera on the north side."

"Wait. She may have been coming in from Jack's place. She told me they met out at Crazy Gal's."

He leaned back in his chair. "Why would Jack kill her?"

I shrugged. "She became a liability? She wanted to get married and have babies, and that's not his style? Or she had a scary husband? I called Jack after Carolyn died..."

"What did he say?"

"He denied killing her, said he had no motive to, because her cash was helping the business. Jack claims that Montoya helped himself to Carolyn's money. He also said, 'I win.' And you know, he has. He earned his stripes by getting into Montoya's assets and his wife's bed."

"Sounds like a sleaze ball when you put it like that."

"If he's right about Montoya, they're both sleaze balls, but I think Jack might be more calculating. I wonder if Montoya was targeted and outplayed by him."

"Could be..."

"Jack could have done it. He's plenty smart enough to pull it off, but then again, Montoya had some great motives, jealousy and money. Is the ME finished with Carolyn's body?"

"No, all that takes more time than it does on television."

"But we know he rammed pills down her throat. I wonder if after he doped her up, she ran for her car, thinking she was getting away from her husband. Then the effect of the pills hit, and she crashed."

"Good theory, but unless the Valium tracks directly back to Montoya, that's going to be hard to prove. Montoya's already dropping hints that Carolyn was going through a rough patch, acting oddly, under a lot of pressure. He's doing everything he can to make it look like she got the Valium."

I shook my head. "The only distress I noticed in her was when she told me she was afraid of her husband finding out about the affair and when I told her about the mess he was in."

"Too bad she didn't clear out." He rose and stretched. "I talked to Aguirre today. He told me he and the buyer agreed on the price for the women and the time for the exchange. You can't tell Taylor. You can't give her any indication when we go. Promise me. You can call her the minute it's over and we've made arrests. Then she can have her story."

"She'll see the email..."

"No, she won't. Aguirre changed the password on the account. Promise me."

"I promise. I want this guy as badly as you do."

***

I slept curled up next to Sam, and I awoke before him thinking how incredibly lucky I was to have found such a wonderful guy.

He rolled over and smiled a sleepy smile. "Morning, sunshine. How's my woman?"

I groaned. "I gotta get up. Benally will be eyeing the clock, hoping to pounce on me for being late."

We had a cup of coffee while we dressed but had no time for breakfast. I drove over the speed limit most of the way to the office and was sitting serenely at my desk when Benally passed by to check on me.

Taylor called to say that the search warrants turned up nothing in Montoya's house or his business. She and Louis had interviewed neighbors about the couple, and they claimed to have never heard any fighting or shouting. "Turning into a dead end. She got the Valium somewhere, but as of yet, we don't know where."

"Who else but her husband and her lover stood to gain?"

"No one we know of."

"And if nothing turns up, her death is ruled an accident?"

"I don't think that will happen. The case will probably stay open because she has those scratch marks inside her throat. Hey, when is Aguirre springing the trap?"

I was glad I could answer honestly. "I don't know."

"I can't wait," she said.

Taylor was counting on me to alert her, but I promised Sam I wouldn't.

When I hung up, Benally stood in the doorway. "Finished with your personal business?"

"My conversation wasn't personal business. How can I help you?"

"You can't. I came to apprise you that I successfully interviewed and hired a new contract counselor. She's the graduate student from down in Phoenix. Really a high-quality hire."

"I'll be happy to help her get settled in at the high school."

Benally sniffed at my offer. "You could learn a thing or two from her."

"What is it that you specifically think I could learn from her? I'm sure she's qualified. We're both graduates of state-accredited social work programs. However, I have two solid years of performance. I have a record for clearing cases, wrote and received a grant for the gang intervention program, and I have good working relationships with professionals in other fields."

Benally's mouth formed a perfect little circle. Her eyes were wide with surprise, and she was blinking rapidly. She was absolutely stunned that I had grown a backbone and jabbed back at her bullying. "I'm just saying..."

"Yes, I heard you, but stating 'I'm just saying' doesn't mitigate the tone or impact of your remarks—or add validity to your opinion."

"You're up for a performance review. I can see to it that you lose this job."

"So are you. Don't forget that caseworkers review the department head. The Navajo Council is interested in the opinions of all their employees."

We had a stare-down and neither of us flinched for a long moment. Then Benally turned and plodded down the hallway to her office. I felt the catharsis of defending myself against a small and petty boss. Even better, I was protected by my opportunity to evaluate her.

I spent the morning sending the draft of our completed curriculum back and forth for comments and revisions to my colleague. At noon, I saved the last revisions and was proud of our work. Both Sam and Agent Aguirre had called. We were to all meet in Aguirre's office late this afternoon. Nothing more was said on the phone.

Chapter 22

Aguirre's assistant ushered me into a conference room filled with several buzz-cut, dark-suited, intense FBI types, Sam and Trace, and Officer Jessica Akee. Long shadows of late afternoon sun slanted in the windows when Aguirre took his seat at the head of the conference table. We all waited expectantly for his briefing.

"You are the primaries on the raid to arrest human traffickers operating on the Nation." He dipped his head at me. "Ms Bia is here as a courtesy because of her initiative and her outstanding work as an investigator in this case."

All eyes tracked to me. I nodded at the faces staring at me.

Aguirre slapped his hand down on the table. "The password to the SilkRoad ad has been changed. No one but me has access. We go tonight."

A young FBI agent cleared his throat, hesitated, then asked, "Uh, anyway, sir, this could be construed as entrapment?"

"Absolutely not," Aguirre thundered. "Placing an ad on the Dark Net to advertise women for sale would *not induce* a law-abiding person to answer the ad."

The agent held out both hands in front of him."Yes. Thank you, sir."

Aguirre waited until the murmuring died down. "Officer Jessica Akee will make the exchange." More buzzing and looks of surprise.

My cell vibrated with a text message. Taylor. I bet she couldn't get into the SilkRoad account. I didn't read it.

Agent Aguirre rapped his knuckles on the table, regaining everyone's attention. "The buyer has moved nearly one hundred thousand dollars' worth of Bitcoins into the digital wallet associated with the IP address at Montoya's home. He's serious. He's got his money ready, but to nail him, we have to wait until he has moved the money into our wallet and takes delivery of the women."

"There's no cell service down there in Honoo Ji. How will we know he's paid for them?" Sam asked.

"There's no *regular* cell service in Honoo Ji", he said smugly. "But Jessica and I will have military-grade satellite phones, and that must be what he's using. When I get the word from our tech guys that the money is deposited, I'll alert Jessica." He turned to Jessica. "At that point, let him take the women. Then the Navajo PD will move in to make the arrest."

Jessica agreed.

Aguirre continued, "We promised him three women and there'll be three female agents in the canyon with Officer Akee."

His assistant turned on a projector and used a remote to lower a screen. A blowup of Honoo Ji appeared with GPS coordinates marked on the map. He talked the officers through the mission.

"Any questions? No? Get your gear and go. You have a job to do."

The agents filed out quietly talking. I cornered Sam and Trace. "I'm going with you."

"You're a civilian. No way," Trace said.

"I had the idea for a SilkRoad ad, paid for it, and without me, we wouldn't be standing here. I can stand still behind a rock and keep my mouth shut."

Sam put a hand on Trace's shoulder. "I'll take the responsibility. She knows the operation. What if Montoya's goons took her now and tortured the details out of her, compromising the mission?"

Trace waffled. "I'm taking plausible deniability on this one. Your ass is on the line, buddy."

***

I hid behind a cluster of hoodoos in Honoo Ji with Sam, Trace, and Nez. The evening was perfect with little wind, pleasant temperatures, and no clouds. I was under strict orders to stay put and be quiet, no matter what I saw. We shifted our weight and did knee bends, trying to ease the muscle strain of standing in place for hours. Agent Aguirre had given the Navajo PD the privilege of making the arrest on the Nation. The federal agents were scattered out of site of the clearing where the exchange would be made. They would move in on Trace's order, but the Navajo PD would be first on the scene.

A sliver of dark moon rose, shedding shards of light between the hoodoos. When the silence was split by the howl of a coyote, I jumped. Sam put a warning hand on my arm and covered his microphone with his hand. He whispered in my ear, "If I don't kill you on this mission, I'm gonna make love to you forever." He eased his hand off his microphone and pointed at it, warning me not to speak. Everyone but me was wired, and all communication was heard by everyone.

I stifled a laugh. As he'd intended, his humor eased my fears.

Officer Jessica Akee waited impatiently for the buyer to appear. She shifted her weight from one foot to the other and stole glances at the rocks we hid behind. She had volunteered for duty, claiming there was no way Montoya would recognize her. Her only fieldwork had been at the high school gang fight, and she had only recently joined the Tuba City station. She paced off her adrenaline, walking back and forth in front of the whorls of rock.

I could see her clearly, though it was hard for me to recognize her. She had rubbed bar soap in her long hair, then drizzled dry sand in it, making it messy and wild. She wore tattered jeans, an oversized battered T-shirt, and dirty white tennis shoes.

Something crashed in the scrubby brush. The noise magnified by bouncing off the rock face, making it sound like an army was approaching. Jessica tensed, and the men around me shifted their weight and held their weapons at ready. Jessica squinted, searching the darkness for movement. A skinny burro bolted out from behind the rocks and skidded to a stop, locking his front legs in surprise when he saw Jessica. He skinned his lips back from his protruding teeth and brayed, tossed his head, and turned around clumsily scraping his hide on the rock as he ran away. Jessica bent over and blew out a huge breath.

"Shit, I nearly shot that ass," Nez said. Trace and Sam covered their mouths, their shoulders shaking in silent laughter.

I fidgeted, kept checking the time, and my impatience grew. The men stayed focused and watchful. As the time for the meeting with the buyer grew closer, my heart began to beat faster. Sam seemed to read my thoughts and patted my shoulder awkwardly with his gloved hand.

The tall gray sage around the fins swayed unnaturally, and footsteps softly thudded on the sand. A man wearing a dark hoodie over his head stepped out from behind the rock fins and swaggered toward Jessica. Sam tensed in anticipation. The man approaching Jessica was taller than I remembered Montoya being, and he moved with the lithe grace of an athlete. His hoodie was pulled forward over his face, casting deep shadows on his features.

He stopped a couple of feet from Jessica and planted his feet wide. "Hello darlin'. Didn't expect such a pretty little gal." He shrugged off his hoodie, and the thin moonlight streamed on his light hair. Texas

Jack stood in front of Jessica, his hands on his hips and a wolfish smile on his lips.

I put my hand over my mouth to stifle any noise at the same time Sam nudged me with his knee without taking his eyes off Jack.

Nez locked eyes with Trace and hissed, “Texas...”

Trace shook his head and drew his finger across his neck, signaling Nez to be silent.

“Show me what you got. I like my deals sweet and fast,” Jack told Jessica.

“Three women for thirty thousand apiece.” Jessica said. “Just like we agreed.”

“Maybe they’re not worth that. Let me see ‘em,” he challenged.

The darkness breathed, and the atmosphere grew heavy. Wet, heavy miasma snaked around the base of the hoodoos. None of the men around me showed any reaction to the whorls of wet mist stealing up our legs. I tapped Sam’s shoulder. He shook his head, dismissing me without even looking, and kept his focus on the clearing.

“Come out,” Jessica called. A young woman stepped out from behind a crevice in the sheer rock walls. She wore dirty, ragged clothes and kept her head down, not making eye contact with Jack. A thin stream of mist coiled around her ankles.

“Come closer.” Texas Jack looked her up and down. “Likin’ what I see. She’ll clean up okay. Trot out the rest of ‘em.”

The other two agents obediently came from behind the rocks and stood by the first woman. Jack’s boots crunched in the rock scrabble as he walked the line, inspecting each woman like a man buying horses.

The earth silently rent apart behind Texas Jack, and foul steam sputtered and boiled out of the Underworld and over the rim, swirling around Jack’s boots, fouling the air with a bitter, acrid stink. Four malevolent figures stalked silently up out of the Underworld on a narrow ledge cut into the side of the fissure. I shook Sam’s arm frantically never taking my eyes off the witches climbing to the rim. Sam jerked his head around to me and put his finger to his lips. He leaned over and in the barest whisper said, “Jack has to take the women before we go in.”

Sam didn’t see the witches. Nez and Trace’s faces showed no signs they recognized the horror unfolding in front of us. No one saw them. Only me. I wanted to cry out, shout a warning, but when I opened my mouth, no sound came out. I was struck dumb and held in place by a force more powerful than my will. I clutched my ghost beads and medicine pouch, unable to take my eyes of the witches.

“We got us a deal. They’re good enough stock,” Texas Jack said.

The witches walked out from the steaming cleft in the earth, taking no notice of our presence, and formed a half circle behind Jack. They faced Jessica and the three female agents, but the girls gave no indication they saw them.

"Steady. We're close. He's going take them." Trace said.

"Roger that," Nez and Sam whispered.

Sam glanced at me, eagerly grinned, and gave me a thumbs-up.

Tight bands constricted my upper body, and my breath came in short shallow gulps. My heart jackhammered in my chest. I feared for Jack, not us. I knew the Holy Ones held us apart from the obscenity I was watching.

A great horned owl lifted off the arm of a witch, silently landing on Jack's shoulder. The bird folded his wings to his body and dug his talons deep, tearing into the flesh beneath Jack's shirt. Blood gushed a red stream down his arm. He grabbed his shoulder and screamed, flailing the air as the owl lazily flew a wide circle over his head. "What the hell?" Jack juked and dived, thrashing the air at the owl. The bird gracefully landed atop a fin, skewering Jack with his yellow gaze. Jack put pressure on his bloody shoulder. "Gimme the women. We're done here."

"Transfer the money, then we're done here," Jessica said.

A quick look at the faces of those hiding with me told me no one but me had seen the owl claw Jack.

The witches shuffled behind Jack, mumbling an indecipherable chant. Texas Jack, still cradling his bloody shoulder, whirled around and saw them for the first time. He glanced over at Jessica with a look of horror just as the owl swooped down and raked its claws across his face. Gourd rattles split the silence, and the witches shrieked evil incantations. Holding one hand to his bleeding shoulder and the other to his bloody face, he gasped and bent over in pain."Gimme the women," he shouted at Jessica.

"Transfer the money to my digital wallet," Jessica said in a normal voice. She waggled her cell phone. "My associate hasn't told me I'm rich yet."

Jack pulled a cell out of his jeans. "Gonna get that money for you right now."

Nez was nearly wiggling with excitement. He punched Trace's shoulder."He's gonna pay."

Without taking his eyes off Jack, Trace nodded his agreement.

Jack fumbled and dropped the phone in the sand, clumsy from his bleeding arm.

"Damn it. Get it done," Sam hissed.

A sudden sandstorm howled through the clearing and swept up sand from the canyon floor, chasing away the wet mist, clotting the air, and stinging our bare skin.

"I can't see a damn thing," Sam said as he pulled his shirt over his mouth.

But I could. Withered, ash-covered hands grabbed Jack, yanking him toward the lip of the gash in the earth. He dragged his heels, kicked and screamed, and fought his captors as the witches pulled him ever closer to the chasm. They wrestled Jack down onto the winding trail that led deep into the dark Underworld where they reigned. When Jack's head bobbed even with the rim of the earth, his shrieks were muted by the walls of stone around him, and when the witches and Jack were below the lip of the fissure, the canyon floor closed over them.

The wind stilled as suddenly as it began. Sand sifted softly to the smoothly scoured canyon floor. Unsettling silence roared in my ears. For a moment, we stood as still as characters in a tableau.

Trace blurted, "Where'd he go?"

Sam shrugged and moved toward Jessica.

Trace yanked his arm back. "We don't know how many guys Jack has with him."

Trace motioned Nez to circle left and Sam right. "Flank 'em and stay outta sight."

The hush was broken by Jessica yelling, "Where the fuck are you?" One of the women agents pulled a gun out of her baggy pants and crouched, slowing turning and scanning the empty space. Jessica rushed behind the fins and then darted out shouting, "Fucker's gone."

A garbled message screamed in Trace's ear piece. He jerked the bud out of his ear and shouted to Sam and Nez, "Aguirre ordered the feds in. Go! Go!"

I stayed behind the rocks as I had been told. The Navajo PD reached Jessica before the federal agents converged on the clearing.

"Why did he bolt?" Jessica asked. "I thought he was hooked. This can't be. He just disappeared." She skewered Trace. "What did you see?" Which way did he go?"

Trace wiped the sweat from his face. "I didn't see anything. He was standing right there, and then the sand was so thick I couldn't even see you."

"Impossible," Aguirre snorted. "Perps don't disappear. You weren't paying attention. She"—he cocked his head at Jessica—"somehow spooked him, and he took advantage of the storm and ran for it. You boys fucked up." He gritted his teeth. "Federal agents woulda taken him down."

Aguirre glanced down at the canyon floor. "Sandstorm wiped out the footprints." He looked at Jessica. "Which way did Jack come from?"

She pointed to a narrow trail between the rocks.

"You two"—he motioned to two agents—"move out that way."

No one was paying any attention to me as I walked over to the spot where the earth had opened and swallowed the witches and Jack. The sand was undisturbed, and no dust drifted in the air. Two perfect owl feathers crossed at the tips lay over the spot the chasm had opened.

"You find something?" Sam asked, coming up behind me. He glanced down at the crossed owl feathers. "The omen of death."

I nodded. "The FBI isn't going to find Jack. No one's ever going to find him." I held up my hand to ward off his argument. "The earth opened, and four witches hauled him into the Underworld."

"Wh-what? You saw them, and you didn't you say anything?"

"I tried. Remember, I kept touching you. But we can see only what we are allowed to see and able to see— never all of reality."

"Why could you see them?"

"The witches wanted me to watch them take Jack to remind me of their power and their presence. They've not forgotten that the Holy Ones held me safe. The witches know humans stand on the ledge between light and dark. They wait for us there."

Expressions of bafflement and surprise flashed across his face. I sensed his Navajo beliefs battling with his rational criminal justice training.

He wrapped his arms around me, clinging tightly. "Are you okay?"

"Yes, I stand in the light of the Holy Ones."

"As I do. You're one hell of a woman."

With his arm still around me, Sam gestured to Trace to join us. He hurried over, a bundle of nerves and impatience.

"What is it? We're in the middle of a man hunt," Trace snapped.

"Tell him what you saw," Sam responded.

I described the four witches coming out of the earth to take Jack. "I knew we weren't in any danger. They came for Jack."

Trace rocked back on his heels. "This isn't all you've seen." He turned to Sam and accused him. "You withheld information from me."

Sam ran his hand through his hair. "I didn't tell you she was a target of witches, but we sure as hell can't share any of this with the FBI."

"You should have told of me." Trace stood firm with his demand.

"So now you know," Sam responded. "Are you gonna share with the feds?"

He shook his head slowly. "No, there're no footprints and no signs of a struggle. At the moment, they think we're incompetent, and I don't have any evidence but two owl feathers to prove we aren't."

"What about Montoya?" Sam asked.

"I don't know yet," Trace barked. He turned his back and joined the search.

"Go back behind the rocks and wait for me. I'll take you home when this is over." Sam kissed my forehead and hurried to join Trace.

Agent Aguirre and the officers combed the canyon as they chattered into their microphones. The two agents returned through the hoodoos from the direction Jack had come from. They had Big Man in tow with his hands cuffed behind his back. "There's a blue cargo van—no windows—parked about a mile back there. He was sitting in the driver's seat."

Aguirre said, "What were you doing out here?"

"Gonna do a little hunting." Big Man said.

Sam guffawed. When Big Man turned his head and saw him, his shoulders slumped.

"This is Big Man, Texas Jack's bouncer, and the head honcho of the Cobras."

"Put him in a car and get him out of here," Aguirre said.

The FBI put out an alert to the highway patrol and Aguirre dispatched officers to Crazy Gal's, but I knew they would never find Texas Jack. The line between good and evil is permeable, and Texas Jack had crossed for the last time.

***

The days after the failed mission were filled with a flurry of questions and chasing leads. I wasn't privy to the FBI post-mission debrief, the endless hours of rehashing, theorizing, incrimination, and report writing, but I knew Sam would tell me what he could. I had told Taylor what I knew, leaving out the witchcraft, and she immediately started working her sources for sound bites for her story.

The day after the failed mission, the county and state had been scoured, Crazy Gal's shuttered, and an exhausted Sam called me. We met for dinner at his house. I brought the pizza; Sam contributed the wine.

He was haggard, unshaven, and his clothes were wrinkled. "Babe, I've missed you." He clung to me tightly, burying his face in my hair. "You smell like the desert after a rain. I probably smell like a dead goat." He stepped back. "Come in. I haven't slept much lately. I'm sorry. I'm all over the place. How are you?"

"Dying to know what you know."

"As you might expect, the FBI hit a dead end hunting Jack. They refer to it as 'planning his exit well.' They're sticking to their version. Jack got suspicious and did a runner in the storm, and not a single one of us Navajo was paying attention. They're covering their asses by blaming us."

"Can this hurt your career?"

"The feds have no jurisdiction over the selection of officers or the management of the Navajo PD."

"That's good, isn't it?"

"Yep, but the FBI does share jurisdiction on the Nation when a major crime is committed, so we'll be still be working together, and that's gonna be hard."

"They aren't Navajo, and they wouldn't understand what happened. If I described what I saw to the feds, and you guys said you believed it, their shrinks would nod sagely and claim we were all sharing the same psychosis."

That earned me laugh.

"What happened to Big Man?"

"He lawyered up and shut up. His lawyer claimed he didn't know Jack was buying women. We let his lawyer talk a good fifteen minutes about Big Man's solid employment history, his clean record, and then we told him..."

"What?"

"Sofia recognized a picture of Big Man as the fat Hispanic man who drove her to Flag in a blue windowless van. She'd never been out of Mexico and certainly had never seen a Navajo in her life."

"What about..."

"Texas Jack? Sofia identified a picture of him and called him Montoya."

"Damn. Jack got Montoya's money, his wife, and framed him for human trafficking—or wait, were they in it together?"

"Montoya claims he knew nothing about the emails, the wallet, the offshore accounts, or buying any women."

"But the Internet traffic tracked back to his home Internet address."

"Yeah, it did, and the FBI seized Montoya's computers and his cell phone. There are no digital tracks on his devices that tie him to the emails responding to the ad." He shook his head. "Nothing."

"So how...who?"

"According to the FBI computer gurus, there are ways to spoof the IP address from where data is coming from."

"Tell me in small words. What is an IP address?"

"A unique list of numbers separated by periods that identifies a computer attached to the Internet, and it's frighteningly easy to steal someone's IP address if the wireless Internet router isn't set up with WPA2 wireless encryption. Montoya's home router wasn't. His network was wide open to hackers. Plenty easy for Jack, who as it turns out, has a Computer Science degree from Stanford. The FBI faxed Jack's picture to the Caribbean bank that wired out funds to what we thought was Montoya's digital wallet. Jack opened that bank account in person with a fake ID, showing his picture and Nathan Montoya's name. The banks in the Caribbean don't ask a lot of questions if you're waving bags of money around you want to deposit with them. Jack had set up the wallet in Montoya's name and from Montoya's IP address."

"Where did Jack get the money he deposited in the Caribbean bank?"

"Trust fund baby. Aguirre talked to Jack's younger brother, and he said Jack and his dad had a falling out. His old man wanted him to bring the family company into the digital age, but Jack wanted no part of it, and that's when he did a runner with his money and turned up here. His family had no idea where he was until I got in touch with his brother. "

"Umm, did the FBI find Jack's computer?"

"Yeah, they found a laptop in his house with his fingerprints on it. Took it apart and guess what? Digital tracks to the Caribbean bank, the digital wallet, and he had answered your ads from his laptop."

"I was sure it was Montoya. Chilling to think how well Jack succeeded in fooling us while he was cranking up the business for himself. If Montoya had gone back to prison, Jack could have picked up the rest of the trucking business for a bargain and had it all. He had the skill set, and he made his opportunity. Remember he called himself a winner? He systematically destroyed Montoya's life, and he didn't even need the money. Screwing his wife was the icing on the cake. "

"No, killing his wife was the icing on the cake."

"Ohh," I gasped. "The autopsy..."

"Think about the struggle you would put up if someone was forcing something down your throat. She had two hairs on her sweater that weren't hers. The FBI lab matched them to the hair in Jack's brush. Both the hairs on her sweater had blood at the root tip which was analyzed for DNA. It matched to Jack."

"I should have helped her get out of here, not just talked about it."

"Don't pick up that load of guilt. She could have made different choices—better choices. You warned her plenty of times. Carolyn was playing way out of her league with those two."

"Jack destroyed Montoya, but he crossed an evil he couldn't beat."

"And he lost. Good riddance. The FBI took cadaver dogs out to search the land around the bar, and they found Juanita's body buried behind the row of shacks. Big Man rolled over on Jack since he's not around to defend himself. He'll still be charged as an accessory to her murder, and he's charged with human trafficking."

"Were the Cobras involved?"

"Yup. Everyone was using everyone else. Jack used Big Man and Big Man used the pee wees and the baby gangers. The little guys made their bones by being lookouts and snitches. Some of the older ones will end up in juvie."

"Were the Dragons tying to horn in on the business?"

"Nah, doesn't appear that way. The Dragons and the Cobras are old enemies. Defending their turf and tagging in each other's territory is business as usual."

"What about Montoya?"

"He's financially ruined. He'll lose the trucking business. His partner is missing, and Montoya can't ask the court to declare him dead for seven years. He can't even sell the property to raise money. He not only has tax problems, his cash cow is dead, and he can't touch what little is left of Carolyn's money until the will is probated. The court has to be satisfied that he's the heir. Montoya will never be off my radar. He's one son of bitch who got used by another son of bitch." He smiled at me. "That make you happy?"

"Yeah, warrior man. It does." I kissed him. "Did Alvin Bryd get out of prison?"

"He's been moved to a comfy prison hospital. He doesn't have long to live. There's no record of any payments into Byrd's bank account. He would have said anything to get of prison."

His face was scrunched with concentration. He sighed and scraped his hand over his rough stubble.

"Are you beating up on yourself because you can't tell Aguirre what happened to Jack?"

His lips curved up. "Nope. I'm tired, not crazy. No Anglo can understand our ways."

He nuzzled my check. "I love you more than the number of stars in the desert sky." We held each other until his head lolled back on the sofa cushion, his eyes blinked shut, and his breathing became deep and slow. His body surrendered to the fatigue, and I tried not to disturb his sleep when I put a blanket over him and left for home.

***

Sam was sheepish when he called the next morning and apologized. "I'm sorry. I was so damn tired. I ate all that pizza and fell asleep. I'm going to make it up to you. Pack up what you'll need for a couple of days. Jeans and boots will be fine. I have all the camping gear for both of us."

"Where are we going?"

"It's a surprise. Tell Benally the office can run without you—you've earned it and we need some downtime. Can you be ready in two hours?"

His talk of camping conjured sexy scenes of us out in the woods, trading bites of s'mores and making love under the stars. "I'll be ready." Just being alone with him would be bliss.

"You're a lucky woman. I'm even a great campfire cook."

"Well, one of us has to be."

He laughed. "See you in two hours."

I told Benally that I was taking vacation time. She held her snark. All she said was that she would put the forms on my desk for me to fill out when I returned. Since I had stood up for myself, our relationship had become more professional. We would never be friendly, chatting around the coffee pot, but we had forged a working relationship.

When he was on his way to pick me up, he called again to make sure I was ready. I dropped my boots outside my front door. When I came back out with my duffle and jacket, Sam's pickup ground into the lot, pulling a heavy horse trailer with two brown tails flying from the rear. He was grinning like crazy when he rolled down the passenger side window.

"Whoa! Cowboy, you've outdone yourself." I dropped my boots and duffle in the pickup bed with his. Through the side vent of the trailer, two gleaming horses stamped and huffed. "What are their names?"

"The mare is Sugar Doodle and the gelding is Cappy."

I stretched my arm into the trailer and touched Sugar Doodle on her flank. She nickered. "When did you get them?"

"Made the deal a couple of days ago. Got the trailer, too, a package deal. The seller swears the mare is a sweet ride. Ready?"

"Sure. Where to?"

"Havasu Falls, the most beautiful place on the Nation."

An hour later we pulled onto a narrow dirt road that tunneled through a thick forest of pine. We broke out into meadow grass undulating in the wind and a thundering waterfall pouring into a boulder-strewn creek that edged the meadow from the forest.

We unpacked the truck and set up our tent to face east. Sam swung a bear bag on a rope between two sturdy pines at the edge of the meadow while I set up a camp kitchen.

"How about dessert first?" I asked.

"You mean you?" He grinned up at me.

"Hold that thought. I'm starving." I opened the plastic grocery bag and pulled out a box of graham crackers, marshmallows, and chocolate bars. "Remember these?"

"Yep. I'll get some sticks." By the time he returned, I had a campfire blazing and he had whittled points onto two small sticks. He bent over to toast the marshmallows, giving me a view of his wide back and muscled legs.

He scraped the hot marshmallow over the chocolate on the cracker, broke off a piece, and fed me. I sucked his finger clean of chocolate. His eyes clouded with desire.

He leaned over, licked the marshmallow off my lips, and nibbled down my neck to the hollow of my throat. When he rasped his big thumb over my nipple, I ached with lust. He laid me on the sweet grass. The sun warmed my skin and the tangy fragrance of the crushed grass wafted around us. He stroked the length of my body with long fluid strokes, setting every nerve alight to his sensuous touch. He teased between my legs, flicking light touches, retreating, and returning until he built the sweet ache. When he plunged into me, I thundered to a climax, riding him hard until he groaned with his pleasure.

We lay snuggled together staring up at the cerulean sky. He placed my hand flat over his heart and then covered my hand with his. "My heart belongs to you. Before I met you, I was armored up and closed off. Your love pierced my shield, softening the brittle shell around my heart, and allowed my love to grow. And my love for you is eternal."

Teaching and shooting news and documentaries took me to work on the East and West coasts, the Midwest, and an island in the Gulf of Mexico. Born a fourth generation Texan, I live in Austin with an energetic mutt that waits patiently every day for me to come home and write.

Connect with me at:
https://www.facebook.com/P.H.TurnerAuthor
https://twitter.com/pht97

Keep reading for a special excerpt of P.H. Turner's

Death & Desire

Ancient rituals. Up-to-the minute deception

Reporter Taylor McWhorter knows something is going on at the newly reopened uranium mine on the local Navajo reservation. The Native workers are being fired. Rumors of bad Native American spirits and shapeshifters mingle with the stink of leach pit mining. The rough red mountains and steep canyons hide more passes and getaway trails than any maze. And Taylor's sources keep turning up dead…

Until she meets Captain Trace Yazzie, head of the tribal police force and plenty to reckon with on his own. The chemistry between them is enough to incinerate Taylor's rule about mixing business and pleasure. But with a murderer on the loose, priceless Navajo artifacts turning up in the wrong places, and Trace's suggestion that spirits disturbed from looted burial sites might be part of the problem, Taylor can't afford to lose her head to lust. This might be the story of the year. But unless she keeps her wits about her, it could be the last one Taylor ever tells…

An e-book and trade paperback on sale now!

Chapter 1

I paced impatiently up and down the sidewalk in front of the 1950s Airstream trailer that had recently undergone a tasteful rehab into the Route 66 Diner. A dry, cold wind whipped around the building and blew red sand in my eyes. Where the hell was he? I looked at my watch and debated going into the diner to escape the blowing grit.

I turned my back to the wind, facing the one-way oncoming traffic on Central Avenue. Niyol was striding toward me wearing a lamb shearling coat and a black beaver Stetson, matching the description he had sent by e-mail. He had straight black hair that hung down past his collar, a turquoise bracelet peeking out his sleeve, and a matching bolo string tie. His eyes tracked to me, his head barely nodding. Tension seeped out of me. He had come to the meet.

I edged toward the alcove outside the diner's front door to shelter from the howling wind. The high-pitched squeal of tires shrieked over the wind. A black Mercedes sedan rounded the corner of Central toward the café. The car popped the curb and aimed straight for him. I dived into the shelter of the doorway. His body suspended in midair before bouncing off the windshield with a sickening, wet *thump*, then tumbled to rest at my feet. The Mercedes swerved back on Central and gunned south out of sight. His unmarred left eye held a look of surprise. Blood from his head dripped into the expansion joint of the sidewalk, forming a puddle around a withering dandelion dying in the crack.

People rushed out of the diner and milled around me. "Miss, Miss, are you hurt?"

I scrabbled to a street-side trashcan for support. "No." I was dizzy and sweating fear. Niyol's body was inches from my foot. The foul stink of death washed over me. Blood pooled near the toe of my left boot. I gripped the edge of the city's trash can, smelled the rancid grease from the remains of too many hurried lunches, and retched until nothing was left but bile.

A woman shouted into her cell phone, begging for help. She tugged my coat sleeve. "Help's coming."

Wailing sirens announced the arrival of the police and an ambulance. A woman in the crowd pointed at me. "She was right by him. Her. Over there," she cried out to the officer. An inner voice reminded me no one in Albuquerque knew I was meeting him. To these witnesses, I was only the person most proximal to him.

An officer bore down on me. "Miss, do you need the EMTs? Need to be checked out?" His badge identified him as Officer Lee Harris.

"No, I'm okay, just shaken up."

A detective joined Officer Harris. "I'm Detective Jorge Gutierrez, Albuquerque PD. You okay to answer a couple of questions?"

"Yeah. Okay…."

He flipped open a spiral. "Do you know this man?"

I squared my shoulders and raised my chin. "I've never seen him before." At least that much was true.

"Tell me what you did see," he demanded.

"I was walking in front of the diner and saw a black Mercedes drive up on the sidewalk and run him down. He was only a couple of feet from me."

"You get the license plate? See the driver?" he asked sharply.

"No. It all happened so fast. One minute he was walking, and the next he bounced off the car. I–I didn't even realize it was a Mercedes until it sped away."

"Look like an accident to you?"

"No, the driver drove up over the curb and ran him down." "Did the dead man speak to you?"

I shook my head. "We made eye contact as we were walking toward each other. He may have nodded."

"We'll have to have you give us a formal statement at the station. Do you have any ID with you?" He held out his hand to me.

I fumbled out my driver's license and passed it over.

He scanned my license and read my name out loud. "Ms. Taylor McWhorter. What were you doing in Albuquerque?" Gutierrez demanded.

"Sightseeing."

He looked at me long and hard. I didn't blink.

"You'll need to make your statement and sign it before leaving the city. The main precinct is at thirty-three nineteen Broadway. Take the first right off Central and head down two blocks. It's on your right." He turned away from me to someone else in the small crowd.

"What did happen here?" I called to his back.

Detective Gutierrez looked over his shoulder at me. "Looks like murder."

An excited older man planted himself in front of Gutierrez. "I was in the diner. Right there in the booth by the window." He gestured frantically. "I saw the driver aim for him."

I turned away without looking back and walked briskly to my car. I wanted to make my statement, sign it, and get on the road back to Flagstaff. I parked a block from the precinct and composed my statement in my head. No need to lie. Niyol Notah was widowed. No wife or kids who might have known he was meeting me. But he wasn't the victim of an accident, which means someone knew where he would be and maybe what he was going to tell me.

I flipped down the visor mirror. My wild, curly black hair was a riot surrounding my drawn face. I fumbled in my purse for a brush and smoothed my hair behind my ears. A pale- faced woman who sported some deep shadows under her blue eyes stared back. *Just make the statement and get out of here.* I stepped out into the wind and cinched my coat around me.

The inside of the precinct house was an institutional brown, the Naugahyde chairs repaired with duct tape. I perched on one until a sergeant beckoned me to join him in a small conference room. A young officer idly tapped her nails waiting to take my statement.

"Will you state your name, address, phone number, and occupation?" the sergeant asked.

I spelled McWhorter for the woman. "I work at KNAZ in Flagstaff," I said without amplifying my work description.

She dutifully typed that in her laptop, and he read into the record his name and rank, the date, and Niyol's case number. No question to me about what I did at KNAZ. I repeated the comments I had made to Detective Gutierrez.

Back in the waiting area on my duct-taped chair, I drank a cup of overly brewed coffee and waited for the statement to be printed for my signature. The whole process took less than an hour. The time had not even run out on my parking meter.

The traffic on I-40W was light in the early afternoon. The first finger of fear trickled down my spine, mingling with my nervous sweat. I looked in my rearview mirror, eying the traffic in the left-hand lane. Nothing seemed out of the ordinary. I dialed the news desk. "Marty, it's Taylor. I'm on my way back, and I didn't get a chance to talk to Niyol. He was run over on the sidewalk in front of me."

"What! You okay?" Marty yelled into the phone.

"I will be," I said grimly. "Someone nearly took his head off. There was blood spattered everywhere." My knuckles were splotched white from gripping the steering wheel. "He died right on the street." My vision blurred to black around the edges.

From down the black tunnel I heard Marty say, "You all right to drive? You sure?"

I shook back the darkness. "No choice. I want to be home in my own bed tonight." I blinked back my tears and steadied my breathing. Better to concentrate on the story. "Listen, Niyol had an older brother on the Navajo Nation near Tuba City. I don't know how close they were, but Niyol told me one helluva story. Maybe he shared some of it with his brother, Bidziil."

I could hear Marty's pencil tapping impatiently on his desk. "You know what the Albuquerque police are calling Niyol's death?"

"Detective Gutierrez says it's murder. Sure looked thatway." "Gutierrez know you're a TV reporter?"

"No. I told them I worked at KNAZ, but they didn't ask what I did, and I didn't offer any explanation."

"They'll find out once they start poking around in Niyol's case. You tell them you were meeting him?"

"No. He didn't ask."

He groaned. "That's gonna come back to bite you in the ass." "I didn't lie. I told them I had never met him."

"Be in my office at ten tomorrow morning. I gotta go. Hell, I haven't completed the run sheet for the six o'clock. You call me if you need anything."

My boss, Marty Cummings, was a seasoned news director, gruff as hell, and had all the sensitivity of a pit bull. KNAZ was the only full-service network affiliate in northern Arizona. My job was to investigate stories from Flag to the New Mexico border. I'd built a nice little life for myself with a snug adobe casita, close friends, and a job with an award-winning news station. Niyol Notah died trying to tell me his story. My job was to get it told.

A semi whipped past me, rocking my Rav4. I kept to the speed limit and punched Louis's number. "You back from Phoenix?"

"Yeah, Eric had a great time. Of course, he could look at every painting in a museum twice while checking his iPad for the painter's life history. Me, I can stroll through an art museum in thirty minutes tops. We did get to play some pretty mean golf. Where are you? Want to come by for a drink?"

Listening to Louis settled me down. The three of us enjoyed each other's company along with some legendary happy hours featuring Eric's gourmet cooking. "Wish I could. I'm on I-40, a couple of hours from home."

"Thought you would be back by now. You talk to Niyol?" "He's dead. Run over."

"Taylor! You okay?"

"Almost, maybe. Marty just asked me the same thing. Better than I was." "Jeez, gal. Take it easy. Who killed him?"

"I don't know yet. Albuquerque PD has me and a witness in the diner who think it was deliberate." I inhaled sharply. "Someone knew he was going to be there and didn't want him talking. I'm meeting Marty at ten in the morning. Can you join us? I want you in on this one."

"Sure. Listen, girl, you need anything—anything at all, even in the middle of the night— Eric and I will be there. Whoever killed Niyol got a good look at you."

"Too bad they don't know I've got squat." I glanced in my rearview mirror. "Thanks, Louis. See you tomorrow."

"Text me when you get home," Louis demanded. "If you don't want to stay in your house, we got a spare room and it's yours."

"Thanks. I think Mac and I'll be fine."

I stopped in Gallup, a major trading town on the edge of the Navajo Nation, for gas. The old Route 66 was the main thoroughfare through town, lined with Indian jewelry stores and run- down motels from the 1940s, still blinking their tourist-court Vacancy signs for those too tired to make it to Flagstaff. Fast-food joints like Denny's lined the old road to lure in travelers for a grand slam breakfast anytime during the day.

An old Navajo man with filthy matted hair and tennis shoes with flopping soles staggered out in front of my Rav at a stoplight. He steadied himself with one grimy hand on the hood of the car, lurched to his right, caught himself, and shot the finger at the Mazda driver who was honking impatiently on the other side of the intersection. He tottered across the street and slumped down on the curb. Holding his head in his hands, he tumbled over in a drunken stupor, half in the gutter and half on the sidewalk.

Chapter 2

Two hours later, the smell of the Coconino Forest pines seeped into the car, and I relaxed for the first time since leaving Albuquerque. Snow-capped Humphrey's Peak jutted through the clouds in the waning light leading me to my casita.

I needed to be alone. Too many people, too many conversations, a shock to my system, and I needed to retreat to my own space and recharge. Renewed, I could happily rejoin the human population and their demands. But now, right now, I craved the sanctuary of the house Eric had found for me. My little adobe house had a wraparound deck with views of the San Francisco Mountains, warm wood floors, and a big kiva fireplace—my little piece ofheaven.

Mac greeted me joyfully, thumping his tail and wriggling between my legs as I dropped the gear bag at the door. I cradled his big black head in my hands. "You're a good boy. I missed you too, fella." I was damn sure Mac had kept the house safe, but I walked through every room, looked in every closet, under the bed, and checked the windows to see they were locked. I tried to convince myself I was acting foolishly, but had no success. Everything was neat and orderly like I left it. Mac cocked his head and gave me his puzzled-doggy look. I stepped into the laundry room, kicked off my boots, and took off all my clothes, even my underwear, and tossed them in the washer on the hottest cycle. I stood there nude, staring at the dried red-brown stain on my favorite Lariats. I poured Clorox on a rag and dabbed at the stain, instantly removing the chocolate leather dye. I scooped them up and tossed them in the trash can.

Mac followed me into my bedroom where I sat on the bed listening for any sound that shouldn't be there. The wind rasped the pinion branches across the roof, sounding like claws scratching the shingles. The horror of Niyol's murder washed over me—his look of surprise, his blood congealing on the sidewalk. I was in my safe space now with no need to show the world my strength and competence. A wave of dizziness hit me, and I almost vomited, my stomach heaving, but it passed before I made it to the toilet. I sat on the closed commode and waited for another wave.

Mac, named for both sides of my family, McWhorter and McMurchie, followed me into the bathroom. He whimpered and rubbed his head on my legs.

"I'm all right, boy." I stroked his black curls, soothing his anxiety. He buried his head in my hands. Mac had a syrupy-sweet disposition that had stolen my heart. His mom was a black Labradoodle who fancied wayward studs. Mac and his two sisters favored their mom, a big frame covered with curly hair. The fourth little guy looked like he had been made from the spare parts. "It's been a crappy day, boy." I rubbed my cheek on his muzzle.

I squinted at my reflection in the mirror, and there I was in all my magnificence—an investigative news reporter sitting on a toilet talking to a dog. And damn it, squinting made the fine lines around my eyes etch more deeply. I reached for the moisturizer.

Mac padded quietly behind me into the bedroom. I threw the bedcovers back and crawled into the safety of my nest. Covered with the filth of Albuquerque's streets, I waited for the fitful sleep I knew was coming. I awoke once, drenched in sweat, dreaming of speeding black cars.

A weak dawn brightened the eastern sky. I stripped my sheets, stuffed them in the washer, and showered. I had my Cheerios while watching KNAZ's early news anchor read the story of Niyol Notah's death in Albuquerque. Not even a picture of him flashed across the screen. He had initiated contact with me less than a month before, shortly after he was fired from Dinetah Mining and Engineering in Flagstaff.

* * * *

I sipped my fourth cup of coffee, waiting in Marty's office for Louis to show.

Louis Dubois was my field producer and cameraman. He and his partner, Eric Jameson, were polar opposites, but made a good team. Louis's Baton Rouge roots gave him his trademark soft slur and courtly manners. Eric was all about his real estate business.

He rushed in, his shirttail hanging out on the left side. "Whew, made it." He grinned as he flopped noisily in a chair and pulled paper and pen from his ratty notebook.

"Glad you could join us ten minutes late," Marty growled. "Let's get started. Taylor, give me your story."

"Niyol Notah e-mailed me about a month ago wanting to talk about the Dinetah Engineering and Mining Company. He moved to Albuquerque shortly after the company fired him."

"He legit? You Google him? Find a phone number and address over in Albuquerque?" Marty barked.

"I did. Even drove by his house early yesterday morning. He has a small stucco ranch house, looked like it was from the 1930s or 1940s in an older part of south-central Albuquerque. I figure that's why he chose the diner on Central for the meeting. But I let him set the parameters for contact. He was skittish. He drizzled his story out over several weeks by e-mail and phone. Albuquerque police have probably pulled his cell records by now."

"So? What have you got?" Marty challenged.

"He told me he was a heavy equipment operator, running bulldozers and road graders for Dinetah. Niyol worked for the mine when Naalish Tsosie ran the operation. The mine was closed for years, supposedly played out, and Tsosie was killed in a one-car crash down in Phoenix right before the mine cranked back up. Niyol got a job running a grader, building a new road to the backside of the old uranium mine. Until he got fired."

"You get the new guy's name?" Marty interrupted.

"Of course," I answered him patiently. "Sancho Chavez bought the rights to the mine." "You mean Chavez bought the mine?"

"No, the mine is on tribal land. The Navajo Nation sells the rights to operate the mine and receives part of the profits. Before you ask, Tsosie's death was ruled an accident by the Phoenix PD."

"You gonna string this out all morning? I got work to do."

I ignored Marty's bluster and continued, "Niyol claimed Dinetah Mining was trafficking in stolen Anasazi pottery looted from the job sites. Heavy equipment turned up the pots and their site foremen collected it on the spot. You can't dig a couple of inches in the sand without finding pottery. Hell, a good wind storm will uncover pottery. Niyol is—was—a traditional Navajo and was offended by the desecration of the burial sites."

"He offer you any proof?" Marty asked.

"He sent me pictures he took on his cell phone, a night scene of a dozer working in a finger canyon, and a man he identifies as a supervisor holding a huge Anasazi pot. He didn't live long enough to share more. Niyol claimed the finger canyons are littered with Anasazi pit houses and burial sites. At night, the bulldozers tore open the graves and men looted the funeral goods. His buddy took the night work for triple-time pay. Not all the operators were asked to work overtime."

"You get this friend's name?" Marty interrupted.

"No, he was giving me the name at our meeting. He did tell me his friend was fired and died within a week in a drunken car crash."

"Anything else to add?"

"Yeah, Niyol saw the foreman of their group hand over pottery to guy who had a truck with a license plate frame that advertised the Ford dealership in Flag."

"Why was Niyol's friend canned?"

"Niyol claims he got the ax because he knew Dinetah was stealing."

"You got any proof he wasn't drinking and driving?"

"Not yet. But I don't think it's a coincidence that Niyol was killed yesterday, and his friend and Naalish Tsosie were also killed in car crashes."

"There's big money in those pots," Louis interjected. "Asian collectors in Southern California and private collectors in Europe, who are none too concerned about provenance, will pay big money for Anasazi pots." Louis stretched his long arms over his head. "Heard the Saudis were getting in the collecting game, too. Paying four hundred thousand a pop for big pieces."

"I know you got jack shit on this story unless you find another source who works for Dinetah. So find something." Marty stood, ending the meeting.

Louis waited until we cleared the doorway to say, "Let's get some lunch over at the Galaxy. Man, I haven't had their wet fries in months."

"I'm there. You realize The Galaxy's wet fries should be on your bucket list once in a lifetime. All that cheese will kill you." He followed me back to the newsroom for me to grab my bag. We left the station by the side door to avoid running into Marty.

The Galaxy Diner was a retro fifties fave of the locals, with a red neon sign in a fancy script over the door. The decor was faux midcentury, heavy on the chrome and cherry red. We slipped into a vinyl booth across from the bar that was rimmed with red barstools. Louis ordered the Galaxy cheesy burger with an order of wet fries on the side and a chocolate milkshake. I had my usual garden salad with a bowl of the day's chicken noodle soup.

"Jeez, Louis, where do you put it all?"I asked him. Louis had to be in his fifties and didn't have an ounce of fat on his lean frame.

"I'm a guy, girlfriend, and pushing all this testosterone means I get to eat more." He dumped a healthy serving of wet fries on my salad plate. "There, you won't starve. Enjoy the fries. You and Mac can run a few miles later if you feel guilty. Now give it up. You didn't tell Marty all you know. Spill it."

I savored the oil and salt on the lethal fries. "I don't want Marty to know until I have a chance to pursue a couple of leads."

"What did Niyol tell you?"

"Niyol was antsy about telling me anything specific in his e-mails. I think if we could have just met, he would have opened up. But here's what I do know. He didn't want to be anywhere near Dinetah after he was fired. Right before he was killed, he snail-mailed me some financial records his nephew Gage filched from the Dinetah office. Gage told Niyol that the mining company was involved in some funky accounting." I sighed. "It's a bitch because I don't want to spook Marty. I'm on a fishing trip for dirt on one of the biggest employers in northeast Arizona. I checked with Linda over in sales and Dinetah buys a lot of advertising time from us. They're a big donor to our 5K Run for the Kids. Our general sales manager will be plenty pissed if the CEO gets mad and pulls their ads."

"What reason did you give Linda for wanting to know how much Dinetah spent with us?" "She was busy putting together the end of the month statements and only half-assed paid attention. I told her I was doing a little research on our major advertisers."

"I can see her buying that."

"Hey, I need your help. You've lived here for decades. I want to be at Niyol's funeral and meet his brother. Do you know any of his relatives?"

Louis scratched his head with one long finger. "Yeah, I went to school with Klah Notah, same clan as Niyol."

"You think you can talk to Klah? Get us to that funeral?"

"Yeah. Pretty sure. Klah lives out by his mother at his family's sheep camp. I'll go by there to pay my respects and ask him if we can come to the funeral to honor his uncle. He'll smooth it over with Bidziil. Niyol was born to the Towering House Clan and for the Rock Gap people. Funeral's gonna be large. Lot of folks in those clans."

"Tell me again about the clan structure."

He mimicked a Scottish accent. "Aye, lassie, you oughta know all about clan structure.

You just visited your Scottish family down at the Highland Games in Phoenix."

“Both the McWhorters and the McMurchies are septs of the Buchannan’s—all of them fought under the same battle flag.”

He grinned. “So that’s a Buchanan battle flag you’re flying off your deck?” “You bet.” I popped a fry in my mouth. “Tell me about Navajo families.”

“A Navajo is born to his mother’s clan and born for his father’s. Navajo’s must marry outside their clans, and the man goes to live with his wife’s people. It’s a matrilineal system. You’ll see how it works at the funeral.”

Made in the USA
Monee, IL
29 July 2022